These short stories were all penned in and around Garry Kilworth's time in Hong Kong.

The collection is split half-and-half into general fiction stories and supernatural tales. They were all inspired by the people and places of that magical effervescent city, not forgetting its surrounding mountains and countryside, and the myriad islands that come within its sphere. There are tales from Chinese viewpoints and stories about the lives of ex-patriots.

If you read no other general fiction stories, then you must try 'Typhoon' with its fearless heroine the indomitable Elizabeth, or the imperturbable reptile catcher from 'The Snake-Man Cometh'. If your taste is not for the fantastic, you would be poorer in spirit for not experiencing the poignancy of 'The Hungry Ghosts' and 'Memories of the Flying Ball Bike Shop.'

If you have never been to Hong Kong, enter it page by page. If you have, retrace its familiar corners.

TALES
FROM
THE
FRAGRANT
HARBOUR

SHORT STORIES OF HONG KONG
AND THE FAR EAST

GARRY
KILWORTH

TALES
FROM
THE
FRAGRANT
HARBOUR

SHORT STORIES OF HONG KONG
AND THE FAR EAST

CONTENTS

| v |

AUTHOR'S SCRIBBLINGS

My wife Annette and I spent several very exciting years in Hong Kong between 1988 and 1992. It was not my first posting in the Far East—I lived in Singapore and Malaya in the '50s and '60s—but it would probably be my last, since we were getting beyond the age where landing good jobs overseas was possible. On this tour it was Annette who had to do the proper day job and I was left free to write, and many of the ideas for stories came from the local scene.

The words 'Hong Kong' (or more correctly *Heung Gong*) are Cantonese for 'Fragrant Harbour', from the time when that still bustling waterway was packed with ships wafting the scent of perfumed tea and oriental spices. Hong Kong was then, and is now, a thriving hive of activity, where East truly does meet West, and the two cultures have surged forward together in a mighty flood of business and commerce. Underneath this striving for the Hong Kong dollar is a world full of mystery and magic. An energetic sub-world where things strange and wonderful occur on a daily basis and small happenings blossom into myths. Even now I never fail to get a great thrill, an electric buzz, when I step off an aircraft that has carried me to Hong Kong.

The first set of tales are Once-told. They are, if you like, everyday general fiction, with no supernatural ingredients. Many of them are *based* on real events, though I stress the word based since there are those who will read these tales and recognise their own experiences which I have taken and wrought, sometimes twisting them into an unlikely and improbable shape. I swear by the old maxim, 'Why spoil a good story with the truth?' As with most characters in fictional tales, those in my stories are an amalgam of several people I may have met, mixed with a good pinch of imagination and fancy. They are not intended to be three-dimensional: I hope they have more corners than that: more idiosyncrasies, more failings, but also more attributes.

The second set of tales are Twice-told, and the supernatural ingredients are an essential part of their make-up. (Nathaniel Hawthorne coined the term 'twice-told tales': stories rooted in myth and folk lore, which have been and are retold time and again). I have always loved ghost stories, fantasy tales, and weird twist endings. Such elements are present in these stories. Again, no writer starts off with nothing. Ideas have to come from somewhere and there are sparks of true happenings in all these tales, no matter how far-fetched they may seem to those uninitiated into Hong Kong life. I apologise to those ghosts and mythical figures who may recognise themselves or events at which they were present, but again I must again admit I have hammered and battered the truth in order to further my literary strivings in the genre.

There are one or two other stories which were part of the same place and time, but they are not included in this volume since they were in another recent collection of my stories enti-

tled *Moby Jack and Other Tall Tales* also by PS Publishing.
They are: 'Black Drongo', 'Death of the Mocking Man',
'Wayang Kulit' and 'Oracle Bones'.

Finally, this volume is dedicated to all Hong Kong friends,
both Oriental and Occidental, many of whom still allow
Annette and myself to visit from time to time, and continue
to treat us with great kindness. You are all treasured people in
our lives and we always look forward to our reunions. I hope
you enjoy these simple tales of that unique, mystical and
enigmatic place which we all grew to love.

Garry Kilworth, August 2007

TALES
FROM
THE
FRAGRANT
HARBOUR

SHORT STORIES OF HONG KONG
AND THE FAR EAST

This volume is dedicated to my great friend and collaborator Robert Holdstock, writer of a unique fantasy fiction which achieved literary excellence.

A generous, inspiring, big-hearted man, Rob sadly died on the last day of November, 2009 leaving many of us bereft.

ONCE-
TOLD
TALES

CHANDLER'S COFFIN

Chandler was an expat European, or gweilo as the Chinese called them, living on Kowloon-side, Hong Kong. He possessed a parcel he had not yet opened, nor ever wanted to. It occupied six feet, by two feet, by two feet of his rather sordid and cramped room.

Attached to the cardboard box, which contained a heavy oblong object in the shape of the wrapping, was a tag which read 'Chinese Rosewood'. This English phrase was followed by some Chinese characters which Chandler had never managed to decipher.

It was time to cut off the cardboard casing and look at the contents beneath. Chandler had his Swiss army knife ready to do the deed, but his hands trembled. It was his firm belief that the cardboard encased a coffin, one given to him by a Chinese craftsman to whom he had 'brought luck'. But Chandler was terrified of death, of the symbols of death, of anything which reminded him that death was not an option, that one day his remains would fill a six, by two, by two wooden box.

Even the word gweilo which literally means 'ghost' invoked unpleasant images so far as Chandler was concerned.

So he wondered whether or not to just walk out and leave the gift behind, where it had lain for 3 months now, occupying almost all the length of one wall of his small room. It had been used variously as a table, chair and even a bed when one night a drunken friend had slept on it. He argued that he was travelling light, that he could not lug such a large package around with him as air freight. Why not just go, leave the thing here, let someone else's body fill it when the time came?

Chandler at this time was living on the corner at the junction of Nathan and Peking Road, Kowloon in Chung King Mansions, a backpackers' hostel and the home of two dozen curry clubs. Chung King Mansions was a terraced building several storeys high sandwiched between smart shops and five-star hotels.

Inside, the building was a rabbit warren of dirty corridors, shops, sleazy restaurants, broom cupboards and rented rooms surpassed only in complexity and squalor by the giant slum known as Kowloon Walled City, where fifty-thousand illegal immigrants sat and waited for an amnesty, ministered to by Jackie Pullinger, the angel of the drug addicts.

Outside, Chung King Mansions was a vertical junkyard of ancient, dripping air conditioners hanging precariously from their rusty cages like oblong bombs waiting to fall on Nathan Road tourists. Dirty electrical wires cobwebbed the facade on which had once been painted in now faint capital letters the intriguing sign: THE FREEZING-HOT BOTTLE COMPANY. The walls were covered in dirt and bird-droppings gathered over countless years of neglect.

In those times there were weekly electrical fires in Chung King Mansions, but none were ever serious because there was always someone around to put it out. Each insect-infested corner of Chung King Mansions was occupied twenty-four hours a day, with its cheap shops, its backpacking boarders,

and its Indian Messes and Curry Clubs which were not allowed
to call themselves restaurants because they could not pass the
fire regulations, or the kitchen checks by the health authorities. Chung King Mansion food was adored by the gweilo rugby
clubs and football teams and that most famous of Far Eastern
ex-pat institutions, the rowdy and enthusiastic Hash House
Harriers, whose members organised cross-country races in aid
of local charities, and who ate curries and drank beer as ener-
getically as they ran through field and street.

Not far away, down towards the harbour on the next
corner, stood the magnificent Peninsula, an aristocrat
among hotels, which boasted opulence rather than modern
decor. There a five string violin quartet played from a small
corner minstrel gallery above the foyer coffee and tea tables,
up amongst the gold and marble of the ceiling. The players'
instruments vied with the crystal chandeliers which tinkled
in the harbour breezes.

It was in the Peninsula that gweilos who had been to a
play, opera or a concert at the Cultural Centre, sat amongst
rich Chinese and sipped chocolate, talking about how terrible
things were in Britain, economically speaking, and how lucky
they were to be in Hong Kong. One of them would be sure
to mention that, really, the latest yuppy-type joke at their
expense—to call them FILTH (Failed In London, Tried
Hongkong)—was quite funny. They were able to laugh at such
things, considering the size and weight of their salaries.

Between the Peninsula and Chung King Mansions were
two famous night spots. One was Red Lips Bar, where it was
said that the girls hadn't changed since the Vietnam War, and
stood toothless and ready to entertain customers half their
age. The other was a great drinking hole called Ned Kelly's
Last Stand, an Antipodean establishment which boasted
good jazz, goodish booze, and a goodly crush of people as
the night wore on.

In another age Chandler would have been called a travelling gentleman, or later still, a hippie. But this was the end of the eighties and people back home in England referred to him as a backpacker. He didn't call himself anything in particular, he simply liked travelling, mostly in the Far East. He had fetched up now, like some loose piece of human flotsam, in the notorious Chung King Mansions.

Chung King Mansions was studiously ignored by its immediate neighbours, who had been trying to have it closed down for years, without success. Its front steps were always occupied by quiet groups of ex-patriate Indian gentlemen, some wearing turbans, some not, discussing business with one another. Most of these gentlemen would thrust a card in your hand as you entered the building, which advertised one of the curry clubs or messes. Pornographic novels, wrapped in cellophane, were sold in the alleys running parallel to the steps.

Inside, the passageways darted left and right, and straight on, through an arcade of Indian food, clothing and spice shops. They did not improve even when you climbed the escalator, which had not moved an inch in many decades. All that happened was the lights grew dimmer as 25-watt bulbs replaced the florescent tubes.

It was a lively, bustling building, perfumed with joss sticks, herbs and spices, where the cockroaches swarmed and the feral cats hunted rats. The backpackers loved it because it was only a few dollars a night and provided tales for home. You could lose yourself very easily in its myriad corridors and Chandler was proud of the fact that he knew them well enough to guide newcomers to likely free beds.

Before landing in Hong Kong, Chandler had been around the world twice and had a suitable number of fairly harmless adventures under his belt to show for it.

In Thailand he had boarded the 6.30 pm train for Chang Mai in the north, just as it was leaving the station five minutes too early, only to find himself accosted by a mild gentleman with a small family who insisted, politely, that the seat Chandler was occupying was his seat. They compared tickets.

Chandler found that though the tickets bore the same seat numbers, he was actually on the 3.30 pm train which had been delayed a mere 3 hours. His own train would not leave (probably) until 9.30 pm. Two ticket inspectors in military uniforms, one large and portly, the other slim and unsmiling, were brought to bear on him. They both wore automatic pistols. They spoke to him in careful broken English and informed him he would have to get off the train.

It was black outside. Jungle swished by.

Chandler panicked and offered to purchase another ticket. The inspectors took pity on him in their unsmiling way. He found himself moved to another part of this half-mile long train at no extra cost. It was no less interesting in its choice of passengers, but it was without air conditioning. Chandler did not care so long as he was not asked to climb down the steps onto one of those deserted lightless platforms bearing names he could not pronounce.

On the return journey, after visiting opium-smoking Akka hill tribesmen and AK47-carrying Karen villagers, he found his seat taken by a young holy man. All young Thai youths do a year or so as a monk, usually travelling the country in their orange habit, and these conscripts to the priesthood were given right of free passage and sustenance on all public transport.

Chandler found to his consternation that he could not shift the youth, who ignored his ticket-flourishing and his pleas, and simply remained in the seat staring fixedly out of the window at the distant mountains. The ticket inspectors shrugged sympathetically. Chandler had to find his way along to the non-air conditioned compartments yet again.

Such were the tales Chandler had to tell.

In Bali he rented a jeep which broke down on the way to Ubud and was soon swarming with local people wielding spanners and screw drivers, all arguing with one another as to who had the right to 'fix it' for the tourist. He abandoned the vehicle and wrote to the hire firm from Australia, telling them where they could find their heap of junk.

In the Vietnam rice paddies he had unwittingly entered a private garden and sat on the grave of a grandfather, only to be chased away by an angry young man wielding a machete.

In Rarotonga he had lost himself in the island's interior and had survived by following a stream down to the shore.

In Sarawak he had played a round of golf with a man he later learned was the chief of police and only by the grace of God had not offered that gentleman a joint.

In Fiji he got coral poisoning from a tiny scratch on his ankle, spent all his money on medicine, and had to last three weeks on a diet of watermelons.

And so on, and so on, over many months and in such diverse places as Malaysia, Japan, Saba, Singapore, New Zealand, Australia, etc., etc.

He had then settled in Hong Kong for a few months, having received some money from his aunt. Hong Kong was electric with interest. Even at the lower end of the income bracket one could visit the street of caged birds, the jade market on the edge of Mong Kok, Happy Valley racecourse, Cat Street antique market, Sham Shui Po livestock market where baskets of live frogs and snakes could be bought, the Golden Arcade computer market where thirteen-year-old whiz-kids could knock you out a computer from spare parts within minutes, Wong Tai Sin temple—beauty in the middle of some scruffy tenement blocks, the extensive country parks in the New Territories—a thousand places.

If you had a lot of money, the choice was even wider. You could make a crossing to Portuguese Macau on the other side of the Pearl River. Macau was in elegant decay, which was never more evident than in the low-priced Bela Vista Hotel, famous for its under-the-carpets and behind-the-wainscot wildlife. If you went only for the day the thing to do was to have a dried-fish lunch and a few hours at the casinos.

Hong Kong was a gourmet's paradise, whose enormous number of restaurants doubled if you counted those on the outer islands like Lamma, Lantau and Chung Chau. Hong Kong was also a gambler's joy and a shopper's heaven. Chandler was no shopper, but he did enjoy food and he liked a flutter on the horses. In Hong Kong he indulged himself. He ate more fish, more shellfish, more pork and chicken than he had ever done in his life before, mostly at Sezchuan and Shanghai restaurants. And he went to the race courses at Shatin and Happy Valley.

Chandler was never very lucky at the races, so he always bet in small amounts on a number of horses in every race. In this way his interest was kept fired. He often won, but usually not enough to cover all his stakes. It did not matter. Chandler enjoyed a true Olympic Games' contestant's philosophy : the fun was in being there and taking part, not in the winning.

He was therefore surprised when a Chinese gentleman in the tote queue turned and said to him confidentially, 'You very lucky man!' and tapped him on the chest.

'I am?' Chandler said. 'Why.'

Again the Chinese man tapped him on the chest. 'You find this number, eh?'

Chandler then realised he was wearing a mock baseball shirt he had purchased in Singapore's Orchard Road. It was striped red and gold and had the number 888 printed on it.

'Eight is very lucky number for us Chinese people,' said the man, insisting on shaking his hand. 'In Canton we say, baat.'

'That's good,' replied Chandler, grinning, 'because my birthdate is 8.8.68.'

The other man's eyes widened. He grabbed Chandler's hand again and shook it profusely.

'You very, very lucky man. I myself was born on day 4 of July. Four is very unlucky number for Chinese people. Sei. Yat, yi, sam, sei . . . One, two, three, four. Sei unlucky number because it is same word as death.'

'Well, I'm not sure I believe . . . ' Chandler began, but the other man had not finished.

'You see power station near Kowloon harbour? It have five chimney. One of the chimney is false chimney. Not used for anything. Just fake. That so we do not have four chimney. Four very unlucky number.'

Chandler was fascinated by Cantonese speakers, who never used plurals or articles. In Cantonese there were no tenses either. When a Chinese person said in English, 'Me go race yesterday,' it was exactly what he would say in Cantonese, a very literal translation.

'I understand,' said Chandler.

They were coming up to the window now and at the last minute the Chinese man turned and thrust some dollars into Chandler's hand.

'You, please? You will buy my ticket for me. Any horse, but not number four. Please?'

The round face with the round John Lennon glasses bobbed in front of Chandler's eyes. Chandler saw that there were three thousand Hong Kong dollars in his hand. Three hundred pounds sterling.

'All right,' he said, 'but you mustn't blame me if you lose.'

Chandler went forward to the window and placed five bets for himself and one to win for the Chinese gentleman. Chandler rarely looked at form or odds. He placed the three thousand dollars on a horse called Golden Stranger, which seemed as appropriate as any other. Gold, he had heard, was also lucky.

'Martin Lau,' said the man, shaking his hand yet again. 'I am carpenter. Make table, chair, cabinet, make even coffin,' he laughed, seemingly embarrassed. 'Chinese man like to buy coffin and keep under bed for when die.'

'I have heard that. Shall we go up and watch the race?'

'Oh, yes. Let us go and win with our lucky ticket.'

Chandler's heart was in his mouth while the race was in progress, for Martin Lau was absolutely convinced he was going to win. It was the last race of the day so Chandler could not offer to make reparations if the man lost. Three hundred pounds must surely have been quite a sum for a carpenter, unless he owned his own business.

As it was, Chandler need not have worried. Martin Lau's horse won by a lip. Even while they waited for the photo, the race being so close, Martin Lau's confidence could not be suppressed. He was certain the horse had edged in front of its nearest rival. There was no doubt about it.

They both went together to collect their winnings, for Chandler had placed a small bet on the same horse. However, the inevitable happened. Martin Lau took him for a great meal at the Seoul Restaurant in Kowloon City, a Korean place where you cooked your own food at the table in between courses of fiery kimshi. Then Martin offered Chandler some of the money he had won.

'No, no, the meal is fine, very much appreciated,' said Chandler, 'but I can't take money.'

'I send you a present then,' cried the still delighted Martin Lau. 'I send it to Chung King Mansions. I not listen to you say no to this. You must take my gift. I send it next week. You very lucky for me. Very lucky.'

And the gift duly arrived, borne by two young Chinese youths in khaki shorts and pure white sleeveless vests. They had placed it where it still lay now. Chandler had lived with it, lived with the symbol of his own death, for three months.

Now it was time to confront it, or not, depending on his courage.

He closed the knife and picked up his backpack, then walked towards the doorway. On the threshold a thought came to him. What if there were a card inside? One of Martin Lau's cards? The coffin might be returned to him, having been left behind unopened by an ungrateful Englishman. Chandler winced at the thought of how he would look to this pleasant, well-meaning Hong Kong man. Was that the impression he wanted to leave?

He really had to open the package and take out anything which would allow the finder to trace the coffin back to Martin Lau.

Throwing down his backpack, Chandler took out his knife again and slit the cardboard box down its seams. He peeled back the edges. The contents were wrapped in bubbled plastic, no doubt to protect the finish on the wood. The shape still attested to the fact that it was a coffin. Chandler could think of no other piece of furniture which was long and boxy. It the width and depth were too small for a sideboard. It simply had to be a coffin.

Yet, when he finally took off the protective plastic, he saw that it was not a coffin after all. He was now glad, very glad, he had decided to look. The object was still strongly connected with mortality and the passing years. In fact there was a song about it and the death of an old man. But the delivery lads had not put it in its correct position. Chandler laughed. The object should have been placed up on its end, standing tall.

It was a beautiful grandfather clock.

SHOOT-OUT IN THE NEW TERRITORIES

Hong Kong's expatriate community was split into two main sets.

There was the 'upper' set, which consisted of the high ranks of the British armed forces, top judges, chairmen of banks and stockbroking houses, and other creatures of their kind. These would be in the governor's circle, going to dinner at the governor's house, and would rent or own apartments and houses in Pun Shan Kui or 'Midlevels' as the ex-pats called it. This exclusive set lived on Hong Kong Island, with addresses overlooking Central and the Botanical Gardens. They lived the high life in Hong Kong, but to be fair they were of that stratum of society who would have lived the high life anywhere they chose to settle, even their old homeland.

The lower set consisted of school teachers, young police inspectors, engineers for China Light and Power Company, long-staying servicemen, architects, speech therapists, educational psychologists and various clergy. This set, in scattered accommodation, lived almost as well as the upper set, having balls and dinners at the many officers' messes, dining out at the best restaurants—these being manifold in the Hong Kong of the 80's and 90's—and enjoying riotous evening junk parties sailing to and from the outer islands. They belonged to such organisations as the Royal Asiatic Society, the Natural History Society, and various exclusive clubs such as the Kowloon Cricket Club and the United Services Recreation Club.

Both these sets had some Chinese and other Indo-China peoples in their circle, but not very many. The Chinese themselves organised their own clubs (perhaps in retaliation) on similar lines. They, for the most part, were millionaires, multi-millionaires and billionaires. They drove Rolls Royces and Mercedes and thumbed their noses at the expat elite, having far more money than most of the colonials, and were able to nurse the knowledge that the westerners' party, however infuriatingly jolly, was on the wane. Time was on the side of the indigenous peoples, even though those peoples were for the most part just as foreign to Hong Kong soil as the descendents of the invaders.

This tale is about one of the lower expat set, an inspector in the police named John Speeks, who was 28 years of age, in good health, and fond of a pint of beer.

Much has been said in the past about minor corruption in the Hong Kong police. That bars such as Red Lips, off the Nathan Road and close to the notorious Chung King Mansions, where the painted ladies who serviced American Soldiers during the Vietnam war still plied a little of their old trade, remained open because blind eyes were purchased.

John Speeks, it has to be said, was not one of those who took bribes. If he did allow Red Lips a little slack, it was because the Chinese madam was putting her son through Cambridge University, and she would amuse him with quotes from Shakespeare and Milton.

Inspector Speeks was a clean, honest young man with a pretty wife who had nursing duties at Queen Elizabeth

Hospital. As a policeman he was considered tough and uncompromising. There was a chiselled edge to his soul. Even his wife was secretly afraid of that hard side of him, not because he would ever do anything to hurt her in any way, but in case she ever made a mistake. She always felt there would be no second chances with John.

The couple lived in a modest flat in Kowloon Tong and were Sunday-only members of Christ Church where the Reverend Jack Jones oversaw his multi-racial congregation.

John Speeks was one of the few policemen who was genuinely shocked when a verdict of suicide was pronounced over a colleague involved in a corruption case. The victim was found dead in his flat, three bullets in his chest and the door to his room locked from the outside. There were secrets wrapped like parcels and there were those who wanted the wrappings to remain.

John Speeks diligently fought great battles with the Chinese smugglers who plied their trade between China and Hong Kong, zooming over the water between in speed boats assisted by three or more high-powered outboards, even though the lines of the law on both sides of the border were blurred and sometimes ambiguous regarding smuggling. His own car had been stolen and later spotted by a friend, being driven in Canton by one of that town's respected officials.

John Speeks did not like the sleazy side of Hong Kong, nor did he enjoy arresting the many boat people who drifted into Hong Kong waters from Vietnam, to be put into holding camps until they could be sent back to their home country. However, though petty crime in public places—pick-pocketing, random violence, mugging—was not high, there was daily excitement to be had with the triads of Kowloon Walled City and with raiding gangsters from over the border in China proper. Brief exchanges of fire were reasonably common between the police and such criminals.

One hot and humid July morning Speeks had finished his breakfast and was walking around his flat calling, 'Lucy, where are you? Come out! I know you're hiding somewhere.'

Lucy was not his wife, who was on duty at the hospital and whose name was Sally, but their flat cat. John did not understand Lucy at all. She frustrated him with her nervousness and strange antics. Lucy was like many things in Hong Kong, she was a complete enigma to John, who liked things clear and unambiguous. He did not understand why half the world chose to live their lives with muddled thinking. Straight, sensible ways were necessary. Anything else was simply confusing.

Flat cats in Hong Kong never left their owners' apartments. In a city where six million people live in cramped conditions, surrounded by fast roads, it was not wise to let cats roam the neighbourhood. Lucy would have lived about five minutes had she left the security of her home. However, like many of her kind, she was totally neurotic, and was forever searching for smaller places in which to hide. If there was an open cupboard she would crawl in and crouch in a corner. If there was a box in that cupboard, she would sneak into the box. If there was an item of clothing in the box, she would hide underneath it.

Sometimes Lucy would refuse to leave her latest security box and enjoyed periods of being pulled around the flat by a piece of string secured to the cardboard. To Speeks this behaviour was totally incomprehensible and unacceptable. It made him angry and edgy, just to have Lucy around. He believed himself to be a strong, hard man, able to cope firmly and surely with any crises or duty, but he detested blurred edges.

John saw that the wardrobe door in the bedroom was partly open. He opened it fully. Inside the cupboard was always lit with a 25 watt bulb to keep fungus from growing on their clothes in the humid conditions. There he discovered Lucy crouched amongst the shoes at the bottom. She stared at him with that half-frightened, pathetic look of hers.

He said to her helplessly, 'Don't you want any food this morning? Your milk is out.'

Lucy glared at him, stretched, peered suspiciously out into the bedroom, then made a quick dash to the kitchen to wolf down her chopped liver. John sighed. Why could she not have simply walked to the kitchen, like any sane British cat? This darting from one dark place to another frayed his nerves.

John put on his peaked cap, and then went to the front door and left the flat. He drove towards Kowloon police station. When he was halfway there he received a call on his radio to say that a robbery was in progress in Mong Kok. Four gangsters, it was thought from the mainland, were holding up a gold shop. They had already shot a customer and one Chinese constable who had run to the scene with a colleague.

Gold shops, where they sold precious metals, jade and jewelry, were prime targets for mainland gangsters.

At that moment cars flashed past him going towards Lion Rock Tunnel. It was a second or two before John realised that it was the gangsters being chased by two police cars. He did an illegal U-turn on the Waterloo Road and sped after the three cars, his heart pounding in his chest.

The chase went up through the New Territories, past Sha Tin and Tai Po, to a country house in a village outside Fanling, still inside the New Territories. For once, and it was unusual, the gangsters had not escaped back over the border into China. Now they were trapped inside a lone house, presumably their hideout before the robbery. They were well armed and a serious shoot-out began between them and the police. John was trying to remember all the right procedures in such a confrontation, at the same time as firing his revolver with a trembling hand.

A senior police official was soon on the scene, followed by a local TV news crew and South China Morning Post reporters. Soon the shoot-out was being broadcast live over Hong Kong TV stations. Senior policemen were concerned about 'doing things properly' in front of such a huge audience. It was a bit like tee-ing off at golf with Lee Travino and Gary Player watching from the club house. The presence of the cameras made everyone nervous.

Just after noon one of the gangsters was shot in the head and fell through an upstairs window to the yard below. There was great excitement amongst observers and participators alike, with the rest of the gangsters cursing in shrill Cantonese voices the police and all who supported them. Shortly after this a second gangster was hit, staggered from through the front door, and was cut down by hail of fire from without. This brought more protests from the two men who remained inside, but who still refused to give themselves up to the police.

The afternoon wore on with sporadic shots being exchanged, but no real damage done to either side. John could not understand why the gangsters were so obstinate. They were bottled up, enclosed in a house from which there was no escape, and if they remained there they would be eventually shot. The mindset of the Asian criminal mystified him almost as much as Lucy's mindset. Any sane Western crooks would have thrown up their arms hours ago, having assessed their chances of escape at nil, and decided that life was sweeter than death. These men were not even trying to bargain their way out.

Round early evening, when the sun was on its way down, one of the gangsters cried out. John's Cantonese was not good enough to understand the harsh request, but a Chinese sergeant translated for him.

'He wants to meet with us.'

'What? What do you mean?'

'He say he meet halfway to the house, sir. One man come out from here, and he will come from the house. He want to talk.'

John's boss asked him for his opinion. John said he thought it was a trick. His boss thanked him for the opinion, but then made up his mind that they would accommodate the gangster, with one small change. John would be sent forward to converse with the man, but would take Sergeant Cheung with him, to act as an interpreter. This was conveyed to the man in the house and a few moments later the crook appeared in the doorway, his hands behind his head. He seemed to be unarmed.

'Go ahead, Speeks,' said his boss. 'The field is all yours. Don't be a hero in front of the cameras. Just remember your training and act with sense and caution.'

'Yes, sir,' replied John, thinking the whole exercise a bad deal. 'I'll do my best.'

He and Sergeant Cheung walked slowly forwards. He whispered indiscreetly to his companion, 'I feel like I've got a bag full of lead fishing weights in my gut.' Sergeant Cheung, his eyes on the windows of the house where the fourth gangster lurked, murmured, 'Me too, sir. He could shoot both of us dead before we get halfway to house.'

The gangster who had walked out of the house stood quietly waiting for them on a piece of waste ground. He was a small man with glinting eyes. When they got closer to him Speeks could smell the man's rank sweat. He too was sweating profusely and wondered if he smelled as bad. Then the man opened his mouth to grin and revealed several gold teeth. His hands were still behind his head, his thin arms forming two sharp, acute triangles.

The man spoke quickly in heavy Gwong Dong Wa—Cantonese—and Sergeant Cheung said, 'He wants to talk terms.'

'Tell him there are no terms. He is under arrest for murder and armed robbery. I have no power to bargain otherwise.'

The gangster looked distressed when this information was conveyed to him and hung his head in a gesture of shame. He spoke again, saying that he did not want to lose face in front of his companion in the house. If the inspector was going to handcuff him, then please do it without any fuss or show.

John stepped forward, reaching for the handcuffs on his belt, when suddenly the gangster sprang at him. Before John had time to do anything more there was a noose of cord around his neck. The loose end of the cord was attached to the pin of a grenade, held in the gangster's hand. These items had been hidden behind the gangster's neck, held in the cup formed by his linked hands.

In that second John knew he was a hostage. If he jerked away he would set off the grenade, which would either blow up in the gangster's grip, or be thrown by that man at John and Sergeant Cheung. Either way there was a good chance that he and Cheung would die with the gangster.

It was a peculiar situation. The gangster was obviously willing to risk his life in order to obtain a hostage. However, it was clear he had not planned the situation very well. It was he who still had the grenade on his person, not one of his hostages. His scheme had been well executed but was warped. It would have been better to have made a pendant of the cord and grenade, thrown the noose over the policeman's head and tightened it, leaving a separate piece of cord tied to the grenade's pin. In this way he would have protected himself against being shot, but left with no choice but to pull the pin, he could have done so and run, leaving the policeman with the grenade pendant.

John was dreadfully upset with his captor, not only because he had tricked him, but because he had not worked out his trick thoroughly. He had not thought things through carefully, the way John would have done. It was a botched job. It was all very upsetting for a police officer who believed in logic and thought everyone else should pay homage to it too.

Cheung was a spontaneous and impulsive young man. Once he had recovered from his shock, he reacted with great swiftness.

He cried, 'Look out, sir!' and drew his revolver to shoot the gangster in the chest at point blank range.

The man fell, fatally wounded, wrenching the pin out of the grenade in the process. The lethal bomb remained in the gangster's death grip. John was terrified. He ran for about five paces then threw himself to the earth, finding a small hollow in the waste ground. Sergeant Cheung was halfway to joining him when the grenade exploded.

The sound was absolutely deafening. John's head jangled, the noise numbing his brain.

When he was able to sit up, he found himself surrounded by policemen. The last crook had surrendered immediately. Someone was inspecting John for wounds, asking him if he was hit anywhere. They could see no signs of blood.

'I—I think I'm fine,' he said, still a little stunned. 'What about Sergeant Cheung?'

'Wounded in the shoulder. Hit by some small pieces of shrapnel. But he should be okay.'

'Good, good,' murmured John, his head only just beginning to clear. 'I'm all right. I'm fine.'

The media were now clustered round him, as his boss slapped him on the back.

'Well done, Speeks. Unusual situation. We'll talk about it later . . .'

His boss then turned to the media, telling them that Speeks was a tough man, one of the toughest policemen in Hong Kong, and that he had proved himself a hero today, along with Sergeant Cheung of course. He said he was proud of both policemen, and the constable who had been first on the scene in Mong Kok. All his men had acted in the best principles of the Hong Kong police, and that there would probably be awards.

John Speeks wanted to talk to someone, tell them how the gangster had fouled up by not thinking things out in a straight-forward and logical fashion. It irked and frustrated him when his boss told him he must not converse with the media. He tried to speak with colleagues but most of them were in a state of unnatural excitement and were talking rapidly, sometimes without a lot of sense.

Shoot-outs of such a prolonged intense nature were unusual and this one had drained their reserves. A few quick shots exchanged in a street was the most any of them had experienced before today. The majority of them had never had to draw their revolvers beyond the practice range. They would listen later, in a bar, or at a social gathering, but tonight they were not completely of this world.

John went back to his own flat, refusing any assistance from medical staff sent from Tai Po hospital.

Sally came home in a state. She had seen much of the shoot-out on television at the hospital. She had feared for her husband's life, had later been assured he was alive and unharmed, and she wanted to hold him. Sally felt he would try to shut her out of this thing if she did not get to him quickly and soften his edges before they closed down on the outside world.

'Darling?' she called, on entering the flat. 'I'm home—I saw it—it must have been awful—you were terribly brave—I was so scared—and proud—oh, where are you . . . ?'

John rarely spoke to her about his work. He kept things to himself and she never knew how safe he was when on duty. For all she knew he could have been through a dozen such occurrences. She was aware he kept things like that from her, to protect her, and normally she would not ask. But this was different. She had seen it and they had to talk about it.

She went from room to room, trying, unsuccessfully, to locate him, then decided he must have gone out. He was probably in a bar somewhere with his cronies. It made her angry that he had not come to her first, for she had suffered too. She wanted to comfort him, even if he did not require it. Such a thing would help sooth her troubled nerves. He might react to such an incident with flinty indifference, but she could not.

Sally gave up calling and went looking for Lucy. After a short search she opened the wardrobe door. Lucy was there, curled amongst the shoes. The cat's green eyes shone in the light from the dim bulb. Sally was about to walk away, to leave Lucy some space, when she suddenly saw her husband.

John was crouched in the far corner of the cupboard.

TYPHOON

Two strong women were about to engage in a short sharp war against each other.

One of these Amazon warriors was called Fiona. Fiona was a typhoon. She had just destroyed the Philippines and was now on her way to wreak havoc amongst the turrets and towers of Hong Kong.

Fiona's opponent was a beautiful young woman by the name of Elizabeth, an expat daughter of expat parents. Elizabeth was about to be married and had recognised signs of those inevitable last-minute jitters in Ralph, her husband-to-be, and was damned if she was going to change her plans—plans that had been long months in the making—for something as insubstantial as a wind, no matter how big.

Elizabeth was aware, through the little icons displayed on the television, that Typhoon Fiona was still increasing in strength. Yesterday the warning from the Hong Kong Meteorological Office had been Number 3. Now it had jumped to Number 8 SE and looked likely to become 9 before the afternoon.

'You can blow as hard as you like, my girl,' said Elizabeth, 'you're up against me now!'

Despite her bravado Elizabeth was anxious, though not alarmed by this threat to the day's proceedings. As a Hong Kong 'Belonger', born and bred in the colony, she was used to surmounting those barriers which the orient could throw in the way of newcomers. Mysteries of the East were easily unravelled by Elizabeth. She saw through the inscrutable to read the secrets beneath. She was also, like most Hong Kong expats, a well-travelled woman. Her speciality was staying at famous oriental hotels that were in a state of elegant decay: the magnificent Kuala Lumpur Railway Station Hotel, its walls whiter than the icing on a wedding cake and its architecture grander than a sultan's palace; the sumptuous Bela Vista in Macau, which had threadbare carpets of Chinese silk and aristocratic mice in the wainscot; that unique and legendary edifice built by a Frenchman in the 1800s, the Continental in Saigon, haunt of war correspondents during the 1960s.

Today the 9th September, 1986, I am getting married.

Another woman, in her situation, might have qualified that statement with a perhaps, but Elizabeth was a resolute woman. Indeed, all other couples, according to the local radio, had postponed their weddings. She and Ralph were the only pair who refused to allow Fiona to come between them. Actually, Ralph would have permitted a delay, if Elizabeth had shown any weakness, which she was not prepared to do. This was her day, not that of some screaming bitch full of nothing but puff and fury. Let Fiona cancel her appointment. It was to be the entrance of the Queen of Sheba, not some hussy hurricane.

The truth was, Elizabeth told herself as she applied her lipstick, it was only today that she felt herself to be totally in control at last. As with many romances there had been rifts and chasms to cross. She recalled one dangerous split, during which she had played the regal don't-care, blowing 2000 dollars on an off-the-shoulder exclusive gown, and dancing all night with British Captains of Gurkha regiments at their Summer Ball. Ralph was there too of course, or she wouldn't have bothered going. She made sure she was looking her beautiful best and had laughed a lot at army jokes. Ralph had been re-captivated sometime during the night, asking her to come back to him over the survivors' Champagne breakfast provided for those who were still there at dawn.

Elizabeth's dogged determination, and it has to be said, very real love for her fiancé, had brought them both within an hour of standing before the altar and taking their vows. She wasn't going to give ground now, especially not to a weather chart.

It has to be said Typhoon Fiona was formidable. She had personally killed over a thousand people on her way through the Philippines. She had snaked across the China Sea, sometimes threatening Macao, sometimes Shanghai, and finally settled on the middle course, for Hong Kong. It simply remained for the people of Hong Kong to discover how fierce Fiona would become. Already her winds were over 180 kilometres per hour, with lashing, driving rains. Aircraft had long since ceased landing at or taking off from Kai Tak Airport. The boat people in Aberdeen Harbour were safely housed on the island. Road traffic was virtually at a standstill.

So, Elizabeth was concerned—not dismayed, merely a little worried—though none of the consternation she felt inside showed on her face. Outwardly, she was calm, completely in control, and had been handing out matter-of-fact commands to her Filipino maid, mother and bridegroom with all the sureness and confidence of one who has seen into the future and knows that all will be well. Typhoons were part of ordinary life, arriving annually, like the cold winds from the heart of the Chinese continent at New Year, and the sweltering, bloody months between winters so humid that documents warped, photos corrugated and untended clothes grew gardens of mildew.

Outside the building, the winds screeched through wires, screamed through narrow cracks, wailed around corners. Fiona's forewinds were banshees, harbingers of death, and their terrible cries were loud and unremitting.

'Your beautiful dress, missy,' said Ada in despair, 'it will get wet and dirty in all this rain.'

Elizabeth paused in her reflections and glanced first at her maid, then at the scything rain that slashed at the bedroom windows of the Kowloon apartment, and then finally down at the extravagantly expensive wedding dress which had transformed her from the daily Elizabeth into the Empress Elizabeth. Elizabeth had a faintly Latin beauty about her, which she knowingly emphasised with a strong eyebrow pencil and swept-back dark hair.

Elizabeth reached forward and took a cigarette from the silver box on the dresser, lit it with the gold lighter Ralph had given her, and made one of her characteristically swift and sensible decisions.

'Ada, fetch me that polythene bag which the new mattress was wrapped in.'

'Missy?'

Elizabeth blew smoke at the mirror in front of her.

'The new king-sized mattress, Ada. It came yesterday, remember? It was wrapped in polythene.'

The Filipina's eyes widened with comprehension.

'Oh, yes.'

The maid ran from the room.

'It'll look like a giant condom,' Elizabeth muttered, 'but what the hell?'

Elizabeth stared at the face of her double in the mirror and decided they both needed to shorten their arched eyebrows by just the tiniest of fractions. Once she had carried out this task she searched the top left drawer of the dresser for the scissors with which she would cut two holes for her legs in the bottom corners of the polythene mattress cover. Through these holes she would put her not unshapely legs before stepping out into the rain. An umbrella to protect her head and shoulders, her body would be encased in polythene, covering the precious dress, which could be drawn up almost to her thighs without creasing it too much. It was crushed silk and could bear a little rough handling.

Since she and Ralph were the only pair, out of four couples, brave enough to go through with her wedding during Typhoon Fiona there would without doubt be a photo of her, almost-thighs and all, in the South China Morning Post, along with a caption praising her ingenuity. The photo would do her no real harm. They were good legs, after all, and it was an unassailable opportunity to show them off. The women would twitch with envy and the men would have longing and deliciously unsavoury thoughts about a white-tulip bride who had innocently bared her long legs.

'Read 'em and weep,' she murmured to herself with satisfaction, and blew another stream of smoke at her doppelgänger.

In the next room a tall, good-looking young man was pacing the floor dressed in an immaculate uniform made for him by Sam's Taylor, of Burlington Arcade off the Nathan Road, Kowloon, outfitter to visiting princes and pop stars, whose photographs adorned his window. The young man's name was Ralph Winston, a young army major in the education corps, keen-eyed and tanned the colour of a copper kettle drum by the suns of Muscat and Oman, Brunei and Hong Kong. His brown leather boots, polished to mirrors, were wearing out the floor in the adjoining room where he had been told to remain until his bride was ready to leave. The weather had forced convention into a corner. The bride and groom were to travel in the same vehicle to the church. The idea being that the fewer vehicles on the road the better. The rest of Hong Kong, apart from a courageous two-thirds of the original number of wedding guests, were already battened down in their apartments, awaiting with trepidation the onslaught of the Number 10—hurricane force winds—and its attendant destruction.

Elizabeth and Ralph were to be married in a small chapel on Hong Kong Island, on the other side of the harbour from Kowloon, some three miles away. Ralph, who had a sudden desperate need to stamp his own mark on a ceremony over which he had gradually been losing control, had chosen the chapel at whim, when they had been church-crawling, looking for a suitable wedding venue and vicar.

'I like the sheep in the stained glass windows,' he had told Elizabeth stubbornly. 'I want the wedding here.'

She had argued but he had eventually got his own way. He could be remarkably obdurate sometimes, even against such impossible odds as Elizabeth. The fact that he had no real preference made his small victory even sweeter.

One third of the guests, including the original Best Man, had cried off. Ralph had quickly chosen a new Best Man from amongst the more stalwart guests. However, privately Ralph himself wondered what he was getting into, marrying this woman of iron will. His own will had never been particularly metallic. It was made of a more flexible material and was not above compromise—when it was permitted to bend. Privately he thought an expedition to a distant church in a typhoon a dangerous, possibly a crazy notion.

Ralph Winston was sincerely in love with Elizabeth. No doubts there. The doubts were concerning the sacred and everlasting institution of holy wedlock.

'I mean,' said Ralph to himself, 'what's that word lock doing there in the first place, attached to wed. Has the sound of dungeons and shackles about it! Wedlock. Dammit, do

I want to be incarcerated in this jail they call marriage? I mean—dammit . . . '

The last minute nerves were jangling like chains.

And what was God trying to tell him by sending this Other Woman to attempt intervention? Stop the ceremony? Fiona had not been invited: she had gate-crashed.

'It's sign,' he told himself, unhappily. 'It's a sign. One should obey warnings and portents, and that sort of thing. Look what happens when you don't! Poor old Caesar, stabbed to death on the steps of—of his own parliament building . . . ' (Ralph's Shakespeare was scratchy at best). '. . . beware the Ides of September, or whenever.'

He stared through the glass-panelled balcony doors at the raging storm beyond, listening to its eerie screaming, wishing he could change his mind about the location of the ceremony. There were much closer churches than the one he had picked, but it was too late to change now. For one thing he had been too firm in his choice and for another the arrangements were all made, there was no altering them now.

There were tree branches swirling in the air after having been ripped bodily from their trunks. There were cardboard boxes, feral cats, bamboo washing poles, clothes, metal cans, and many other objects hurtling through the atmosphere beyond the windows. On receiving the Number 8 signal the majority of the 6 million inhabitants of Hong Kong would have removed all plant pots and chairs from their balconies, rolled up their carpets, placed their furniture in the middle of their apartments and taped their windows to minimise the catastrophic effect of flying glass. They would then have prepared a spot for the family somewhere away from air conditioning units, which were likely to be blown inwards, often causing almost as much damage as a shell fired from an artillery piece.

Elizabeth had allowed none of this to take place in her apartment, for that would have been conceding something to

Fiona, whom she was going to defeat. come what may. Showing contempt for Fiona's destructive force served to play down the typhoon's importance on this, Elizabeth's day. Elizabeth would not allow any rival to steal limelight on the occasion which belonged to her, and her alone.

The phone rang, jerking Ralph out of his reverie.

He picked up the receiver and said. 'Hello?'

At that moment Elizabeth's mother, frowning heavily. entered the room. Ralph put his hand over the mouthpiece of the phone and said, 'It's Father Devlin,' which caused the frown on Doris's brow to deepen even further.

Ralph said, 'He wants to know if he should come here, instead. and perform the marriage ceremony in the apartment?'

With his hand still over the telephone mouthpiece, Ralph stared at his future mother-in-law. The looks they exchanged in silence were utterly comprehensible to both, since they signalled identical information. They each knew the answer to the question without consulting Elizabeth.

Ralph took away his hand, sighed heavily so that Father Devlin should know his true feelings, and said, 'It's very kind of you to try to save us the trouble Father, but we feel that we must have a church ceremony. A wedding here at the apartment would not be the same.'

Ralph replaced the phone gently on its cradle and Doris left the room, her heels clacking on the parquet tiles.

As a wedding guest, stepping out into the driving rain, I looked in vain for an ancient mariner to grasp my arm in a claw-like grip and keep me there with some wild tale about a sea voyage. until the wedding was over. There was no wizened elder in sight. The streets were empty of people of any age. I climbed aboard the army coach with a feeling of inevitability in my chest. We were all going to have to go through with this ceremony towards which Elizabeth, niece of the Commanding Officer of Kowloon Barracks, had been steering the whole of expatriate and army society since the announcement of her engagement.

The colonel himself had been called away, to an emergency conference on the colony, in England. He must have climbed aboard the plane taking him back to the UK with a great deal of relief, having stated that he would not hear of a delay to the wedding simply because of his absence. The plans were to go ahead without him.

As the Colonel's niece, Elizabeth was a powerful woman, hence my presence at a wedding, otherwise I would have cried off like most of the civilians. As the Colonel's adjutant I was his stand-in. It would have been impossible for me not to attend. The rest of the wedding guests were made up of army officers and their families, some of whom welcomed a bit of excitement and some of whom felt that since the C.O.'s adjutant was going, they would risk it too.

We were all travelling together in one coach to the small church in Central. At least there would be no traffic snarl-ups at the entrance to the cross harbour tunnel when we drove to the island. Normally it was a free-for-all and added at least thirty minutes to any journey.

I nodded to the Chinese corporal sitting in the driver's seat of the coach. He looked quite unhappy and I couldn't blame him. Out of all of us he was perhaps the only one present who had no choice in the matter at all. He was there by command: orders were orders. The coach itself was rocking back and forth violently under the onslaught of gusts of wind, but the occupants, decked out in various pieces of rainwear, seemed reasonably cheerful.

'Everybody here?' I called, rather pointlessly.

Captain Chuck Wilson, shouted, 'Everyone who's going to be. Come on, let's get this show on the road.'

Chuck was a Gurkha officer, famous for once having telephoned a Welsh regiment and requested the use of their regimental mascot, a billy goat by the name of Taffy. 'Just for tomorrow.' Chuck had told the Welsh, 'it's the Gurkha festival of Divali, you see.' The Welsh officers were furious with him, once they learned that Divali was when the Gurkhas traditionally beheaded sacrificial goats.

'We've got to wait for the bride's car,' I said, 'then we'll follow on after.'

After ten minutes, during which someone tried unsuccessfully to start up a sing-song, the wedding car appeared. One of the decorative ribbons had been torn off already and the other snaked like a kite's tail from the front of the Rolls. Our driver hastily pulled out behind the passing vehicle and we had begun our three mile journey.

'Wonderful,' muttered a lieutenant's wife, sitting opposite me.

The Rolls at first tried to travel reasonably fast, and we did likewise, but the huge pools of water in the empty streets made high speeds dangerous. While we were driving down the Waterloo Road, the car suddenly aqua-planed in front of us, its wheels buoyed by wind and water. A precious hubcap was scraped against the central reservation barrier, when the car's driver lost control of the steering, and sparks streamed from the point of contact.

After this, the Rolls slowed to around twenty mph.

Side winds lashed at the coach causing us to skid every so often and I noticed that the coach driver's face was set in that oriental fixed stare which meant he had consigned his soul to Fate and anything that happened was in no way his responsibility. So far as he was concerned there was no free will left in him and events were now controlled by the gods.

During our slow progress along the Waterloo Road from Kowloon Tong we had to divert several times, to small side-streets, in order to avoid obstacles blocking the main highway. The Rolls seemed to be ignoring no entry signs, so we did the same, travelling in the wrong direction down one-way streets. I had to order the corporal driver to break the law, otherwise he would have halted the bus and refused to proceed any further.

The rain was hard and white, hissing in huge dense clouds which sometimes reduced visibility to several feet. We passed Christ Church Kowloon, just half a mile from the barracks. I understood that Ralph had specifically requested the chapel on Hong Kong Island, and Elizabeth staunchly supported this desire. A great pity, for it would have saved us a terrible journey into the unknown had they been prepared to compromise.

When we reached Mong Kok, the most populated area of the earth, we entered the land of tall buildings. At this point we went up on to flyovers. Tremendous gusts of wind came from between the skyscrapers. They were appallingly savage. They screamed at us in a dark, unknown language, furious that we had dared to venture out while they were in town. Even though the driver had taken to using the centre of the road we were still blown towards the adjacent parapets, alternately, as the winds came first from one side, then the other.

Every so often the car in front swerved to avoid some object in the road and the coach of course followed suit.

Several times we went over the top of something—an abandoned motorscooter, a bag of rubbish—when we were not quick enough to take avoiding action. In consequence, passengers of the coach were tossed upwards, as well as sideways, and people had stopped making jokes, preferring to concentrate instead on retaining their grip on the edges of the seats.

It was impossible to remain dry, even inside the coach, for water was forced through every tiny crevice, every fissure, in the vehicle: around the windows, the doorway, through the front screen. A fine spray, like the most delicate of Irish drizzles, filled the interior of the bus, gradually settling and soaking everyone inside, even those with rainwear.

The Rolls in front, less subject to the winds than the high-sided coach, bore resolutely on, seemingly ignoring the wails and howls of the inclement animalistic weather. I imagined the car being powered, not by a Rolls Royce engine, but by Elizabeth's will alone, for it seemed invincible. We in the coach were surviving by a series of miracles, while the car seemed invulnerable to everything that was thrown at it by Fiona, resisting and repelling, rather than absorbing the blows.

As we continued into and along the Princess Margaret Road, I saw a whole network of bamboo scaffolding being torn away from the side of a half-built skyscraper. Something flew from the sill of the building and struck the roof of the coach, causing a bump to appear in the coach ceiling. Thirty pairs of eyes stared at the lump for a moment, then immediately turned their attention to the driver, who cried out in alarm as the windscreen wipers were ripped away from the windscreen before his very nose. The rain continued to pelt at the glass, making it impossible to see anything except the distorted shape of the Rolls in front, as it swept onto the Hong Chung Road and down towards the tunnel.

'Can't see, Sir,' cried the driver.

At any moment I expected him to let go of the steering wheel, consign his soul to the Otherworld, and bury his face in his hands. However, he bravely stuck to his post, steering blindly into the white, needle-sharp rain that attacked his windscreen, seemingly oblivious of the banshee howling of Elizabeth's adversary.

'Keep going, corporal,' I said in my calmest voice. 'We'll be inside the tunnel in a moment.'

The harbour itself was in turmoil and I noticed junks and cargo ships alike being tossed around on monstrous waves. The Star Ferries had stopped running when the Number 3 had been hoisted of course, but they were still there, moored to their jetties on both sides of the harbour. On the island side I could see the tall hotels swaying, sometimes a few feet at their tips, backwards and forwards in the typhoon. Tourists trapped inside them would be wishing they had gone to Spain instead.

We got through the tunnel quickly, the usual bottleneck being free of traffic. No one was really in the mood to appreciate it though, since we had still a third of the journey to go, once we reached the island. We whipped into the semi-darkness of the interior, after the Rolls, glad to be in the safe womb of Mother Earth for a few minutes.

On the other side of the tunnel, we emerged into the mêlée again. The air was full of unidentifiable flying objects, which struck the coach on all sides. Fortunately the windows were protected by wire netting—anti-grenade screens—so nothing broke except one or two spirits. To the right and below us I could see sampans and junks crowded into a typhoon shelter close to the harbour wall, their rigging and stays whipping invisible demons with a fury surely unmatched by any supernatural forces. We swept on, protected a little from the sideswiping winds and rain on this side by the clusters of tall thick buildings and the bridge-work between them which allowed for no narrow passages of air. Once again we took to the airways of the flyovers, trusting our souls to the Lord in our desperate voyage through Fiona, as she screamed around the corners of our vehicle.

I staggered along the aisle of the bus as a sailor might down the gangway of a ship in a storm.

'Nearly there, everyone,' I said. 'Almost made it. Just another half-mile. Well done. No panicking, was there? Creditable show everybody.'

The white faces, white knuckles, belied the last two sentences, but no one was going to argue with me.

Finally, we drew up outside the church, the rain still furiously lashing at our nearside windows, but curiously less potent than when we had started out. The driver pulled on the handbrake and gave out a little sigh. He looked soaked in sweat and his eyes gleamed with an unusual light. I smiled at him, weakly I think, and he returned this in kind. I believe at that second he wished all gweilos in hell and I can't say I blamed him for that. The bus still swayed and rocked, but we were safe, for the moment.

Outside, the bride was leaving the Rolls, which had been parked under the building overhang. She was sheathed in a glistening polythene bag from which her shapely legs protruded. Ralph was directly behind her, his eyes fixed to those flashing white thighs. Lord knows what he was thinking at that precise moment.

Just then the bridegroom glanced up at me, as I peered through the window, and there was something in his eyes which sent a jolt through me. There was a kind of resolution there. not too difficult to define. It was the sort of determination I had seen in men who had been through a hellish battle and had come out unscathed but positive of one thing, that they were going to get out of the army as soon as possible. Instantly I knew we were going to have trouble inside the church, with at least one of the two main participants in this marriage.

Once within the church walls, we adjusted our wet clothes and emptied our soggy shoes while congratulating each other on our courage. The roof to the church was leaking, moisture-filled wind was whistling like steam between the leaded joins of windows, and the rattling doors needed two strong men to open them against the draught. There was a layer of rainwater on the floor. One window, covered in pictures of distorted sheep, bulged inwards as if about to burst.

Little we cared! Here we were, by royal command, and we had made it!

'An adventure to tell the C.O. about, eh David?' murmured Chuck Wilson. 'At least it's all going through.'

'Rather,' I acknowledged, 'providing it does go through.'

Chuck frowned and glanced in the same direction in which I was looking. The bridegroom was coming towards me, with the Best Man in tow. There was a sickly smile on the groom's face.

* * *

Ralph had not enjoyed the car ride to the church. There had been times during the journey when he had been sure they were all going to die. In fact it had not been a journey, it had been an odyssey. The Rolls had seemed so vulnerable. Buffeted by the winds, lashed by the rains, the vehicle had jumped and skipped its way to its destination. Ralph had been too frightened to talk very much on the way over and had simply answered people in grunts.

Having survived and cheated the gods of his death Ralph was determined that the life he had saved would remain a single one. Had the ride been a gentle one along flowering English country lanes, past breeze-blown hedges in June, towards a peaceful village church, Ralph's last minute worries might have been quietened and put to rest. But the flight through wild chaos had completely unnerved him. Fiona's fury had convinced him that he was not the marrying kind.

'Standish,' said Ralph, addressing the Colonel's adjutant. 'I'm ducking out. You'll have to tell the bride I can't go through with it.'

Ralph's tone was jocular, for the only way he could deal with unpleasant tasks was to inject humour into them, but he let Standish see by his eyes that he was serious. He clasped his hands behind his back and widened his smile as he waited for the Standish's answer. Standish was only a captain and Ralph expected him to do as he was told.

Standish smiled too, but there was no merriment in his eyes. It was the fixed grin of a corpse.

Ralph realised that Standish was no fool and would probably recognise his hysteria for what it was, no matter how deeply it was buried. They did not know each other well, being from different regiments, but army men could sense battle fright in each other. Ralph was past caring about things like that though: he did not care how transparent he was.

'Me?' laughed the adjutant. 'You've got a bloody cheek. She'd eat me alive. Come on, everyone feels like this at the last minute. Did myself, dammit. Doesn't mean anything.'

Ralph faltered before this unexpected refusal but maintained his shallow effort at kidding. He turned to his friend.

'Well, what about you, Chuck?' he asked. 'Will you save me from a fate worse than death?'

Chuck appeared to understand what was going on too.

'No chance, sunshine. Elizabeth, well, she'd skin me alive. I like my skin, old son. She's your girl. Aren't you fond of her?'

Ralph snapped. 'Of course I'm fond of her—I love the bloody woman to bits. But what's that got to do with marriage?'

Ralph turned to his Best Man, who had already raised his hands in self defence.

'Nor me,' the Best Man laughed. 'Personally I think she's a very lovely girl . . . '

'Well, you marry her then.'

'She doesn't want me—she wants you.'

'Fine,' growled Ralph, 'Looks like I'll have to go through with it, unless I jilt her at the altar, doesn't it? Thanks a bloody lot, the whole pack of you. Join the army and make good comrades. Ha!'

Ralph strode from the group towards the back of the church, where he lit a cigarette with trembling hands and tried to gather himself together. He told himself he had been in worse situations, though he couldn't recall any just at that moment. He knew one thing, he wasn't just going go meekly like one of those lambs in the church window. He'd walked away from her before and he could do it again, wedding or no wedding. Elizabeth was used to having her way, but he, Ralph, had shown her more than once that he was no weakling.

Before he was halfway through his smoke, he heard the

music—Handel's Arrival of the Queen of Sheba—and knew she was on her way down the aisle. He trod on the cigarette butt quickly and made his way to the altar, where the Best Man was already standing, waiting, looking anxious. Ralph could not let Elizabeth reach the altar and find him missing. If he was going to escape this marriage thing (who invented it anyway?) it would have to be a last minute effort.

Ralph was after all a spontaneous creature, when it came down to it, and nothing threw the opposition more effectively than unpredictable behaviour. She thought him soft and malleable, but in fact he could be hard and unbending when it became absolutely necessary, when survival was at stake. His battle over the sheep had proved that.

How about after 'Do you take this woman . . . ?' a stunning 'I'm sorry, I don't' and then a swift retreat? No, that would be too crass. Perhaps a quiet word with the Elizabeth and the priest, right there before the altar, would be best?

When she was about halfway down the aisle Elizabeth saw Ralph slip between some empty pews and join the Best Man at the altar. She wondered what he had been doing, but guessed he was nervous and had gone for a cigarette. When she actually reached him, the smell on his breath confirmed her assumption. The panic in his eyes was so vivid she smiled in an attempt to calm him. Prenuptial nerves. He was thinking about losing his Freedom. Elizabeth was wise enough to recognise these surface signs and knew them for what they were: evanescent, transient, fleeting feelings that she had suppressed in herself, but which were running riot in the breast of her intended.

Ralph did not look at her, even when she moved close enough to his side to touch him with her dress. She touched his hand with her fingers, lightly, making sure he was actually there, then congratulated herself inwardly. After all, she had insisted there was no danger in venturing out into Fiona's blast and she had been right. Everyone had arrived safely at the church, Fiona was on the wane, and the wedding was about to begin. Elizabeth had almost conquered the Big Wind that frightened so many Asians and Europeans alike. She narrowed her eyes, staring at the window at which Fiona was still ranting and railing, but the threat was weakening—gradually, slowly dissipating.

'So much for you,' she muttered fiercely at the waning Fiona. 'Nobody gets the better of this girl.'

It was at that precise moment that Ralph had turned towards her a little and seemed about to say something, but her timely utterance had, it seemed, caused him to be struck dumb. His first shocked expression gradually changed to one of uncertainty. He stared at her and his lips parted slowly. A worried look appeared in his eyes.

'What's the matter my love?' she whispered, as the priest began to approach. 'Anything wrong?'

'Look, Elizabeth . . . ' Ralph faltered, but he was interrupted by a slight sound from above and in front of them.

The stained glass window depicting the Virgin Mary, situated over the altar, rattled feebly as Fiona gave out a last desperate sigh. Ralph's attention was drawn to this window at which the vanquished typhoon, subdued by the victorious Elizabeth, breathed its last. There was a final shudder of the glass, then all was still.

Ralph then glanced again at Elizabeth and suddenly let out a very loud snort of laughter, startling the solemn priest.

'What?' asked Elizabeth, smiling.

Ralph filled his chest with air and let out sigh.

'There was another typhoon,' he explained, pointing at his own chest. 'In here.'

Elizabeth smiled. 'And?'

He laughed again. 'It seems it died with its big sister.'

THE SNAKE-MAN COMETH

Everything was ready for the colonel to begin his briefing of the coming exercise: the illuminated roll maps, the slides, the flip charts, the video and television screen. One of the main reasons for Exercise Hightech, though the army needs little excuse for war rehearsals, was to test some of the new sophisticated equipment and weaponry recently received from the United Kingdom. There were new rocket launchers with missiles that could be guided through a specified window of a skyscraper from five miles away; there was a pocket-sized electronic navigator which communicated with satellites, providing a soldier with his location, speed and direction to within a hundred feet of where he was positioned; there were scopes that banished the blackest night, giving their users clear vision in the darkness; there were computerised assessors of enemy strength; many other new or improved devices. The wonders of the technological age were legion and killing had been made easier than ever before in the history of warfare.

Colonel Feversham's regiment was not one of the famous regiments, though it had seen one or two glorious moments, chiefly in the Boer and Crimea wars. More important these days was to survive the drastic cuts imposed upon the army by politicians. The more famous your regiment's name, the more likely you were to be heading the list of those to fall under the axe. The Argyll and Sutherland Highlanders, for example, had been one of the first to go, despite a list of achievements that stretched back six hundred years. The brass could hide a regiment few had heard of, whereas the well known regiments immediately came to the minds of those compiling inventories of expenses.

Nonetheless, he was of course proud of 'his boys' and wanted them to do well in the coming exercise. They were all seated before him now: smart, poker-backed, keen. That was the best thing about a professional army: there was no one who did not wish to be there. Conscripts would be draped over their chairs, dreaming of whatever such men considered more important than the defence of their country.

'Now chaps,' began the colonel, 'here's the drill . . . '

Colonel Feversham stopped in mid-sentence and frowned. He was about to be interrupted by a Chinese mess orderly, who had quietly opened the door and stood waiting at attention just outside the room.

'Yes, what is it man? Can't you see I'm giving a briefing?'

The orderly took fright at the colonel's aggressive tone and disappeared. The colonel's mild annoyance turned to exasperation. It was this damned face thing. You only had to give them a hard look and they would run off, no doubt to plan how they would get back at you for it and recover their dignity. The colonel had heard said that they would wait patiently for years for the right moment to deliver the return blow.

'Come back here, man,' cried the colonel. 'Sarn Major, find out what he wants, for heaven's sakes.'

The Sergeant Major disappeared, then reappeared a few moments later with the information.

'It's a cobra, sir. Gone up the drainpipe outside.'

The colonel considered this carefully.

'Well can't they get it down?'

'Not at the moment, sir. They're worried it'll get into the air conditioning ducts and drop on someone's head or something.'

There was a shuffling of feet as a tremor went through the room, not unlike that which goes through a herd of antelope when a predator has been sighted. One or two soldiers actually had the temerity to glance up at the ceiling, which earned them a bark from the Sergeant Major.

'Oh well,' said the colonel, 'better clear the building I suppose. Send the men back to their billets until we've caught the beast.'

The soldiers were marched out, leaving Captain Selhearst and the colonel alone.

'Come on David,' said the colonel, 'let's go and see what's happening with this little beggar.'

Despite himself the colonel felt a trickle of excitement run through him. He had never seen a cobra, not outside a zoo at any rate. Snakes did that sort of thing to you, he told himself. They were sinister, cryptic creatures. They reached back into man's ancestry to the beginning of the world and the first great betrayal. He was fascinated by snakes, especially poisonous ones. Someone once told him that ten thousand people died every year in India as the result of cobra bites. Difficult to believe, but he was assured it was a fact.

Once the drainpipe had been pointed out to him Colonel Feversham immediately assumed command of the situation. They, everyone else, expected it of him. He was the senior officer present. He ordered an apprehensive-looking Sergeant Major to stand by the drainpipe with his pace stick, ready to clout the snake once it emerged. The colonel wondered whether it was a protected species. Perhaps they were supposed to put it back onto the mountainside wilderness of Tai Mo Shan, in the New Territories, from whence it had no doubt come.

'Is the snake still up the spout? Hasn't crawled out along the gutter I suppose?'

'No sir,' said the orderly. 'Corporal Chueng is on roof.'

The colonel looked up and saw that there was indeed a man on the flat roof of the building. The corporal held a garden rake awkwardly in one hand. He wondered how Corporal Chueng was feeling, up there, and guessed he would be preparing to jump into the hibiscus garden should the cobra's head appear out of the top of the drainpipe, rather than remain trapped on the roof. Corporal Chueng was certainly very close to the far side of the building.

'Good. Good man,' said the colonel.

Now, what to do about it.

'Any chance of getting a high-powered hose over here, David?' he asked Captain Selhearst. 'Could wash the bugger out then.'

'Actually sir, believe it or not the fire wagon's out on an actual fire. One of the married quarters. Soldier's wife left her chip pan on the stove.'

'Warned them about that,' muttered the colonel, then remembered it was his own wife's amah that he'd warned, not the wives of his soldiers. He did not correct his mistake.

'Has anyone tried a few puffs of insecticide?'

This was taken as a command. A runner was sent to the mess kitchen, always infested with cockroaches in Hong Kong, and a canister of DDT obtained. It was thrown and deftly caught by the man on the roof, who approached the top of the drain-pipe warily, gave the dark hole a long squirt of vapourised fluid, and then hastily retreated to await the outcome. This exercise was repeated several times, without result.

Next, a bucket of ice water was attempted. This too was a failure.

'You sure there's a damn snake up there?' asked the colonel.

No one answered him, which meant they were.

He considered a number of other plans—a brick on the end of a rope lowered into the pipe; a fire underneath the pipe; a long bamboo pole shoved down the pipe like a chimney sweep's brush. None of them seemed really satisfactory.

'Try dropping a rock down the hole,' he said at last.

A suitably-sized smooth stone was obtained from the Officer's Mess rock garden, thrown up to Corporal Chueng (who was getting braver and visibly more casual by the minute) and this was dropped down the pipe. It rattled to halfway down the pipe, then seemed to jam. Nothing. At least they knew it was in the bottom half of the pipe. The colonel did not again ask whether there was a damn snake up there, though he was tempted to. He was also tempted to drop a hand grenade down the pipe and blow the bloody thing to pieces, but this too he resisted though the mental image of the explosion satisfied temporarily his lust for positive results.

Just then the mess orderly pointed towards the main gate, where some commotion was in progress.

'Snake man come,' he cried, forgetting the obligatory 'sir' in his excitement.

'Who sent for him?' asked the colonel, knowing as soon as the words were out of his mouth that he was wasting his breath, for no one amongst his Chinese staff would admit to taking initiative, even were they responsible.

The Chinese were brilliant imitators, quick learners, but not good on initiative. The colonel believed it had something to do with having a picture-language, instead of an alphabet code. They had to learn to recognise a complete word by rote, not make one up from small characters, or determine meaning from the order of those characters. They had no concept of encoding and decoding language, only of identifying set figures. He had often voiced this theory of his, to his officers, when they were clustered around the bar.

'Oh, go and help him through the gate, Sarn Major.' he added. 'They'll be there all day otherwise.'

The Sergeant Major hurried off, no doubt happy to be relieved of his duty of knocking the snake on the head with his pace stick.

When the snake man was presented to him, Colonel Feversham found a short, bandy-legged Chinese standing before him. The snake man had cropped hair, with irregular bald patches showing through the black bristle, looking rather like scars. He had on a dirty singlet, and a pair of khaki shorts two sizes too large for him. Tucked in the waistband was a worn motorcyclist's gauntlet. The crotch of the shorts was level with his kneecaps. On his feet were two worn rubber flipflops. In his right hand was a long thick stick. In his left hand was a sack.

So this is the fearless snake catcher? thought Colonel Feversham. It just went to show that looks weren't everything. Now what did this chap think he could do that the army hadn't already done?

The colonel turned to his mess orderly.

'Does he speak English?'

'No sir,' replied the mess orderly, without even consulting the snake man. 'I will interpret for you, sir.'

'Good man. Ask him if he wants anything.'

At this time the snake man had gone down on his hands and knees before the pipe and to the consternation of everyone except Colonel Feversham, he was peering up the hole.

'Good lord,' said Captain Selhearst, 'he'll get bitten if he's not careful.'

'No, he's not that stupid, David. I'm sure this isn't the first cobra he's been asked to catch.'

In fact, thought the colonel, he knows that the snake went up the pipe, and therefore its head pointing to the top. The pipe was too slim for the cobra to turn round. It could probably travel backwards, but only tail first. The man was definitely not stupid.

The snake man straightened and smiled at the colonel, and asked him for something. The colonel knew enough Cantonese to know that the drawn-out aaaaaa terminating the sentence meant it was a question.

'He wants long piece of string, sir,' said the orderly. 'I get him some.'

The orderly disappeared. In the meantime the snake man inspected the ladder used by Corporal Chueng to get up on the roof and apparently approved of the design and strength of the device, for he gave the colonel the thumbs up. The colonel smiled inwardly, though his face remained impassive.

The string arrived. A whole ball. The snake man cut a short and a long length of string. With the short piece he tied the opening of the sack securely around the bottom of the drainpipe. At the end of the long piece of string he made a noose, and this he slipped around the sack, close to the top. Then he climbed the ladder with the end of the string in one hand and his stick in the other.

At the top the snake man paused dramatically, then began to hammer on the pipe with the stick.

Within a short space of time something fell into the sack and began to writhe. The snake man pulled the noose tight, descended the ladder, and untied the sack from the pipe. He held it up, the creature inside wriggling and squirming.

Captain Selhearst took an involuntary step backwards. The orderly clapped his hands. Corporal Chueng looked relieved.

'Well done,' said the colonel. 'Can we see the beggar?'

The orderly said something to the snake man who pulled on his gauntlet, reached inside the sack, and produced the snake.

It was indeed a cobra. The snake man held it close to the head and the coils wrapped around his bare arm. He looked the cobra in the eyes and said something to it, then laughed.

The orderly did not interpret the sentence. The colonel however had heard the words 'sik faan' and knew enough Cantonese to guess that the snake man was going to eat the snake later. It was said that the Cantonese ate anything with its back to the sky, and certainly snake soup was a winter delicacy. The cobra, being a highly poisonous snake and therefore regarded with some awe, was especially sought for the pot. Along with the banded krait its gall bladder was eaten raw, fresh from a live snake, in the belief that it possessed magical qualities which would be transferred to the devourer. This was one snake that would not be returned to the wild, whatever its status in the eyes of the government wild life department.

Whatever it was that the snake man had said to the cobra, the colonel did not request a translation. It was better to remain in ignorance. Any order by him to do the right thing by the creature would be like blowing in the wind.

The cobra went back into the sack, which was then fastened with some string. The snake man produced a piece of paper. He peered at it closely and then handed it to the colonel.

'What am I supposed to do with this?' asked the colonel, staring at the Chinese characters.

'He wants you to sign it, sir, so he can get his money from the government department,' explained the orderly, who followed this explanation with an 'Excuse me, sir' and reached over and turned the paper upside down. The orderly coughed. 'Wrong way up before.'

Colonel Feversham signed the piece of paper, then said, 'Right, get the men back here Sarn Major, on the double. We've got a briefing to do.

The Sergeant Major marched away.

The colonel said, 'Showed a bit of initiative, that one, David.'

'The snake man, sir? Oh, yes, I thought so too.' Captain Selhearst grinned. 'Bang goes your theory about learning characters by rote, and coding the alphabet and all that.'

'Oh no,' replied Colonel Feversham quietly. 'Not at all, David. You see, the fellow was illiterate. Never learned to read or write, in Chinese or in English. So his brain is quite unhampered by either.'

'Sorry?' said the captain, looking quite puzzled.

'You saw the orderly turn the piece of paper the right way up? Snake fellow handed it to me upside down. He didn't know which way round it was supposed to be, any more than I did. Chap couldn't read his own language, you see.'

Captain Selhearst's expression changed.

'Good lord. You're quick, sir.'

'Have to be David. I'm the colonel.' He stared after the snake man, thinking, I liked that chap. Had a bit up top.

To Captain Selhearst he said, 'Now let's get in there and get on with the briefing. Back to the twentieth century, eh? All that electronic wizardry. All that sophisticated weaponry. Make the mind spin, don't they? The wonders of the modern world?'

'Yes, sir, they certainly do,' replied the captain.

MOON DAY

Ha-lo met us at Tai Po KCR station. She had brought with
her, her son Chang Ko who was 15, her adopted daughter
Tai Song who was 13, and an elderly lady she introduced
to us as 'auntie'. Jill and I gave Ha-lo a hug and shook
hands with the rest. Chang Ko smiled shyly and Tai Song,
a bit bolder, nodded. Neither had much to say to mother's
gweilo friends. Was it because we were uninteresting to
them, or did they hold us slightly in contempt? Perhaps it
was Jill's bright red hair and freckles, or my own six-foot
frame and bushy beard streaked with white which made
them ill at ease?

Ha-lo was a part-time cleaner, who went through our apartment like a whirlwind two mornings a week, and who had
subsequently become a friend. She was self-motivated and she
owned a quick enquiring mind. Her pleasant features were
as round and soft as a dim sum dumpling. We dreaded the
August Moon Festival when she would bake for us expensive,
but traditionally solid-rice moon cakes, and wait for us to eat

them. They were like lead cannon balls. If dropped, I swear a moon cake would be dense enough to go straight through the magma to the earth's centre.

When I offered her a piece of one once, she wrinkled her nose and said, 'Oh, me no like.'

On Chinese holidays, especially New Year, we would be invited to Ha-lo's rented flat in a high rise block at the back of Ti Po near the Lam Tsuen River, to join in the festivities. We felt very honoured. Hong Kong Chinese, prefer to meet even their closest Chinese friends at a restaurant, rather than in the cramped confines of their homes.

In Ha-lo's ten-by-ten foot flat lived Ha-lo, her husband, and the two children. They shared a minuscule kitchen, two very narrow bedrooms and a living-room which could be crossed in one stride: not unusual in a small city of seven million souls. A visitor from the USA once remarked to me that there were more people on Nathan Road at ten in the morning than in the whole state of Nebraska at any time of the day, month or year. Certainly this same man had been further amazed by more than 50,000 Filipino maids at Chater Gardens, where on Sundays they gather like sparrows to chatter to their friends until dark.

The train for Shenzen eventually arrived and we had to stand, the train already being full of people going to visit their families in China. When we reached the border we found a few more thousand people in and around the station area, waiting to go through into the People's Republic of China. It was a frightening experience, being part of that crush funnelled through about ten gates, into the immigration area. I dreaded the thought of a panic.

At immigration we had to part with Ha-lo and her family and proceed through a different channel. There we had to sign forms to swear on oath that we had not had diarrhea or a skin disease within the last twenty-eight days. (Does one admit to

such things, even when interrogated by the Chinese Government?)

We then saw an unsmiling Chinese official who asked us
where in China we were going. He had a sharp, narrow face
and dull-grey eyes: probably an imperious Han from the
North with a high-latitude disposition, unhappy amongst
the squat southerners with their harsh language and stri-
dent tones.

'Shenzen,' we said.

He stamped our visas SHENZEN ONLY, in Chinese and
English.

Once released on the other side we found Ha-lo fretting
because we had been a long time.

'You bin long-long time,' said Ha-lo in the pidgin which
assisted our conversations. 'Udder one make trouble?'

She meant the officials.

'No,' I replied to Ha-lo's question. 'No big trouble.'

She smiled. 'You come then. We go brother housey.'

The whole point of the visit was to go to Ha-lo's old village,
where she had been raised until the age of 16, to see her older
brother. Her older brother's daughter, Ha-lo's niece, had just
had a baby and it was the baby's Moon Day, when it was first
allowed out of the house where it was born and given a name.
For the first month of its life the baby had not existed, during
the most dangerous period when it was most likely to die, but
now it had made it through and was shown officially to relatives and friends.

An ancient van of unknown manufacture was waiting with
a niece and nephew to take us to the village. Showing off
my hard-learned Cantonese I asked the niece her name as we
bounced along, at first on the nice new roads of Shenzen—
the Chinese doppelgänger of Hong Kong—onto the terrible
country roads outside, and was ticked off by Ha-lo. Apparently it was not good form for middle-aged men to ask young

girls their names on so short acquaintance. I apologised as best I could in my faltering Chinese.

Suddenly, as we sped along, Jill hissed to me, 'We've just been through a check point . . . '

I went cold and looked back. We had indeed just left the Guongdong Economic Zone. There were fences around it to keep out Chinese from other provinces. I asked Ha-lo how many kilometres we were travelling and she replied cheerfully, 'Oh, fifty-sixty.'

Fifty-sixty? Our passports were stamped with great red letters SHENZEN ONLY and we were now well outside our permitted visiting area. We were illegally in another China province. It was at least a prison sentence, with many written apologies to boot.

'What do we do?' I whispered to Jill, who did not panic as much as I did on such occasions.

'Forget it.' she said, characteristically. 'We're in now. Let's worry about getting out later.'

The van gear-crashed on, weaving through the multitudinous road works, and I tried to put it out of my mind. There were no checks on leaving the economic zone, but there would certainly be a filter point going back in again. I just hoped there would be a huge queue at the barriers and they simply waved us through. Anything else was too horrible to contemplate.

We arrived at the village: an alley separated by two rows of grey terraced houses, not all identical. The doors and windows were painted in dark colours which had peeled and blistered with the heat and damp. Only the pretty red-tiled, sweeping roofs saved them from being completely ugly. There was a fat sow at one of the low windows, her trotters on the sill, looking out as if she were expecting a parade to pass.

Surrounding the village was a low area of paddy fields, gradually sloping upwards like a bowl into gentle hills. The air was remarkably clear above the paddies, creating an atmosphere of level, green tranquillity. I had no idea whether serious fighting had ever occurred in that area, but you could not imagine a battle taking place there. The spirit of the land was too peaceful to have been blooded by war. At the same time you couldn't call it beautiful, not like Guilin with its mysterious, awe-inspiring hills, despite its rural persuasions.

There was livestock cluttering the alley, and the inevitable bicycles leaning against walls. Children ran around, noisy and underfoot, seemingly uninterested in visitors. Chief amongst the various odours was a thick compound of cooked food, damp stone and rotting cabbage stalks. You could have formed pots out of the smell and baked them in the sun.

The whole village was involved in the Moon Day, but in stages, so many people were still in or around their houses. The adults tried not to stare at us as we walked between them, and the children continued with their games.

One thing struck both Jill and I as very curious and we had no answer for it. Ha-lo had told us that Chang Ko and Tai Song had not been back to the village since they were infants. Ha-lo herself had been back several times to see her brother and nodded and smiled to old neighbours and relations as she passed, but no one spoke to the two children, though they must have known who they were and why they had come. No one rushed forward with arms open crying, 'Is this little Chang Ko? Is this my niece Tai Song? My, haven't you both grown?' There must have been aunts and uncles, cousins, perhaps even brothers and sisters in Tai Song's case, but no one came forward to greet them. Shyness? Contempt for city folk? Some cultural ritual we knew nothing about? It still remains a mystery to us.

There was something else which concerned us both, something quite sinister, but we didn't mention it until later.

Ha-lo's brother greeted us with great enthusiasm and showed us chipped Formica tables laid with newspaper and covered in plates full of things to eat. Some people were already feasting. Jill and I sat down and looked at the food, our fearful expectations being met. Chinese village food often smells of rancid fat, has a grey nebulous appearance, and tastes strongly of long-dried meaty-fishiness.

If a Chinese eats fresh fish or meat, it is alive just before it hits the boiling water, but grey bean curd forms a great part of the villagers' diets, and the meat and fish is often dried. We had nothing fresh before us except some choi sum greens. We ate sparingly, having been told that human faeces was used as fertilizer in China, hoping that we would not have to lie on our forms about not having diarrhoea when returning to Hong Kong. The rice was as usual good, but we despaired at the amount of other dishes that lay awaiting us on the table top. It was quite different from the food we were used to at Ha-lo's house, in Hong Kong, where the relatively high salaries enabled people to fill their tables with fresh fare.

In fact, we need not have worried, for when we announced we were full, the dishes were whipped away with a smile and presented to villagers outside the communal kitchen (opposite the brother's house) for sharing out. It was not a poor village, having its own flour mill, but it was not rich either. Immediately after the meal we were actually taken to the 'rich woman's house' who showed us her bathroom with its hot water taps, making us turn them on and off to show they worked, and a real flushing toilet. The rich woman was an old friend of Ha-lo's, who opened her house to all sorts of people for mah-jong and other activities, and she laughed a lot.

After visiting the rich woman we wandered through the village a couple of times, our earlier suspicions and fears taking firm hold, and then back to the brother's house to see the new baby.

The family was, like all families, allowed only one child. It struck me at the time of the student killings in Tiananmen

Square in '89, but did not seem to register with the media, that a whole generation was wiped out with each single student's death. One baby to each couple meant that every crushed or bullet riddled student was an only child, carrying all the hopes and aspirations of the family crashing down onto the bloody concrete flagstones with them. Indeed, the same could be said of each young soldier who died in that confrontation.

This new baby was full of light and promise however.

The infant was wrapped in a lovely silk shawl of red and gold: lucky colours. One of my meaty hands could have held that tiny, fragile form. Its eyes had that permanent look of enquiry which is peculiar to most month-old babies. A boy, it was passed to Jill to hold. I told the mother in Cantonese that the baby was ho leng, very beautiful, and she asked me for a European name for the child.

This stumped both Jill and I for a few moments, not being prepared for it. I searched my mind for a name which would be easily spoken in Cantonese, rather than grab something out of the air, like Roger, which would tongue-tie them all. Eventually we came up with Alan. 'Al-lan,' we said.

The mother was delighted.

'Ah-lun. Ah-lun. M'goi lei,' she thanked us.

The name we had given the baby would not be its real name of course—I believe it was just a nice gesture on the mother's part—but we all went away feeling happy and honoured on both sides and the baby would have a story to tell.

After holding the Moon Day baby, Jill was given another family's eighteen month old son to hold. Like all its contemporaries, it had no nappy on. Instead, it's trousers had a hole cut out of the bottom, so that it could do its business when it wished without soiling its clothes. Jill had had similar experiences in Borneo, when we stayed at Dyak longhouses on the Rajang River. It was customary to give a woman a baby to hold, possibly as sign of trust. I was glad I was not a woman. Jill looked very vulnerable in her white slacks, bouncing on her knees a baby that might at any moment erupt from the rear.

Chang Ko and Tai Song had until this point trailed around with their mother, aunt and us, not saying a word to anyone. They both looked ill at ease and out of place, especially the willowy, delicate Chang Ko, with his crimped hairstyle, fussy shirt and expensive Reebok trainers. He looked what he was: a Hong Kong trendy.

His short, chunky country cousins had pudding basin haircuts, well washed ill-fitting clothes, and hands engrained with soil. Their skins were swarthy and dark, from working out in the paddy fields, unlike Chang Ko's which was creamy. They had muscles where he had soft-looking silky flesh.

One of these country cousins came to us while we were drinking Cokes at an outside table. He was a big lad in braces and laceless boots and he carried a .22 air rifle. He spoke to Chang Ko rapidly, and fiercely, and I vaguely understood that he wanted his city cousin to go out in the fields and shoot the gun.

The terrified Chang Ko looked around for his mother, who had gone off with the auntie somewhere. Then he turned to me, to whom he had not spoken more than ten words in two years, and grabbed my sleeve.

'You come too,' he hissed at me in English. 'I want you to come with us.'

Apparently he felt he had more in common at that moment with an adult 'foreign devil' than he did with his young relations.

So we went out into the fields to shoot the gun and had a marvellous time. Chang Ko didn't want to go back when the lead pellets ran out, so we borrowed some bicycles and went riding around the countryside together, along the paddy field paths and through the bamboo groves. We became, not surprisingly, quite good friends after that incident.

That short cycle ride gave me a real sense of that part of China, as a spiritual landscape.

My visit to Guilin, the memories of which I now treasure, had left me full of images. There had been the people doing tai chi around the lake in the early morning; the duck seller with his bicycle festooned in living creatures; the truck drivers who refused to budge from the middle of the road; the oxen in the wet fields pulling ploughs; the ceramic works with the yard below their windows piled high with broken shards of pottery; the cormorant fishers on their slim bamboo rafts, sending their birds down into the grey depths of the murky river; and finally, the strange limestone mountains which had been carved out of the landscape by water, sometimes evident as tall spires of craggy rock with stunted pines spurting from fissures halfway up, and occasionally helmeted by a small temple or house.

In Guilin the mystique of the landscape went so deep I could not meet it. It could be appreciated from a spiritual distance, but an outsider, especially a westerner, could never hope to join with it. The landscape around Ha-lo's village however was not so awe-inspiring, did not have the same impenetrable face, and was more yielding. I felt I could have been a boy there, running around the paddy fields, cycling along the paths, cutting bamboo staves for a multiplicity of purposes in and around the home, being scared by snakes, shooting rats, bringing in the harvest, being a boy and close to the earth. I felt I knew it a little, through my association with my own East Anglian marshes, which must surely have been a geophysical cousin of these flatlands.

When we got back with the bicycles, it was time to go, and we said goodbye to Ha-lo's brother and her relations. It was time to face the border guards ringing the economic zone. The journey in the van seemed to take many hours, though it was probably only about one.

It was getting dark as we came to the check point. There was a queue at the wooden boxes, not unlike those in which the guards stood outside St James's Park barracks in London, which housed the usually sour-faced Chinese officials. We joined one of these queues, our thumbs covering the words SHENZEN ONLY on the visas stamped in our passports.

When I reached the box there was a severe, hard-faced woman inside who must surely have been a dogma-yelling banner-carrier during the cultural revolution. I could see her kicking and scratching intellectuals, fired to fever pitch by Mao's sayings, chanting abuse onto her former school teacher's bowed head. I tried to look like the English peasant I really am, so there was some bridge of commonality between us.

She looked at my passport for a good two minutes, stared me in the eyes for another one, then flicked her head for me to go through, all without a change of expression. I heaved a sigh of relief. Jill followed me just a minute later, wearing her couldn't-care-less-if-I-do-get-caught attitude. I wished I could be more like Jill, but my mind and body are used to these crises where both go rigid with tension, then relax into jelly with the euphoria of escaping discovery.

When we reached the border proper, we simply went through the motions again, and were passed over to the Hong Kong Chinese immigration officials in their smart uniforms, interested only in illegal immigrants, illegal live plants (Jill was carrying a bonsai tree given her by someone in the village and hidden under some sandwiches in her carrier bag), and forcing all gweilos like us, with no Hong Kong residential status, to fill in immigration forms. Jill always resented filling in the forms and made a great fuss about it, while I as usual did as I was told.

We said goodnight to Ha-lo, her auntie and the kids, at Tai Po and thanked her for a wonderful day. It had been a wonderful day. It was a day full of experiences for us and one that would be treasured amongst other rare days of our lives. We were grateful and we felt privileged.

Only one dark spot in the day, which we had met while wandering through the village alley, remained with us. There may have been an innocent explanation for it, or not, but during our time there we had seen plenty of boy babies, and infants careering around the alley, but no girls. The only girl child we saw was about six years of age, helping her mother carry water from the standpipe to her home. The only one.

FACE

The knifegrinder's call decorated the evening, so low and unmistakable that those who were in the apartment blocks within earshot of the sound could not fail but to stop and consider it. Some shrugged their shoulders and continued with their tasks, others settled into their leisure; Wong Sin-saang took down a heavy-bladed butcher's knife from its hook on the kitchen wall. He travelled by lift down thirteen stories and stepped first into the hallway, then the street.

Around him was a forest of square concrete sequoias, but in a clearing in the middle, by the children's playground, stood the knifegrinder.

'How much to sharpen this knife?' Wong Sin-saang asked the knifegrinder.

The artisan inspected the blade and saw that it was a good one, made of the finest Japanese steel. The dying rays of the sun snaked along the well-honed edge, which through long use and sharpening was now like a sea-wave curling along a beach of dull-silver sand. The knife was still in prime condition, however, and the knifegrinder could see how clean the striated blade had been kept. Though the metal was scored and no longer shiny, there was no rust nor any pit-marks on its surface.

'This is a good knife,' said the knifegrinder.

'I know,' said Wong Sin-saang. 'I used to be a butcher and I used this knife all the time. Now I have my own business and do not need to cut the meat myself. I have others who do that for me.'

'You are a very successful man,' acknowledge the knife-grinder, who was a recent immigrant to Hong Kong from mainland China. 'I hope one day to be just as successful, for I am a businessman too.'

Wong Sin-saang nodded at this statement, seeing a world of difference in himself and this old man plying a fading trade, but saying nothing which would offend the dignity of the knifegrinder, for he did not wish the man to lose face.

The craftsman then took a second look at the blade, made some mental calculations, and gave Wong Sin-saang a price for sharpening the implement. A little haggling took place according to established rules and finally the amount was agreed, without any loss of face on the part of either man.

The knifegrinder, who apart from whetstone blocks, owned a grinding wheel propelled by a bicycle chain, cogs and pedals, proceeded to hone the edge of the steel, comet tails of sparks flying from between the metal and stone. Changing after a while to the whetstone, he worked as carefully and earnestly as a clockwork watchmaker, attentive to the fineness of his craft. The blade had to be as keen as possible, without wasting any more metal than necessary. Knives were expensive imple-ments and the whetting of them an art.

'So,' said the knifegrinder, his words keeping time to the rhythm of the swish, swish, swish, of the smooth steel on the shallow whetstone, 'this is the first butcher's knife I have had to do for a long time. It is usually housewives' scissors, which need setting as well as sharpening, or the pocketknife of a triad gangster who wants to kill a rival (I know these things you see, Sin-saang), or perhaps a family meat cleaver. I do not often get to do an instrument of quality like this.'

Wong Sin-saang nodded.

'May I ask you, Sin-saang, why you do not get the knife sharpened by one of your butchers, at your shop?'

'Since you ask,' said Wong Sin-saang, 'I will tell you. I need the knife to use in one hour's time, when I go to meet a young Australian man who works with my daughter.'

'Ah,' said the knifegrinder, obviously catching the air of intrigue, 'this gweilo has done something to offend you?'

'He told my daughter he would like to strip her naked.'

'I understand,' said the artisan, carefully inspecting the edge of the blade in the dying light, 'it is a matter of face.'

It was indeed a matter of face. The young man in question had made many unwelcome advances towards Wong Siu-je, the pretty seventeen-year-old daughter of Wong Sin-saang, and tired of his insinuations and lewd suggestions, she had eventually told her father. Having done so they both knew, father and daughter, that action must be taken.

Her father at first complained to the management of the firm that employed both his daughter and the young man, but they confessed that though they were sympathetic they were unable to do anything about it. The young man in question was on contract work for a year, in a senior position, and any unprovable accusations from the management might result in a law suit against them. What their employees did outside of work was legally none of their concern, so they said, and perhaps Mr Wong should request the help of the police? Wong Sin-saang said he had taken advice and did not wish to use the police, for the man had done nothing to break the law, and it would mean going to court and obtaining an injunction. Since this would expose his daughter to unwelcome media attention, he did not wish to do this either.

So Wong Sin-saang then asked his daughter for the best place to meet this gweilo and she had informed him that the man always took the same lift as she herself took, down from the seventh floor of Pacific Ocean House, when work ceased at the end of the day. He waited for her to leave and would follow her to the MTR underground station. When she was alone he would whisper things that only she could hear. If she had a friend with her, he would simply remain a few paces behind, staring at her back and other parts of her body as she walked ahead. If she turned, he would be there, with his lewd stare.

Her father asked her if there were many people in the building at that time of day and she replied that though the particular lift she used was a private one, owned and used only by the offices of her firm of architects, and often almost empty, the foyer below was crowded with lower level shoppers and people on their way home from work.

This sounded like the ideal place to meet the gweilo.

The knifegrinder handed the implement back to the ex-butcher and received his payment. As Wong Sin-saang walked away, the old man's cry went out again, like the sound of someone in need of assistance.

In approximately an hour, at the appointed time, Wong Sin-saang waited on the sixth floor of Pacific Ocean House, outside the lift used by the firm of architects. He did not look out of place in the smart modern building. He wore an English blue Worsted suit, a white shirt and a silk tie. In his left hand he carried an American leather briefcase. He was a businessman now, and looked every inch of it, from his short well-groomed hair to the soles of his Italian shoes. His spectacles were designed by St Denver of Paris and his underclothes came from the expensive though not exclusive Marks and Spencer Store in Harbour City.

Up his right sleeve was a broad-bladed butcher's knife, honed to perfect sharpness by the knife-grinder.

He did not press any buttons, but let the lift go up and down in front of him, as he watched the numbered lights on the panel go on and off. His daughter would stop the lift at his floor on her way down from the seventh, accompanied by the young man who had been bothering her for so long.

Wong Sin-saang did not have wait for very long. When the doors to the lift opened, his daughter stepped out quickly, and he stepped inside, blocking the young man's exit. The doors closed behind him. There was no one else in the lift except this tall brown-haired gweilo wearing dark glasses. Wong Sin-saang did not have to ask who this man was, for his daughter would have told him had this not been the person who had been insulting him and his family.

The lift began to travel down to the ground floor and Wong Sin-saang dropped his briefcase and allowed the knife to slide down his sleeve into his well-practised butcher's cutting hand. He informed the young man who he was and that he was here to gain face.

The young man's eyes widened on seeing the blade and he began yelling and screaming. This was very bad, for an oriental knows that such behaviour is a terrible loss of face and in no way serves to open any discussion. There was nothing else that Wong Sin-saang could do.

He went to work with the knife.

When the lift arrived on the ground floor and the doors opened, a shocked crowd stepped aside, some of the women covering their faces, some of the men averting theirs. Several of the females screamed, unused to such sights in the rush hour of Hong Kong. Others simply stared in astonishment.

Out of the lift, weaving helplessly between the people, came a completely naked young man attempting to hide his genitals with his hands. Though his body was not marked in any way, he had been stripped clean of any clothing. He ran through the foyer and through the double doors, out into the street, where shrieks and eventually some laughter travelled in his wake.

Next out of the lift stepped a smart businessman, Wong Sin-saang, whose former skill and dexterity as a butcher had not failed him in gaining face. In less than a minute-and-a-half he had stripped the young man clean of every stitch of clothing, using the blade sharpened the evening before by the knifegrinder, without so much as scratching the man's skin.

It was a feat of which any butcher would have been proud.

MR. HO

During the Second World War, Gun Club Hill was an internment camp run by the Japanese equivalent of the German
Gestapo. Tortures took place there, forms of cruelty best
forgotten, and many deaths. A place of terrible pain, of
darkness and despair, of horrors that soaked the hill in evil.
It might have become an ugly place, drenched in twisted
souls. It might have become one of those areas which cause
a shudder to run through a visitor, even one ignorant of its
history, if it had not been for the children. Ghosts in torment
cannot suffer where children run, said Mr Ho, for the laughter
and innocence of children lend them peace and keep their
agony at bay.

Mr Ho had a large moon-shaped head with a beaming
face. In fact, having been told his name at a party, what
with the background chatter and my poor hearing it went
right past me, and for a long time I thought of him as 'Mr
Moon.' Then one day I was invited out to dim sum, by Dan
Sethers, one of the teachers who had formed a friendship

with the school janitor, and I felt that since I was to meet him properly I ought to use his right name, even in my own thoughts of the man.

We met in the Golden Dragon Restaurant behind the Gun Club School where both Dan and Mr Ho worked. Mr Ho's favourite dim sum restaurant was a jau lau, crowded and monstrously noisy with Cantonese diners who find it necessary to shout at their neighbour from two feet away. Trolleys with individual dim sum dishes—shrimp balls, pork balls, barbecued pork dumplings—were wheeled between the round tables that seated a dozen people at once. The trolley ladies yelled out their particular wares—'Siu mai! Siu mai!' 'Ha gau!'—and the diners held up fingers for the number of bamboo steamers they wanted.

'How do you do, Mr Ho,' I said, when Dan introduced us.

His hand enveloped mine, for though he was not a tall man, Mr Ho was large. His palm was calloused and rough: the tough skin of a manual worker. I guessed his age to be around sixty, though gweilos like me are notoriously bad at judging the age of orientals, who often look younger than their years to western eyes.

'Please to meet you,' he said, his English unfaltering. 'You Mr Sether's friend?'

I said that I was.

Mr Ho then ordered some dim sum dishes for us and we tried to converse, though I found it difficult to hear him, his voice being unusually soft for a Cantonese speaker. The noise around was almost alarming: children running and screeching; plates being clattered; trolley waitresses yelling; families shrieking at each other. An occidental hearing a tape recording of a jau lau at dim sum time would be forgiven for thinking that they were listening to some playback of a disaster: a fire in a crowded building, or people fleeing from an earthquake.

Eventually the restaurant thinned out and I was able to put some questions to the janitor.

'Mr Ho,' I said, 'I don't know whether you know, but I'm a newspaper reporter. I work for the South China Morning Post. I'm interested in your story. I understand you can't get British citizenship, though you worked for the British Navy?'

Dan Sethers said, 'A stoker. Mr Ho was a stoker in the Royal Navy for twenty years, and yet the bastards won't even entertain the idea of giving him a passport.'

Like many Hong Kong Chinese, Mr Ho wanted to emigrate before 1997, when the British left. I don't suppose he was so much enamoured with colonial governors, as concerned about what the Beijing Government would do with someone who had worked for British Navy.

Also like many Hong Kong Chinese it was possible that he looked with apprehension towards the day when the mainland Chinese would begin imposing their will upon the territory. It was the bureaucracy Hong Kong feared the most: the interminable forms to fill in for the most minor things. It slowed business down, stifled it. Hong Kong's success depended largely on the incredible speed at which it moved: shifted its imports and exports, made deals, raised buildings, built roads, transported merchandise. They knew the snail's pace of business life in China, the mountains of paper needing to be stamped with chops and processed through innumerable corrupt officials, and many had fled to Hong Kong because of the frustrations it caused.

They had a phrase for it: 'the dead hand of China'.

Even people like Mr Ho, at the bottom of the heap, are affected by the wealth, or lack of it, of the whole territory. Mr Ho loved to gamble at the racetrack: he loved the horses. He also enjoyed his food. The wealth of Hong Kong allowed him to indulge his pleasures in these directions. No doubt he feared the mainland Chinese would take these away from him.

'I was in navy, yes,' he smiled, his round face crinkling. 'I was on board H.M.S. Gallahad when she sink in the Falkland's War. Very cold in water.' He laughed. 'Antarctic ocean very cold.'

'Man's a bloody hero,' snapped Dan. 'Makes you sick, doesn't it, the way we treat them?'

Dan was a Yorkshireman carved straight out of Yorkshire stone from the crags of Gordale Scar: dark-bearded and dour, blunt, no-nonsense. He had the blood of lead miners in his veins, and not a little of the native aggressiveness of his county. I had been born in York but raised mostly in the midlands and the south, I used to joke that we were soul mates, but my own personality was entirely more frivolous than Dan's. I envied his pragmatism during those times when the darker side of my imagination emerged, and he viewed my occasional obsessive behaviour with unvoiced suspicion.

'Twenty years service, and they won't help?' I said. 'It does sound a bit rough.'

'A bit rough?' snorted Dan, and pecked viciously at a prawn ball with his chop sticks.

Mr Ho shrugged his shoulders at me and smiled, that moon face of his breaking into tiny wrinkles. The word 'Ho' means 'good' in Cantonese. It can mean other things too, depending on the tone used, but 'Mr Good' was how I thought of him at that moment. He was essentially a good person: you sensed it as soon as you met him. He was gentle, kind and thoughtful, and I knew he valued loyalty and friendship very highly. Those teachers at the Gun Club School who had befriended Mr Ho, had nothing but praise for him, and in Dan's case, respect.

Loyalty. He had been loyal to the British and now it was their turn to reciprocate they had reneged. The waters of British bureaucracy can be colder than the Antarctic Ocean and they had frozen Mr Ho's application for British citizenship. He had filled in the forms and heard nothing more, ever.

A deputy head at the school had attempted to break through the ice floe, and had been summarily rebuffed. It was clear that the Immigration Service wanted nothing to do with an elderly ex-stoker with no money, no sought-after skills, and only his history to offer. With a British passport Mr Ho could have gone to the International School in Singapore, where the old Gun Club deputy head now worked, but not without it.

'Mr Ho,' I said to him, 'I would like your permission to write up your story, in the newspaper. It sometimes makes a difference when the media makes a fuss. The only thing that shifts these faceless characters in the civil service is the fear of adverse publicity. Some politician will be bound to see it as a good vote-catching cause, and take it up.'

He smiled again and shook his head.

'No thank you. I thank you for your kindness. I know what you try to do, as a friend of Mr Sethers, but I think better not.'

I was disappointed and he saw it in my face. It obviously distressed him, for his face immediately took on an earnest expression. Then he leaned over towards me and said conspiratorially, 'I tell you another story you can print.'

'What's that?'

'Gun Club School,' he whispered, 'has ghosts. Yes, really. At night I am sometimes afraid of the noises. In the day the children are there. Ghosts no stay where children run.'

'What are these ghosts then, do you think?' I asked, knowing that the Cantonese took the supernatural very seriously.

'From the war,' he said. 'The Japanese kill many people at the school house. Shoot them. Torture them. Chop off heads with sword. They still there. Ghosts.'

'Were you here in the war?' I asked. 'In Hong Kong?'

'Young man,' he smiled. 'I take food to prisoners.'

Dan nodded grimly from the other side of the table. I read a lot into that. Mr Ho was obviously one of those many Chinese who smuggled food to British soldiers, when Hong Kong was under the occupation of the Japanese army. Was this yet another example of unrewarded service? There were probably many more. I didn't really want to know. I already felt dirty.

At the end of the meal I shook hand with Mr Ho and we parted.

Of course, I could have written up the story without his permission, and in many cases would have done, but Mr Ho had already experienced betrayal from my nation. I did not want to add to the crimes. Dan Sethers told me, as we left each other, that he believed Mr Ho was afraid of the publicity. His job, and indeed his home, for he lived in the storeroom at the school, was too much to risk. He was afraid that the school authorities might sack him, if he became the centre of an emigration controversy. Indeed, I would not have put such treatment past them, for many were of the same ilk as the bureaucrats.

I heard nothing more of Mr Ho for about a year, except for Dan Sethers' occasional mentions of him in passing.

Then towards the end of January '91, Dan Sethers came to me in high temper.

'They're trying to sack him,' he fumed. 'They want to sack Mr Ho. It's the bloody accountants again, trying to save money by cutting out what they call frills. They're worried about a measly four thousand dollars a month.'

Four thousand dollars was less than a quarter of what a teacher at the school was paid.

'What are you going to do about it?' I asked.

'What can I do? Make a protest, of course, but a bloody lot of good that will do.'

Dan seethed, in that dark, quiet Yorkshire way. He would shake a finger or two in someone's face, I knew. Dan wasn't afraid of authority and had suffered because of it. He was regarded by his superiors as a 'bloody nuisance' because he used his initiative and spoke his mind at staff meetings. But this made any intervention by him a destructive business, and tended to make those in power dig in their heels.

I went about my own business, writing up stories, getting flack from various sources as is usual for my line of work. I was due to leave Hong Kong in February and return to England to sort out some domestic affairs there which needed my attention. I doubted I would return. The night of my flight out of the colony Dan called me on the phone.

'That business with Mr Ho?' he said. 'It's been settled.'

'He's been sacked,' I said, taking my cue from the grim sound of Dan's voice. I should have known better. I should have guessed that good news differed not the slightest in tone from bad news when it came from Dan Sethers.

'No, no,' that strong Yorkshire dialect on my ears, 'quite the opposite. The teachers threatened industrial action if Mr Ho was given the boot. The management backed down. He's safe for a while, is our Mr Ho.'

At last. At last Mr Ho had had a glimpse of what I considered to be at the roots of decent caring people from my country. I could leave the territory with a little less shame staining my nation.

'Was he pleased?' I asked.

'You'd think he'd backed the winner of the Gold Cup,' Dan replied. 'You know that smile of his?'

'I remember. I just wonder what it would have been like if we had rewarded him as he deserved, for his service, rather than merely correct what would have been a wrong. What do you think?'

There was silence as Dan considered this, then he said in that blunt way, 'No bloody different, I'd say. Mr Ho is Mr Ho. He gives you back full measure, whatever you do for him. No less for a small favour, than if you'd bought him his own stable of racehorses. He's a one off, is Mr Ho.'

I agreed with that.

'What sparked off this sudden display of loyalty amongst the staff?' I asked. 'I thought they were scared of making waves in case they lost their contracts?'

'Dunno,' said Dan. 'We had a meeting there one night, to discuss it, and though they all started out by saying there was nothing anyone could do. We stayed until after dark—Mr Ho's right by the way—it is a spooky place. Anyway, by the end of the evening there was a change of mood—they finished up saying they would go all the way for him. I was surprised too.'

'You think you persuaded them?'

'Something did—I don't know that it was me.'

When the plane took off, I looked down on the coruscating colony of Hong Kong and managed to pick out the dark patch that would be Gun Club Hill. Its ghosts would be roaming, without the children there to keep their misery back.

Mr Ho would be in his bed in the storeroom, perhaps feeling anxious by every little noise. He need not have worried, I was sure. It was the ghosts of bureaucracy, the faceless ones behind the paper walls, who were his real enemies. Chinese, British, whatever. They were the ones to be feared.

The real ghosts, the ghosts of those who had died there, were on Mr Ho's side.

CHILDREN OF THE VOLCANO

We let Fritz hire the bemo for us. He was one of those people
that plan everything meticulously, down to the last tiny detail,
leaving nothing to chance. Although we had all met only three
days previously, in a restaurant somewhere along Monkey
Forest Road, Greta had already decided that Fritz must be
extremely bored with his life. 'How can you not be bored
when you know everything that's going to happen to you?'
Since we were all backpacking around Indonesia, I tended to
agree with her. One doesn't backpack unless there are expectations of being surprised, or of falling into unusual situations, otherwise why not stay in a Bali beach hotel? Ubud,
a small town full of local artists and wood carvers, was in a
hinterland valley surrounded by terraced hills and duck-filled
paddies. The package tours tended to visit for a day, but not
remain overnight, which suited us fine.

I was the only English person amongst the group, though
there was another native speaker of my tongue: Shelly, the
wife of the Swiss architect, Dieter, was an American. Dieter

was a German-speaker. Kathe and Fritz were Austrian. Greta came from Bavaria, and the natural leader of the group, Renarta, was Prussian. Since I only had limited German the group spoke mainly in English, which was extremely kind of them. Kathe was the only poor English-speaker and she made no objection.

Finally Fritz agreed on a price of ten thousand rupiah with the driver of the bemo, to take the seven of us to Lake Batur, nestled between two active volcanoes. Fritz had developed a local reputation for driving tough bargains and most of the bemo drivers, though they pestered the life out of the rest of us, stayed clear of the Austrian, who bludgeoned them with short solid blows—not more than a hundred rupiah at a time—until even the most haggle-hardened of the Balinese went down under heavy Germanic insistence. You could see them wincing as the words thudded into their skulls, their eyes blinking with each fresh blow, their simple open faces revealing the strain.

'So!' cried Fritz, turning to the group and gesturing with his fingers. 'It is settled!'

'Well done,' Renarta said, 'wasn't it?' she asked of us, but I hadn't then got over feeling sorry for the bemo driver, who looked as if he had just betrayed his mother, albeit under torture. He tilted his head and fiddled with his keys, gazing off into the distance beyond his battered minibus, as if he were now sorry he had ever decided to leave the paddy fields to go out into the world to make his fortune.

We set off straight away. Renarta occupied the seat where normally the tour guide would sit and she fell into the role immediately, but her information was of a general nature, and she always deferred to Fritz on details of history and local culture. In fact Fritz supplied most of Renarta's monologue, though he never usurped her position, releasing the information through her. Kathe sat quietly beside her knowledgeable, competent companion, staring out of the window through round-lensed glasses, looking like Heidi lifted from the mountains and dropped into a bewildering foreign city. Kathe relied utterly upon Fritz for all things, including which brand of toothpaste to use. They had met in Innsbruch just prior to departure for the Far East, and Kathe had clamped herself to her fellow Austrian. Kathe was searching for herself, using Fritz as an unknowing guide.

We bumped along the badly-maintained roads, northwards towards Batur, absorbing the beautiful scenery that we had heard so much about and which had not failed to disappoint us. Bali was a natural park, hastily laid out by a busy God, but subtly improved upon by a people who had a flair for landscape gardening and dramatic colour. There were feral blooms growing in the hedgerows that any gardener back in Europe would have given his fingers to see flourishing in his own flower beds. There were tiered fields of fresh green rice, which fed each other from the top with slim waterfalls. A pale wind exposed the undersides of leaves and blades of plants: a softness sweeping over the fields gently smoothing the fine sea of green.

During one of Renarta's rare pauses, Dieter talked excitedly about 'vernacular architecture', which he explained was architecture without an architect.

'. . . their traditional huts, for example. Not crude dwellings—they have sturdy hardwood frames, and you notice how they use palm trunks for the pillars? When a palm is live the pith fibres allow the water passage upwards, through the bole, to the leaves. The Balinese builders turn the trunk upside down, so that rainwater runs down the pillar into the ground below. They've been building to the same design for centuries, perhaps thousands of years, perfectly, but without any plans, any drawings and perhaps very few tools.

'You see the same sort of vernacular architecture everywhere in the world: the huts in the Swiss Alps, the Scottish crofts, Arab dhows, Maldivian dhonis . . . '

Most of us remained fascinated, even after Renarta, who was a doctor, interrupted with thoughts about vernacular surgery, and Greta surmised wildly on the possibility of vernacular people.

Shelley, possibly defending what she saw as her husband's territory, said, 'What's that supposed to mean? Vernacular people?'

Greta explained.

'From what Dieter has been saying, vernacular architecture involves the use of local materials to make a standard design, is that correct Dieter?'

A nod from the Swiss.

'So, the builders take items from the landscape—trees, reeds for the thatch, raffia binding for the joints—and redirect their natural functions—the reeds shed water, the hardwood supports weight, the palm transfers moisture—in the creation of a new object composed of natural things.

'Humans have gone through the same transformation as plants into huts or boats. We are not doing what we were originally designed to do—hunt, fish, gather. But no one has planned what we have become. God did not redesign our purpose. We have done that ourselves, without resorting to specific blueprints, just utilizing the natural materials, using each other as models, and turning the human body into something more suited to the world we have reshaped around ourselves. Don't you agree?' Greta always needed confirmation for her ideas.

Renarta laughed, as if to say that's a little too heavy a discussion to get into on an outing to a volcano.

It was a rare Kathe, a Kathe who for once did not look at Fritz before speaking, but took the idea further on her own. She spoke German, which I followed with difficulty.

'By the same token, then, the process could be reversed?'

Dieter, once this had sunk in, shook his head violently.

'You can't take the tree and the reeds and replant them, expect them to flourish again.'

'No,' interrupted Fritz, coming to his companion's defence, 'but it can be returned to its original place in nature, though it fails to function exactly as it did before. The landscape can reclaim it . . . '

We lapsed into silence after that. This was the normal effect of Fritz speaking directly to us all, rather than through Renarta. Absorbing his words was like digesting a large starchy meal. It left you feeling lethargic and heavy, with a strong inclination to rest.

On the descent to Lake Batur, our driver ran the gauntlet of wood-carving vendors, who would even follow you into the toilet, murmuring into your ear, trying to convince you that your life would improve if you bought their wares. They ran alongside the bemo, waving their goods, thrusting crudely-hewn images of animals through windows that refused to shut, seemingly uncaring of the fact that they might go under a wheel at any moment. We left these people behind once we reached the winding lake road at the bottom where we picked up speed.

The first thing that struck us was the vastness of the lava ash plain from the volcanoes Abang and Batur, which took us fully half-an-hour to drive through. It was a most depressing place of black and grey dust, with sparse vegetation—there were some shrubs with berries—and ugly bubbled-rock projecting from the level surface. In the centre of this was the lake itself, like a pool of black water from some mythological dead place, which souls had to cross to reach some kind of underworld. Even Renarta was stunned into silence.

When we pulled up at the edge of the lake, the choking black coal dust billowing around the bemo, we alighted to find that our feet sank into the soft ground. It was not a comforting texture.

The driver of the bemo, no less sullen than when we had begun the journey, pointed to a stream which oozed out of the dark earth, forming a separate pool close to the main lake.

'Hot water,' he murmured, then having shown us the warm spring which we had come to see, climbed back in his vehicle to go to sleep in the front seat.

'Come on,' cried Renarta, trying to inject some enthusiasm back into the party, 'let's go for a dip!' and with typical Western European lack of modesty, stripped off her shorts, T-shirt and underclothes, and ran to the spring, diving in. Others followed her example, though Shelley and I did so with obvious shyness. Once we were in the water we thrashed around 'enjoying' ourselves, splashing companions and making silly noises supposed to resemble seals.

Suddenly, in the middle of the flurry, Renarta said, 'Look there. Children.'

Standing not a hundred metres off was a small band of youngsters, ranging from four or five years old, to ten, perhaps twelve. They were covered in the black dust from head to foot, and stood watching us, silently. None of them smiled very much, though one or two had their mouths open.

'Where on earth do they come from?' said Greta, and when we had all looked around, seeing nothing for miles but the dark peaks and lava plain, her puzzlement became infectious.

'Maybe someone dropped them here?' suggested Dieter. 'Left them here to play?'

Greta snorted.

'Who would do such a thing? To play in this place? That would be criminal.'

'Well, what then?' asked Shelly.

We received part of the answer when one of the children came forward a few paces and held up a string of small fish. Everyone groaned. The vendors were even out here, in this forsaken black pit. We ignored the gesture, renewing our squealing and splashing, and even when the child started to cry and eventually ran back to be comforted by her companions, I swear none of us felt very much. After weeks on Bali we had become immune to these kind of tactics. The locals used their children to reach inside us, forcing pity out of little hidden pockets. We had really had enough.

Once we had exhausted our water play, we had a game of tag on the shore of the lake, running after one another, tapping a shoulder, falling on the soft dust, getting blacker by the moment, until the eyes and teeth were stark in their faces.

We stayed until evening, lying at last in quiet under the dying sun, and Renarta said, 'Look, I'm exhausted. Why don't we stay here the night? It's so warm and peaceful . . . let's send the bemo back?' Whether she was joking or not hardly mattered a few moments later, because when we looked round for our driver, he and his vehicle were gone. Perhaps he had at last taken offence at Fritz's meagre offer and had decided to abandon us, to teach us a lesson? Whatever the reason, he had left us here, with the darkness falling.

We all dressed again in the half-light and then took stock.

It was Kathe who took the initiative, and that worried me even at that point. I wondered to myself why this uncomplicated person, this simple female, closer in spirit to the biblical original than any woman I had ever known, was prepared to assume responsibility for anything.

She said, 'I'll go and ask the children if they are being picked up. Those that want to go back to Ubud can pay for a lift . . . ' It would be expensive. It was we who were at a disadvantage now, not the vendors.

As we watched her walk towards the children in the gloaming I knew something strange was happening, something beyond our control. The light was wrong. How this had come about, I had no idea: it was just . . . wrong. I wanted to shout a warning to her, but the words were like pebbles that rattled in my throat.

She reached the children of the volcano and they clustered round her, murmuring. Then she disappeared down in amongst them, as if she had fallen into quicksand. I suppose she must have squatted, to be more on their level, so that she could speak with them more intimately, but she had gone down too far, below the shoulders of the tallest children.

'Too far . . . ' I managed to blurt, but no one paid me any attention, their eyes were on the children, the now excited children, who squealed and shrieked, much in the same way as we had been doing earlier.

Kathe had not drowned in black quicksand. She emerged, twice more, the first time laughing and shouting, 'They weren't selling the fish—they were giving them to us . . . ' and submerged again each time, but never more fully, only to just above their shoulders. The last time she did not come up for ages and again I thought, has she suffocated? But then, finally, she was there again, her head having bobbed to the surface. When she finally came out of them completely, she was different. She began walking back, waving for the others to follow her example, and jumping and skipping, like the other children.

Renarta went, followed by Dieter and Shelley, and Greta ran to catch them up. Only Fritz and I remained behind.

'Shall we go?' he asked me, and I was shocked by his tone which carried the revelation that he too was malleable, ready to be remoulded. His precise fastidious plans, from which he rarely deviated, protected a vulnerable soul.

'Are you coming?' he repeated, almost angrily, as if I were holding him back.

Terrified of what was happening to them all, I shook my head. As I was pulling on my shoes, Fritz suddenly raced across the black shore and his dark-dust form melted with the children and the shades of deep evening.

Once the shoes were on I felt safer, less insecure, but I still stayed where I was, afraid to venture too close to the children. It was fear that saved me, nothing else. It was the kind of fear that kept me from drinking too much alcohol, or from becoming a junky, for I was frightened of changing myself into someone else. I realise now that I was the only coward amongst them. That panic ensured my denial of the same urge that had drawn the others forward, because my terror was greater than any curiosity, greater than any wish to experience new perceptions or dimensions, greater than any desire to return to some forgotten state of being.

Darkness came to the lake, touching the darkness of the shore and plain. The great brother volcanoes had disappeared, but I could feel them there, their presence imposing itself upon my spirit very strongly, hardly understanding how I could resist them. I honestly believe that if I had not put on my clothes and turned my face towards the road and set my feet walking, I would still be there beside the lake, with Renarta, Shelley, Fritz, Greta and the vernacular Kathe. I would be there, playing games, gathering berries, eating fish.

The last words I heard, as my feet found the hard dust of the road in the darkness, was Renarta's voice, shrill, excited, quite young, revealing the beginnings of leadership qualities, saying, 'What shall we play now?'

BLOOD ORANGE

An expatriate 'gone native' was something of a cliché just after the war. Some of us just could not go home: would have found it impossible to face relatives and friends. Some of us stayed in Singapore because we were not the same people that had been sent out there. Internment had changed us drastically and we knew that we fitted into life more easily in the east than in our birthplace. Some of us, those like me, simply could not let go of the small patch of soil which had forced such dramatic changes upon our lives.

So we had stayed on, poverty ensuring that the only way we could do so was to live simply, in the most primitive conditions. It was because of our meagre pensions that we lived like the natives, not because we were ascetics or had found the secret of the Orient.

When I was released from Changi POW camp in 1945, 1 was twenty-four years of age. The hair on my chest had gone white and crisp. I was thin, wasted and hollow, both inside and out. I moved only two hundred yards from where I had slept for four years, to a hut in the kampong immediately outside Changi jail. There I stayed and here I will die.

One aspect of Japanese life I have adopted from my captors: a strong sense of ritual and a respect for symbolism. It is necessary to point this out, in order that I am not considered mad when I say that, every morning, I devour a child of the sun.

The earliest light of the day is filtered greenly by the canopy of palm leaves above my rattan bed. Half an hour later the sun's rays strike my face and I know it is time to rise. My bed is situated on the veranda of my hut and the first thing I see, as I search for my sandals with my feet, is a narrow, worn-earth pathway through a long arch of vegetation, at the end of which stands Changi jail.

It has of course reverted to its role as a civil, and military, prison, but it has changed little from the days when Japanese soldiers manned its pointed watchtowers. I suppose I could best describe it as looking like a Turkish fortification. It has a Middle Eastern appearance about it that is a little incongruous among the Singapore temples.

Over the pathway bats glide, seeking diurnal resting places after the night's hunting. There are insects, too, the size of hummingbirds.

Cultivated flame trees fill the morning with scarlet blossoms and there are other rich colours on the bushes that line the walk. Singapore is only just saved, by the sombre dark green of the more prolific wild palms that serve to dampen down what might otherwise be a vulgar show.

I rise from my bed and take my breakfast, which is always the same: an orange—a blood orange, if I can get it. It is a fruit that seems to be available the whole year round in these times of plenty.

I begin the ritual by peeling the object, placing the skin aside for afterwards. Then I split the flesh into segments, to destroy that appearance of a human brain. I form a line of them on the dish. I eat the segments slowly, crushing them with my toothless gums to release the lifeblood of the fruit. Finally, once all the segments have been devoured, I break the rind into small pieces and swallow them.

This morning the ritual is a painful experience—spiritually painful—and I do it because I deserve to suffer. A sense of betrayal needs sustenance to stay alive, like anything else. I feed it daily.

Daniel and I were interned together, when the Japanese overran Singapore in 1942. We were both twenty years of age and bewildered by the predicament in which we found ourselves.

For two years we had been enjoying the heady atmosphere and freedom of an exotic island, with its liberal—no, licentious—attitudes and its mystical culture. We had been drugged by the place, the lion city, with its temples, erotic carvings and bars full of girls. That we should confuse culture, religion and sex, and not see the pathos beneath the glitter of the night life, the sad plight of the females with whom we consorted, was barely excusable by our youth. We took things at face value, being shallow boys looking to enrich our experience of life. Of course, we looked in the wrong places, boys always do. Sensitivity is a gift of the older, more reflective man. Sensuality governs the young.

We were totally unprepared for the privation which was to follow such an uncontrolled existence. Of course, we told each other at the time, there was no question that we would not survive. We would see each other through. There were others who would not make it, because they could not rely on the support of a friend.

Daniel and I had been raised together from the age of four. We had attended the same schools—not very good ones—and had joined the Air Force together as mechanics at the age of eighteen. We were totally committed to one another.

It is true we quarrelled on occasion: most close friends do. Such comradeship is like a marriage, excluding the physical element. Certainly we had shared the same bed with each other, and our girlfriends, uninhibited by the presence of a friend.

Daniel was the more outgoing personality. He was not the brash extrovert who bores his listeners, but a youth with many social graces, and I was a little jealous of him at times. The ease with which he communicated with others left me feeling quite inadequate. Being the quieter, I clung to his coat-tails on social occasions, standing by his side and only injecting a remark into the conversation when there was a lull. Strangely, I was thought the cleverer, because of this, but it was essentially a cheat. Whereas Daniel was fair and lively, I was dark and moody, and in allowing him the floor most of the time, I had the leisure to form some witticism in my mind and to insert it at an appropriate point.

Daniel was always the first to praise such witticisms, always carefully placed, and would put his hand on my shoulder, saying. 'You've got to get up early to catch this lad. He's as sharp as a razor.' Thus, quite wrongly, I earned the reputation for being a street intellectual; someone who said little, but when he did open his mouth, by God something smart came out.

The other area in which I was envious of Daniel was sport. He had an athletic body which he used to its best advantage. He was a brilliant swimmer, could dive to competition standard, boxed very well and was in the Far East rugby team. Those were only his major achievements: he could play most sports and games to a reasonable level. Consequently, he was very successful with girls: the two often go hand-in-hand. The daughters of older, married-accompanied servicemen sought him out at functions and dances. Strangely, he was a rotten dancer. I was much better. I had a natural feel for the rhythm and my loose-limbed frame seemed fashioned for movements put to music.

* * *

This made little difference to Daniel's standing amongst the young females. They dragged him on to the floor and insisted on trying to teach him the rudiments of dancing, and his awkward, jerky steps, instead of frustrating them, merely amused them and endeared him to them.

Daniel's quick thinking saved my life on two occasions in Singapore. Once, ignoring his advice, I swam too far out into the straits and got into difficulties in the fast currents of those dangerous waters. He coaxed and bullied me back to shore, refusing afterwards to consider his efforts to have been of any consequence. Instead of chastising me for my stupidity, he praised my stamina and endurance, saying that if he had had a cramp in such circumstances, he could not have remained as cool and clear-headed as I had done. But it was only his presence that had prevented me from succumbing to panic: his calming influence. I had not had cramp and pure funk had caused me to struggle at a time when I should have acted rationally, thus causing myself to get caught in the mainstream of fast-flowing water.

On the second occasion, we were walking across Changi golf course, myself in the lead, when a cobra reared up not a yard in front. I froze as the snake sat, swaying its hooded head before me. I think it would have struck had not Daniel thrown his shirt over it, like a gladiator's net. We left the shirt where it was, and ran.

Daniel was shrieking with laughter, while I shook in terror at the thought of what might have happened. It was as if he had just performed some schoolboy prank. It was not nervous laughter. Danger to him was an exhilarating experience. It was fun. It acted on his body like breathing pure oxygen. He got high on it. His eyes would sparkle and the excitement would be apparent in his whole demeanour.

Whenever he retold this story, he maintained that I had deliberately distracted the cobra long enough for him to remove his shirt. I was the hero, not him, because my part was the more dangerous of the two.

I almost came to believe this version myself, he recounted it with such conviction, his hand on my shoulder and his pride in me evident in every word and gesture. Yet when I recalled the incident, truthfully, I remembered that he had not been wearing his shirt; he had removed it earlier to improve his tan. It had been draped over his arm when we were confronted by the snake. But Daniel was like that. He preferred to share the glory, even to the point of giving me the major role.

I hated Daniel for his selflessness, his modesty, the purity of his friendship. He turned truth into a lie which I had to live and act. I had to pretend to be this person he had made me into—brave, clever and the perfect friend.

I lived in constant dread of being exposed as a fraud, of Daniel turning to me one day and accusing me of all the falsehoods with which he had moulded me. He never did. Always his shoulders were there, ready for me to climb upon. Always his hand was willingly extended to pull me up beside him, to share in any glory. I hated him for it.

When the Japanese arrived we were ordered by our officers to parade on Changi airstrip. The first enemy soldiers I saw were riding bicycles: small, wiry men looking as if they were on their way to work at some factory. They took little notice of us, but dumped their machines before lining the route along which came one of their high-ranking officers in a staff car.

I was not afraid at that time. I certainly had been, before it was obvious that we were going to surrender and not have to fight to the last man to defend the island. After which, I relaxed and prepared for the inevitable. Daniel did, at one point, suggest taking a boat and trying for one of the many islands that lay south of Singapore, but I persuaded him of the futility of the scheme. The Japanese would certainly have found us.

We were herded into Changi jail, which became a prisonerof-war camp, and we very quickly realised that our lives, henceforth, were to become one long fight against the ravages of malnutrition and disease. The Japanese guards became almost superfluous: there was nowhere to run to, even if we did escape, and the real enemy had become hunger exacerbated by dysentery. All talk centred around the stomach and bowels. Personal possessions—watches, pens, lighters—became the currency with which to buy food, and we found that this was best achieved by forming groups and pooling our resources.

I was forever on the brink of starvation and on the edge of some indefinable illness. Until you have known such unrelenting hunger and the violent misery of constantly inflamed bowels, you cannot imagine what despair the spirit suffers. It is an oppression which seems eternal. Hell could devise no worse punishment for its inmates. Around me, all the time, men died of broken spirits. They simply gave up, realising that death, whatever it was like, must be better than a life spent in constant worry about finding something to put in at one end of the body which would cause agony, later, at the other end.

It was indeed an attractive thought, that one could leave all the wretchedness behind simply by ceasing to breathe. To drift away from that detestable body and its functions, its interminable craving for nourishment, its whining, whimpering, self-pitying spirit, seemed like a sensible and blessed act.

But Daniel would not countenance surrender to the body. He insisted we fight against such considerations, our combined strength helping each other through.

'I want to live,' he said. 'And you, too. We'll prop each other up. Support each other. One of us, alone, can't make it—but together we can do it . . .'

This was a daily lecture, and indeed, such talk kept me from suicide in that humid, heavy climate that pressed down on one's soul, squeezing it dry of will and purpose.

Through guile, charm and artful manipulation, Daniel

managed to get us a job, cleaning out Lieutenant Matsumara's quarters. For this work we each received extra rations, directly from our patron, though this was kept secret from the other prisoners and Captain Yakusha, the camp's Deputy Commander. It was only light, domestic housework, but it left us feeling enormously fatigued. At the end of two hours of sweeping, dusting, scrubbing and washing clothes, we would be exhausted. I complained bitterly about this fact to Daniel, quite forgetting that we were in a privileged position and receiving more than most other prisoners. Daniel rarely commented on these outbursts from me, knowing that they stemmed from something beyond that which could be put into words.

When Matsumara returned, to inspect his rooms after our cleaning sessions, Daniel would always be smiling, to show his gratitude; an attitude which seemed to please the Japanese officer. He appeared to like Daniel, though his expression never revealed such feelings, and he was fascinated by our close friendship.

He would say to us in his broken English:

'Which one you is the strong?'

Daniel would reply, 'We support each other. Our strength is in our unity.'

Once, probably one of the only times I spoke to Matsumara without being asked a direct question, I added, 'We would die for one another.'

Matsumara was impressed, but whether it was the words, or merely because I, the silent one, had uttered them, I do not know.

He said to me, slowly, 'You would die for your friend?'

'Yes. I would give my life for him, if I had to.'

His keen, Oriental-brown eyes studied me for a long time, while Daniel smiled, looking from one to the other of us, and finally, Matsumara said, 'Yes, you would.'

I would give my life for him. The words had not been spoken

in truth, but because they had been expected of me, at some time, by my friend. I was still playing the role he had written for me, encouraged me to act. I must have been good at it, for Matsumara accepted it as fact.

Matsumara was a young officer who had recently been promoted from the ranks: a field promotion, for valour, he told us. He was in fact a fairly ignorant man—not unintelligent, but unlearned and lazy. His father was a peasant farmer, but Matsumara had distinguished himself on the field of battle and had brought himself to the notice of his superiors. He valued, above all things, courage. He was not a happy man. Most of his fellow officers were from high-born families and his lack of education was apparent—I believe he was held in scorn by his contemporaries. I was convinced he could hardly count and said to Daniel that any figure past the number of six left him confused. Why I chose this figure, I do not know, for I had no proof of it being the threshold of his mathematics, but for some reason I needed a simple encapsulating definition of his educational weakness. Whenever Daniel started defending the Japanese lieutenant, I would always fall back on my dismissive statement: 'The man's a dunce. He can't even count past six.'

Once, Daniel said, 'Does that matter?' But I was so angry with him for questioning my judgement, he never again gave me any argument. He realised, I suppose, that I was grasping at some irrational means of identifying Matsumara. In order to bring the man within my sphere of contempt, I reduced him to something smaller and more insignificant than myself. It was necessary to me that I could look down on the officer who terrified me.

Oh, yes, I was afraid of him. I did not understand the man or his culture. I thought him unpredictable and unreasonable. To me he had a lunatic's eyes and mannerisms and I could not trust his moods or rationality. No doubt he was as sane as any man caught up in a war, but I always felt insecure in his pres-

ence and worried that at any moment he might turn on me
with the impulsiveness of a wild beast.

Matsumara was, like many Japanese officers, fascinated by
his sword. He would be forever cleaning the blade, or honing it
to a brilliant sharpness. He doted on it, lovingly, telling us as
we cleaned around his desk that it was a shinshinto blade—a
new-new sword—dating back only to 1860. It was a katana,
a long sword, slung from the waist and worn with the edge
upwards. He showed us the undulating temper line and the
tight itame grain. There were stylised Sanskrit characters on
the steel which he translated for us.

'Yamano Nagahisa: cut through two bodies.'

'Yamano Naganari: cut through three bodies.'

These were the weapon's previous owners. Matsumara often
said, rather wistfully, that he had not yet had the opportunity to test the weapon's strength on a man. He wanted his
own inscription on the blade. This was another reason why he
terrified me. I felt that he only needed one small excuse for an
execution.

The months passed and somehow Daniel and I survived.
But we sank ever lower,body spiritually and physically.

Matsumara, anxious to be of active service to his Emperor,
became irritable at being left in the stagnant backwater of
Changi POW camp. He took out his frustration on us, sometimes beating us with a bamboo rod when the cleanliness of
the hut was not up to his standard, which varied from day
to day. He seemed forever dissatisfied with everyone around
him, complaining about the prisoners, the guards and his
fellow officers. As things went, his treatment of us was
comparatively humane. Other Japanese were far more cruel
in their disciplinary punishments. Then, suddenly, Matsumara found a new, subtle torture, a game, which seemed to

satisfy his need to strike deeply into our spirits and helped to
alleviate his bitterness.

He received a gift from his father in Japan: a box of oranges.
Each day he would put three or four out in a bowl and then
excuse himself while we cleaned his rooms. Just the scent of
those fruits was enough to make my head reel and drive my
senses crazy. I slavered over them, as I polished the desk top
and touched their textured forms with aching fingers.

I dreamed about those oranges every waking and sleeping
hour. They were the children of the evening sun: spherical
golden objects full of goodness. One of them, just one of them, I
convinced myself, could prove to be the panacea for all my bodily
complaints. Rice and biscuits were sawdust in comparison to
those beautiful, succulent fruits that adorned Matsumara's desk
top. I was driven mad by their fragrance, by the sight of them.
I tasted the juice, the flesh, in my dreams—burying my teeth in
the segments, letting the amber liquid run down my chin, lapping
it back into my mouth with my tongue. I tormented myself with
thoughts of how I should peel the fruit, working slowly from
the top. Then I should break it, first in half, then in quarters,
admiring the grain, the golden threads of flesh. Then to shred my
first segment, placing it between my teeth, sucking the wonderful
fluid down, feeling the citric acid stinging my parched throat. My
body would tingle with the electric sensation of vitamin C, as it
worked its way through my torso, driving out the inflammation,
the ulcerations. It would find my limbs and cure the external
sores, the swellings, the constant fever. No longer would I shake
and shiver, sweat and overheat, in my bed at night. The orange
would wash away the malaria. The mere odour, as I pressed it
to my mouth, would clear my head of the demonic ache that
plagued me from morning to night, from dusk to dawn. Just a
single one of those oranges held the combined secrets to perfect
health of all the wizards, physicians and sorcerers, collected since
the beginning of time.

Matsumara knew. Oh yes, he knew. He would watch us as we cleaned, noting when our eyes strayed to the bowl, for Daniel was just as obsessed by the fruit as I was myself.

The Japanese officer knew also how to increase the intensity of that obsession. He would pick one up, turn it over in his hand and sniff it with those wide nostrils, then rub it against his cheek. Then the ritual would start.

He would begin by peeling the object, placing the skin aside for afterwards. Then he would split the flesh into segments, forming a line of them on his dish. He would eat the segments slowly, crashing them between his lips to release the lifeblood of the fruit. It would dribble down his chin and he would wipe it back into his mouth with a stubby finger. Finally, once all the segments had been devoured, he would break the rind into small pieces and chew them, before swallowing.

The ritual was a painful experience for me—spiritually painful—and I suffered with every mouthful that he took.

Afterwards, he would give us our oatmeal biscuits—the payment for our services, knowing that they would taste like ashes in our mouths after his exhibition.

He knew the depths of his cruelty, the depravity of his actions, but when I think about it now I believe he could not help himself. He was desperately lonely—a peasant officer among aristocrats—and he wanted to be where the fighting was, out in the Pacific. He had been dumped and forgotten, and it gnawed at his spirit. Rejected by his fellow officers, out of contact with the rankers, left to rot in a prison camp, he was boiling with contained anger. He had no release valve and turned that emotion to poisonous pleasure. He needed to hurt, and we were available. I do not, now, believe he was a naturally vindictive man, but his situation produced something from the corner of his soul, blew it up, expanded it, until his spirit became a balloon full of nothing but foul gases.

Always there were only three or four oranges in the bowl.

There was no way we could steal one without Matsumara knowing. The penalty for such an act would be death. So we continued to stare dumbly at the wonderful spheres and suffered the distress of watching them disappear down Matsumara's throat, one by one.

Despite Matsumara's new torture, he was as talkative as ever with Daniel. He told us, for I was always there to listen, of stories of courage amongst Japanese heroes. Daniel, in his turn, would contribute one of his own tales, and in most of these it amused him to make me the protagonist. It gave my friend a kick to see Matsumara's eyes stray to my silent form as he related some courageous incident in which I was the hero and, quite often, Daniel was the man rescued from drowning, or saved from the deadly bite of the cobra. It was in Daniel's make-up, his personality, that he could not keep a good story contained. He had to tell it, if the opportunity arose. But he was too modest to make himself the hero of the piece, even when that was the fact, so he switched the roles around.

Matsumara would look in my direction, as I swept the floor, or dusted his military reference books, and say, 'He is brave man. I see it in his eyes. I feel it in my heart. He speaks little, but his courage is strong.'

One day there were seven oranges in the bowl. Matsumara had left us alone. I stole one of the fruits.

Daniel said, 'Don't be a fool. He'll know.'

'He can't count,' I said, the hand holding the orange trembling violently. 'It'll be all right.'

Daniel protested, pleaded with me, getting angry. I stood there, strangely impervious to all his arguments. He could have taken it from me by force, but he didn't, and finally we heard Matsumara's footsteps on the front porch. I ran out of the back door and hid the fruit at the bottom of a pail, covering it with cleaning rags. I still had the bucket in my hand when I was called inside.

I went into the hut and found Matsumara confronting Daniel. The lieutenant was in a terrible rage. His face was ugly with wrath as he screamed at me to stand beside my friend. He could hardly get the words out, he was choking on his anger.

He thrust his face before Daniel's.

'Someone has eat one orange.'

Daniel said nothing. I waited and waited, my heart thumping and my legs shaking so badly they would hardly keep me upright, but no words came from the mouth of my friend. Out of the corner of my eye I could see he was white with fear and this increased my own feelings of terror. I could sense a wetness in my shorts.

'Speak!' screamed Matsumara.

But for once Daniel was silent. He stood there, in his stained khaki shorts and dirty vest, and his mouth remained tightly closed, though his eyes were still full of panic. The lieutenant sniffed his breath, then mine, and shook his head in frustration. We both had gum disease and the foul breath that went with it.

Matsumara drew his sword. Its glinting hurt my eyes as the rays of the sun from the window struck the blade. I could see the edge, brilliant in its deadly beauty, as the light seared along the honed temper line. I could not take my eyes from the weapon. It seemed to have a cold personality of its own, like a shark whose purpose blinds it to all but death.

The savage face was now before my own.

'You! Did you steal orange?'

Even now I cannot recall why I answered as I did. At the time I believe my consternation was so great that I hardly knew where I was, let alone what I was saying. It was not courage, that much is certain. It might have been that his fury filled me with dread, and like a recalcitrant schoolboy, faced by an enraged master, I wanted only to soothe, to appease the man. This is not altogether satisfactory and I only use it as an excuse in my most desperate moments of guilt, when

I am overwhelmed by the horror of my betrayal of my best friend. In my more truthful moods I admit to myself that, deep down, I knew how my words would be taken. I knew that Matsumara considered me a selfless, brave man and the perfect friend. I knew that he admired such things above all other attributes in the character of a man.

I was aware that my hand still held the bucket which contained the stolen fruit. I placed it down, carefully.

'I stole the orange. I am the thief,' I said.

He stared into my features, for a long time, and then at Daniel, who remained unmoving, a slight, sickly smile forming at the corners of his mouth.

Then the lieutenant took Daniel by the hair and dragged him from the hut. I followed, stumbling down the wooden steps into the sunlight, as Daniel was forced to his knees on the hard-baked earth. My friend's head was bowed and he remained perfectly still, silent.

I saw—a dream-like scene—Matsumara raise the sword. It flashed once. There was a terrible sound. Daniel's head rolled at my feet, the neck raw and bloody.

That evening, I took the orange from its hiding place and went into a remote corner of the camp. I peeled it quickly and then broke it in half. Inside, there were red veins—blood-red veins—that ran through the raw flesh of the fruit, making it appear like an open wound.

It was a blood orange.

I stared at it in the dying light of the day. It was Daniel's head. I was holding Daniel's head in my hands.

I buried my mouth in the neck and sucked the blood from the severed veins. I remember I was crying. At least, I think I was crying. God knows, I tried hard enough. But it tasted so good. It tasted so good.

WALKING CAGED BIRDS

The Sunday market at Sham Shui Po was responsible for filling several streets with a solid mass of people, struggling and writhing through each other. Children were lost somewhere, below the shoulders of the adults, and parents relied on keeping the small hands within theirs. Impossibly, the jostled stalls that lined the curbs remained upright and untrampled.

The attraction of Sham Shui Po is in the variety of its cheap wares. There you can buy anything from snake meat to transistor circuits to 100-year eggs. It is one of those Asian bazaars that sell matrimony vine, yam beans and angled luffa, as greens to go with your pork chop and mashed potatoes. Where live, grey catfish bubble like lava in old oil drums, and Cantonese chestnuts are baked in charcoal.

It was down one of these streets that Phillip came across a stall selling caged birds and wondered whether to make a purchase.

He stood there for a few minutes in the boil of people, being nudged and pushed from all sides, finding it difficult to remain still so that he could study the birds.

From what he could see there were dozens of different types of songbird, none of which he recognised, ranging in prices from a few dollars to a thousand. They were small creatures, some of them not bigger than a wren, most with a bright patch of colour somewhere on their plumage or beaks.

The preferred cages, at least by the Chinese customers, were rounded and made from bamboo. These too, were small, and reminded him of the kind of cages he had seen in pictures of Victorian drawing-rooms. Metal cages, like those occupied by budgerigars back in England, appeared to be less expensive, and certainly not as popular. He guessed the smallness of everything had to do with the lack of space in Hong Kong, the woodenness to do with the humidity which caused metal objects to rust very quickly. Apartments were tiny rooms in tower blocks, often occupied by three generations. Perhaps the lack of living space can be best underlined by mentioning the fact that there were places called 'romantic hotels' in certain areas of the city, where young married couples rented beds by the hour in order to start a family of their own in some kind of cool privacy. Under such conditions a pet would have to take up as little room as possible.

The reason he was considering buying one of these captive singers was that his wife had left him.

It was not the only reason of course. Back in England Phillip had been the deputy head of an Essex village school. He and Rita had lived in a cottage and the loudest sound they heard was the bark of foxes calling each other, or the screeching of squirrels quarrelling with magpies. In Hong Kong, where he was headmaster of a much larger establishment, there was the constant sound of traffic, aircraft flying overhead, jackhammers on every street and pile drivers on every spare piece of ground. Consequently, he was always trying out schemes of introducing pieces of his old way of life into the apartment overlooking Tai Po Road. One of the reasons Rita had left him, he was sure, was the fact that she hated the noise. She was still close by, but up in the New Territories, living with Arthur Gordon-Williams, the President of the Cricket Club. It was quieter on their Spanish-style suburban estate, up in the hills, in a house Phillip could never afford in a million years. Rita had the gall to suggest he got himself a 'nice young Filipino girlfriend' which caused him to remark that his wife had acquired some rather strange morals since she had been in the Far East.

Rita's leaving had come as a bit of a shock: she had always seemed so contented, humming away as she did things around the flat. Even now, when he thought about it, he was a bit bemused by the change that came over her. Or rather the change that did not come over her, since when she met him at the club, she seemed the same as always. Smiling, and cheerful on the surface at least. She had simply told him one evening as they were getting into bed, 'I'm going to live with Arthur,' and then switched out the light and went to sleep. It was not until he came home the next day that he realized the remark was serious. Gordon-Williams was a bachelor and though he hadn't yet said as much, Phillip suspected that Rita's defection was a bit of a shock to him as well. He clearly hadn't been expecting her to descend on him, suitcase in hand. It was all a bit bewildering.

It was difficult, living alone in a colony where all the ex-pats and other gweilos were partying most of the time. He was invited out, of course, but he suspected on sufferance, and it was little fun being out with several couples knowing you had to go home alone to a small empty apartment at the end of the evening. The trouble was, he was trapped by circum-stances. You had to get on in the world. It was expected of you, by everyone, and the only headmaster's post he had been able to get was in Hong Kong. Perhaps in a few years, when he'd danced enough to the right tunes, they would offer him a post in a school in England. Until then, he was caught in the same net that held a lot of others like him.

Company was a problem. He had purchased a spaniel in the first instance, possibly to spite Rita who disliked dogs, but found the strain of the animal's presence too much. Rabid creatures wandered over the border from China from time to time, sending a ripple of fear through the colony. He had found himself staring into the hound's liquid eyes of an evening, wondering if he would recognise rabies in time to avoid being bitten. What if those soft brown eyes suddenly turned hard and vicious and Goldie leapt at him with slavering teeth? Several painful injections and still a good chance of dying in agony. Goldie was sold to a local pet shop, and no doubt went to a family, hopefully on one of the islands where there was a better chance of controlling the disease which sometimes had the army out on (unthinkable in England) dog shoots.

'How much?' he asked, tentatively. 'Er, ngoh yui er, yat bird. Gei do chin—a?'

He pointed to a caged bird. It stood so stiff and still on its perch, as it warbled its sweet song, it could have been one of those mechanical toys the Chinese used to be so clever at making.

The stall owner moved out into the mainstream in front of his wares where Phillip was trying to maintain his balance against the constant conflicting currents of people. Reaching up with a pole the little man unhooked one of the many cages.

Brusquely, he said, 'This one? Fiffy-dolla. Okay, you want?'

Phillip had to make up his mind fast. It was not like the old days when they needed gweilo custom to make a living. These days they were just as likely to get impatient with you and wave you away with the contempt you probably deserved. Phillip found the typical brusque Cantonese manner intimidating anyway.

'Yes, well, I want it. But it seems a little cruel. Haven't you got a larger cage. Bigger cage? Look, what about that one . . . ?'

He pointed, but the man shook his head, his mouth a thin line.

'No, no change, no change. You want this one? Fiffy-dolla. No change.'

Phillip was sweating. The little man must have thought he wanted the same bird in a bigger cage for the same price. He tried to explain.

'No, this one too small. Bird unhappy, see?'

Now the Chinese smiled and waved a finger.

'Bird no happy, bird no sing.'

Was that true? Phillip doubted it.

He made his decision.

'All right.' He handed the man a hundred and got five filthy ten dollar notes in change. Sometimes he thought they kept the dirtiest money just for him.

'Bird happy,' assured the little man cried, smiling, as he moved with the flow. 'You walk him, bird happy.'

'I wish I was,' thought Phillip.

Phillip fought his way to Sham Shui Po railway station and out of the masses, before he thought, walk the bird? Of course! He had seen them, in the park of a Sunday morning, strolling around with caged birds held up by one hand. They showed them to each other, perfect strangers (probably) stopping to let the birds introduce themselves, the owners not speaking, but allowing the songsters to give each other a trill. They walked their birds as Englishmen walked their dogs. Today was Sunday.

He got off the train at Shek Kip Mei, not really knowing the district but having a good idea that there was a park nearby. He left the railway station and began walking along the street, holding his bird out in front of him. Although he felt a little self-conscious, no one laughed at him, or even looked his way especially. He passed another man carrying a similar caged bird, but the Chinese did not make any move to introduce his pet, so Phillip kept on walking. Eventually he came to a large colonial-style house with gardens all around it. There were one or two couples strolling around, between the bushes. A park, if ever he saw one.

He went through the gates and under the flaring canopy of the flame trees, looking for a bench on which to sit for a while. His bird was singing, sweetly.

Phillip found a seat under a sweet chestnut tree and sat down. The bird continued to warble to the world. Along the paths which wound in and out of the shrubbery were other birds fanciers, walking with caged songsters held out in front of them. Hanging in the trees like lanterns, were still more cages, all containing birds. Their owners sat around beneath them, talking in a tonal language full of chirrups. The scene was rather like a surreal movie during the shooting of which the film maker Werner Herzog had sought the advice of the painter Magritte.

Phillip put his own bird on the grass in front of him and then closed his eyes and listened to the sweet sounds.

When he opened his eyes again, he became aware that someone was sitting next to him. He glanced across and was confronted by a young Asian girl with wide eyes and a broad, open-mouthed smile. She looked from Phillip to the bird, without losing her grin.

'Yes,' said Phillip, 'nice little chap, isn't he? At least, I call him a he. She could be a she.' He laughed and the girl laughed with him.

Encouraged, he continued to talk.

'Of course, I think the smallness of the cage is a little cruel, but the man at the stall said, 'Bird no happy, bird no sing.'' He frowned. 'I'm not sure about that. I mean, what about black slaves? They sang all the time, but I shouldn't think many of them were happy. Do you see what I mean?'

She swung her legs under the seat, still smiling at him.

'And if you think about it,' continued Phillip, 'I mean, I'm no ornithologist but as I understand it, birds mostly sing to define territorial boundaries. There was a thrush that used to perch on our television aerial, in England. He used to sing all the time, but it was only demarcation. He was warning away other thrushes. Nothing to do with being happy or sad or anything like that. We've got to be careful not to anthropomorphise such creatures—' he stopped, realizing she probably wouldn't understand the word. 'I mean, give them human feelings and reasons for their actions. Maybe that sound he's making isn't singing at all, not to other birds. Maybe it's a harsh unpleasant language to other birds and grates on their ears. Perhaps the sounds he is using are dark oaths, bloody threats . . . I'm sorry, I wasn't swearing you understand. I meant ugly threats, full of menace.'

Phillip warmed to his idea.

'When they meet each other in the park, one bird is probably saying to another, 'If I could get out of this cage I'd peck out your eyes,' something like that. And all the while their owners are grinning away, and not understanding what's going on between them.'

The girl's smile did not waver. In fact it seemed fixed in some disturbing way.

'I've come to the conclusion,' said Phillip, 'that we understand very little about our fellow creatures, especially birds.'

At that point, the girl began to stand. At least, she was assisted to her feet by a man sitting on the opposite side to her. The Chinese gentleman and the young girl walked off, slowly, along the path towards a car park half-hidden by some trees. The man was holding the girl's arm. She looked back, once, still smiling. He realized she hadn't once offered a remark to him, and came to the conclusion that she only spoke her own language.

'Funny thing,' thought Phillip. 'In the beginning I could have sworn she was following my English. Just goes to show. I must have sounded like some sort of simpleton, stupid grin on my face and wittering away in a foreign tongue.'

He picked up his caged bird and strolled across the grass towards the car park, hoping to find a toilet there. An orange juice he had drunk earlier in the afternoon was beginning to wreak havoc on his weak plumbing.

Reaching the cars, he began to cross the asphalt when he saw the young girl again. He realized then, that any language might have been unintelligible to her. She was in a line of others, all being assisted up the steps of a coach. Several of them wore a similar smile, the smile that said they were locked up inside their own heads.

'What a shame,' thought Phillip. 'She seemed so happy . . . '

His bird chirped away, as if in agreement. Phillip looked down at the cage in his hand. After a few moments thought, he crossed to the trees, set the cage on the ground and opened the little door. Then he walked away from it, without a second glance. He felt pleased with himself, for having been able to draw an analogy between the young girl and the bird in the cage.

On reaching home he put the key in the lock and opened the door, only to hear noises coming from the bedroom. For a few moments tremors of fear went through him as thoughts of burglars worried him. Then he recognised Rita's perfume.

'Is that you, my dear?' he called.

A second later the bedroom door opened and Rita stood there, with an armful of books.

'It's me, but I don't think I'm your dear any longer,' she said, heaving the books into a cardboard box on the floor.

'These are mine,' she explained. 'I'm shipping them back to England.'

'Whatever for? You can come and use my library whenever you want, you know that.'

Rita's eyes were colder than he remembered.

'Because I'm going home soon,' she said.

Phillip considered this carefully, before saying, 'But Arthur's tour of duty isn't due to be completed until next year.'

'I'm not interested in what Arthur's doing.'

'But aren't you two . . . I thought you left me for him.'

She stared at him frankly.

'I don't want to hurt you Phillip, but I left you for other reasons, certainly not for Arthur Gordon-Williams, who is no improvement on you. I used him for a while, to collect my thoughts, that's all.'

'You used him?'

'You're not shocked, are you? It happens all the time you know, people using each other.'

He regarded the cardboard box.

'Yes, I suppose it does. But you always seemed so, oh, I don't know. Anyway, what do you mean,' he realized he should be bristling, 'no improvement on me? What's wrong with me. I always treated you well. I never knowingly hurt you in any way.'

She sighed.

'No, you never did that. You're not a bad person, Phillip. You just . . . don't understand that's all. You think that if you take me out once in a while, I should be happy. There's more to it than that. I don't expect you to understand. You've never understood how trapped I felt.'

'But I do understand—now.'

'I'm sorry,' she said, closing the lid of the box and carrying it the books towards the door. 'It's too late to go into it all again. I tried telling you before, but you wouldn't listen.'

Rita went through the open doorway.

Phillip stood in the middle of the room and stared at the spot where she had been standing.

He remained there for a long while, before saying to the empty room, 'It's not that I didn't listen. It's just that I didn't understand the song . . . '

TRIADS

Lee Tam Cheung was an eye-eye, an illegal immigrant, and he lived in the massive slum known as the Walled City. Cheung had come to Hong Kong at the age of fourteen, not on a traditional junk, but on a smuggler's craft: a sleek launch with three huge outboard engines designed to outrun the customs' boats. He had at first stayed with an uncle in Kam Tin, a Hakka village in the New Territories, but when it became too hot for him there he fled down into Kowloon and entered the Walled City.

Inside the Walled City an eye-eye was safe, since this piece of land in the centre of the colony still belonged to China, though too far from Beijing to be administered or policed. Only when he left the slum did Cheung risk being stopped by the police and sent back to China. Not that the risk stopped him or his friends from going outside the Walled City.

Actually, there was no longer a wall around the ancient city of the Manchus, but it was still just as impenetrable to strangers. An area the size of a large football stadium had filled with boxy slums, built haphazardly, side by side, one on top of the other, until it was now a single unit, a labyrinth of dark tunnels and stinking corners. People within had to call to those with dwellings on the edge to find out if it was night or day, raining or fine. It was said that the 'ghost children' born in the gloomy tangle of tunnels and cells asked the eternal question of all oubliette prisoners: Who stole the sky?

Bundles of electric wiring ran in tangled loops alongside dripping hose pipes carrying the city water supply, to junction boxes with no lids and silver paper in place of fuses. There were people living in cupboards, running fish-ball businesses. There were large families in tiny single-roomed flats. There were over fifty thousand people, crammed in a place without natural light, with fetid air, and crawling with wildlife.Cheung did not mind the darkness, dirt and squalor. He expected them in a place where the Hong Kong police could not enter and lawlessness flourished. The Walled City was a place of prostitution, heroin addiction, drug smuggling, extortion and fear, run by the Triads of which Cheung was a member. Cheung was a tin-man-toi for the 14K, a watchman for one of the most notorious of the Triad gangs. He had a tattoo on his left shoulder to prove his allegiance, for the members of a Triad gang are not all known to each other on sight. They work mainly in groups of three: hence their generic title.

Cheung, at eighteen, was a strong youth, good looking and as yet unscarred by the knives or choppers of rival gangs. Cheung enjoyed his privileged position as a Triad member, the camaraderie of his friends, the young prostitutes who liked his hard body. Cheung thought he was satisfied with his lifestyle.

Then he fell in love.

It was on a balmy evening in November. The last of the typhoons had swept through the colony and had gone its savage way up into China. Cheung and two friends were sitting on the harbour wall, Kowloon side, watching the light-encrusted craft weaving in and out of each other—the banana-shaped junks bobbing high on the water, the innumerable ferries, the lighters, the barges, the sampans, the jetfoils—laughing and joking, when an expensive white yacht passed with a young girl on the deck. She looked up from a magazine she was reading and stared right into Cheung's eyes. The two people, youth and girl, were only a few feet apart at that moment.

Cheung was immediately smitten by her beauty. She looked so clean he could have eaten her like ice cream. Her thick, black shiny hair hung down her back and as she turned shyly away from his glance he could see that it was cut in the straightest line he had ever seen, just at the point her tiny waist met her small hips. Her eyes were like black gems; her teeth as delicate and white as eggshell porcelain; her nose a neat button on her perfectly heart-shaped face. She was, he guessed, seventeen or eighteen years of age.

Without saying a word to his companions, Cheung stood up and began running along the harbour, keeping pace with the boat. The girl looked up once, and then down at the deck immediately, but he could see she was smiling. Once, Cheung had to dash out into the busy streets because his way was blocked along the edge of the harbour, but he shot back to the water's edge again as soon as he was able. Then the yacht pulled away from Tsim Sha Tsui and began to cross the harbour to Hong Kong Island.

Cheung ran to the Star Ferry, managed to pay his sixty cents and jump on a boat that was just leaving. The yacht was slightly faster than the ferry, but still it had only just berthed at Queen's Pier when the ferry docked. Cheung raced down the gangways and reached Queen's Pier just as the girl was getting into a Rolls Royce. He hailed a taxi. When he could not get it to stop, he jumped out into the road in front of the next one. The driver leaned out of the window.

'What are you doing, you little fool? Get out of the way.'

Cheung said, 'I need to ride.'

'Go to the taxi rank then,' screeched the driver, an old man with a dark patch of skin down his cheek.

Cheung pulled out a knife and pointed it at the old man's throat.

'You take me or I'll kill you,' he said, savagely.

Not waiting for an answer he wrenched open the back door. A frightened-looking Filipino passenger opened the far door and scrambled out into the road. She ran towards a policeman, standing by City Hall. Cheung growled, 'Drive,' at the old man, who hastily put the cab into gear and shot forward.

'Follow that Rolls,' snapped Cheung. 'Don't worry old man, I'll pay you your fare.'

The driver seemed to relax after that, only occasionally glancing into the rear view mirror at his passenger.

Once out of the fast-moving traffic of Central, and on the winding roads of Midlevels, the taxi managed to keep in touch with the Rolls. Finally the Rolls stopped outside a block of luxury flats. Cheung heaved a sigh of relief. At least she didn't live in a house with high gates and dogs. He paid the taxi driver and ran towards the Rolls, stopping and slipping into the shadows of roadside bushes when a man got out of the driver's side.

After a few more moments, the girl got out. She was wearing a tight black dress, a single string of pearls, and smart leather shoes. She carried a Gucci handbag. She could have been any one of ten thousand Hong Kong girls. Even the Gucci bag did not need to be real: there were copies to be had of designer bags and watches all along the Nathan Road.

The man got back in the Rolls and manoeuvred it slowly down the ramp below the block of flats. Cheung came out of the shadows and ran up to the girl.

'Do you like me?' he said, startling her. 'I like you. Can I meet you? Where can I meet you?'

She stared at him with round eyes for a moment, then she said softly, 'Saturday—I'm going to the theatre with some friends. Meet me in the interval, in the Cultural Centre coffee shop . . .'

'I'll be there,' hissed Cheung, fiercely, and then he was gone, back into the shadows of the foliage. A few seconds later the man returned. He was smart, slightly corpulent, wearing a business suit. He carried a black briefcase. Cheung could see he was a successful man. Her father, no doubt. The pair went arm in arm up the steps, into the hallway of the flats, to be greeted by a watchman. Cheung stared at them, visible through the glass doors, as they took the lift. She looked back once, blindly, into the night.

On the way back to the Walled City, Cheung told himself stories about his future.

'I could be successful too. I could be a businessman, if I got the chance, later on. What I would like to be is someone like Jackie Chan—a film star—or Andy Tam—a pop singer. People have said my voice is good. Yes, I could be a pop singer. You have to be an old man like her father, to get respect in the business world, but pop singers need to be young. She won't marry me yet, I know that, especially if she finds out where I live and what I do, but if I get to be successful, then she'll think about it I'm sure. I'm good looking. She likes me, I can tell. All it takes is a little money.'

When he arrived back at the Walled City his daih lo asked him where he'd been.

Cheung studied a rat that was crawling into a crevice while searching his mind for a reply. It would not do to lie— he had been with two of his gang when the yacht passed. But they would laugh at him, maybe even be angry, if he talked about love.

'Following this rich girl,' said Cheung. 'I—I can get some money out of her.'

'That's dangerous,' said his Triad big brother. 'It's better stick to shopkeepers and tradesmen.'

Cheung nodded. 'This is a sure thing though. She likes me. I'm going to milk her with her consent. There won't be any real trouble, you'll see.'

That night, watching the Jade Channel on TV, the local news showed a shoot out between police and Chinese mainland crooks. The gangsters had robbed a gold and jewelry shop at gunpoint, in Mong Kok, then sped away in a stolen car. Unable to get back over the border, they had holed up in a village in the New Territories. Some Hakka fishermen had given them away to the police, for a reward. The crooks were armed with Chinese pistols and some grenades, and the police with revolvers and rifles. One policeman was wounded and two of the crooks shot to death, right there on the screen. It was very exciting.

'We're gangsters, aren't we?' said Cheung to his closest friend, Fat. 'We're like them.'

'No,' said Fat. 'We get rich slowly and carefully. They try to do it all in one go—and they either die or retire—one or the other. We're not like them at all, really.'

'Maybe I'll be gangster, when I'm older,' said Cheung. 'I don't care about dying.'

Fat chuckled grimly, 'You'll probably be dead anyway, before you're much older, my friend. The Big Circle will catch you one night, when you're alone, and chop you to bits.'

Fat himself had once been caught out alone by the Seui Fongs. Since they were working on constructing bamboo scaffolding at the time their weapons were bamboo staves. They spotted him running down an alley and chased him. Fat found himself trapped, and had sat down cross-legged and bowed his head, waiting for the staves to fall across his head and back. They beat him until he was close to death. The scars were now a badge of honour and Fat never lost the chance to remove his vest and parade them in front of people.

'Not if I get out of here,' muttered Cheung.

'What?' asked his friend.

'Nothing—just talking,' answered Cheung.

She was not there on Saturday. Cheung was furious and went to her block of flats. He waited. When she did not appear, he kept going back. Finally, when he saw her, she was going into the flats, carrying a small suitcase. She had obviously been away with her father, who accompanied her up the steps to the building as before, carrying the rest of the luggage. Cheung used a pair of binoculars to watch the lift lights and discover which floor she lived on.

He waited until she came out again, then followed her on a stolen motor bike. This time she was driven by the chauffeur. The car went to Kai Too, where she got out and entered a department store. Cheung ditched the bike and followed her.

He caught up with her in one of the aisles, in the perfume department.

'You promised to meet me,' he said, grabbing her arm. She looked frightened and about to scream, so he let her go again. 'You promised,' he said with grief in his tone.

'I—I don't know you,' she faltered, looking around at a counter assistant who was watching them.

'Yes you do, you promised to meet me,' he said, helplessly. 'Why didn't you keep your promise?'

He waited for her answer, a little giddy with the cloying fragrance of the perfumes.

'I—it's—it's very difficult,' she murmured, looking down. 'Let's have coffee here.'

Suddenly, he was elated. She did like him, after all. It was going to be all right. She was just a bit shy, that was all, a bit scared of her father. Once she knew how he could arrange things, meetings and things, and give her a good time, then she would trust him more. They would have a fine time together.

and he would work towards becoming more respectable, so that they could eventually marry.

'Do you like Andy Tam?' he said, following her to the department store's coffee shop.

'I adore him,' she said, her eyes sparkling. 'I met him once, you know.'

'Really—you really met him?' He was a little crestfallen by this news.

'You're a lot like him,' she said. 'I think. You look like him, only tougher. Tough like Bruce Lee.'

Cheung's heart immediately swelled in his chest.

'My name's Lee too. I can do martial arts,' he said. 'I've done that.'

'I could tell,' she smiled.

They ordered coffee and cakes, and she questioned him all the time, about how he came to Hong Kong, where he lived, what he did. Cheung answered her with a mixture of lies and truth, trying to hide the worst of his background, but bringing out some truths, making them sound more romantic than they actually were. She was such a delicate creature, so well-formed, so beautiful.

'Perhaps you would come with me to Wong Tai Sin Temple,' he said rashly, stirring his coffee, unwilling to drink it quickly. 'We could ask the fortune tellers if—if we are matched.'

'Matched?'

'You know what I mean.'

She laughed. 'You're an eager boy, aren't you? I don't think I could do that . . . '

He flared in annoyance. 'Boy? I'm a man.'

She smiled and shook her head. 'Seventeen, eighteen?'

'Oh, yes, and how old are you?' he snorted.

'I'm twenty-six,' she said, laughing.

He was stunned for a moment. He didn't believe her. The girls he knew of that age were past it. They had skins like roasted duck. They had worn eyes in worn faces. They looked like his mother. She—her complexion was so smooth, like silk, and everything about her seemed young and fresh.

He looked at her hands. They were slim and tapering—smooth, unblemished. Still, she had led a closeted life. She hadn't had to sell fish or frogs in Sham Shui Po live market, or skin snakes with a razor blade before boiling them in fat, or spend hours binding the claws of green crabs with raffia. Her hands were made to lift bone china tea cups to her rosebud lips, where that little pink tongue nestled. Her cheeks had felt nothing but soft pillows. The clothes she was wearing looked flimsy and needed to be handled with care. She was a fragile doll, made by an artist with an eye for perfection, dressed in diaphanous silks and satins.

'Twenty-six,' he repeated. 'Well, I'm twenty. That's not much difference . . . '

She accepted this lie without a murmur, though her eyes were full of amusement. He wanted to challenge that amusement, tell her this was serious, that he was in love with her, but he knew that would be a mistake. He was balancing on a wire at the moment. Once he got to know her better, then would be the time to argue with her over such things.

'I have to go,' she said, suddenly getting up.

'I'll pay,' he said. Then he remembered something. 'What's your name?'

'Sophie,' she replied, pulling on her lace gloves. 'Goodbye.'

'Wait,' he cried. 'When will I see you again?'

She fluttered a gloved hand at him and smiled, then walked quickly from the room without looking back. Cheung paid the bill, then rushed out after her, but she was gone, lost in the crowd. Still, it didn't matter, not that much. He knew where she lived. One step at a time. He was progressing. He had never had a girl with a gweilo name before. That was posh. Well, just once he had been with a girl called Celery Woo, but she was a prostitute and that didn't really count.

The next two weeks were long ones. Cheung's duties as a tin-man-toi kept him busy at the Walled City. A big drug deal was in progress which the Big Circle Triad wanted to be part of, but the 14K had rejected the partnership. This meant that Cheung was needed as a watchman almost twenty-four hours a day, to warn of any attack by the Big Circle. He sat in the dark, damp recess of the alley which led to the 14K's section of the vast warren which formed the interior of the Walled City and reflected miserably on the fact that she was probably out with her friends, laughing and having a good time.

Cheung looked around him in disgust, at cobwebs dripping from the mass of dangling wires; at cardboard, corrugated metal and boxwood rooms around him; at the rats around the rubbish; at a dripping hose pipe joined with sticky tape. Was this his destiny, to live and die in this place? To breathe the trapped, stale air of this sordid ghetto? And the smell? Was he supposed to live with the smell of damp rot, cooking and sewage forever? The only people who were probably worse off, were the Vietnamese refugees, in the various camps around the colony.

There had to be an end in sight, when he would be able to wear expensive clothes, walk around without a knife in his pocket, go into a classy restaurant . . .

Something moved in the net of shadows at the end of the alley.

Cheung leapt to his feet, a butcher's chopper in his hand.

'Attack!' he screamed. 'Attack!'

The Big Circle came out of the darkness then, yelling and shrieking, their faces contorted. Cheung's warning had been timely and he was soon reinforced by his own Triad. The alley was so narrow it only took two or three of them to defend it against the invaders, though of course being at the front Cheung had to withstand the brunt of the slashing knives and choppers. He received a long gash on his right arm, but his adrenalin was high and he went into a kind of trance as he traded blows with his enemies. Strangely, there was no fear in him. He felt invincible. He was lord of the alleys. They would not pass him. Not while he was on his two feet. Not while his arm swung the chopper with such skill and accuracy.

When it was all over, and the Big Circle had fled, there was the sweet smell of blood in the gamy confines of the tunnel. One youth had been seriously wounded, was perhaps dead: a member of the Big Circle. They had dragged him away with them. Cheung was not sure, but he thought it was a blow from his chopper which had been decisive: after which the Big Circle had retreated down the crooked alleyways, back to their own territory. Others had various wounds, including the slash Cheung himself had received. He and his comrades laughed and joked with each other as they made their way through the wormery of the Walled City to one of its illegal doctors.

'Did you see Cheung?' cried Small Ng, the third member of Cheung's cell of three. 'He was a real warrior!'

Cheung felt like a giant. His feet seemed to float over the flagstones of the lower level alley. He had fought a battle and had emerged victorious—not only victorious, but a hero. He was a bandit from the water margin, a freedom fighter who had vanquished the foe! Mandarins would tremble at his name. Warlords would beg him to fight at their side. Mystical mountains would whisper his deeds.

He knew from experience that his part in the fight would be exaggerated, until it reached legendary status. Promotion in the 14K was assured now. He had proved himself. The pain in his arm was welcome to him, adding to his glory. It would have been a lesser personal victory, had he come away unscathed. Now he would have the scar to show enquiring younger members of the Triad, when they asked if it had been a fierce fight.

The doctor stitched his wound and Cheung told his friends he was going outside.

'What for?' asked Fat. 'Aren't you going to stay and drink beer with your friends? We should celebrate our victory.'

'Later,' Cheung said. 'I have something to do first. I'll meet you in Kowloon City—in the Korean Bar.'

Cheung was risking his newly-earned prestige by not following the rituals of a victorious battle, but he had to see her, he had to see Sophie, while the lustre of achievement still shone from his form, while he still felt omnipotent, god-like, immortal. He just had to see her, now.

'Well don't be late,' Fat warned. 'Diah-lo will want you there.'

'Tell Big Brother I'll be there,' he assured his friend. 'Don't worry about me.'

Cheung drifted like a phantom out of the Walled City, into the streets of Hong Kong, his arm a throbbing pleasant reminder of recent events. First he went to a hardware store in Kowloon City and bought a length of nylon rope. Then he took a taxi all the way to Midlevels. Once outside the block of flats where she lived, he waited for a car to arrive—any car— hiding close to the garage. When one came, he slipped into the garage while the electronically operated door was open. He let the car's driver use the basement lift. When it returned, he used it himself.

He knew that the garage lift would go to the tradesmen's entrances to the flats. The door to Sophie's flat, like all Hong Kong flats, would be protected by a metal gate. The front door, reachable only through the lobby lifts, would also be rein- forced by protective steel cage doors difficult to force without a great many tools and a lot of uninterrupted time. There was another way in though, via the balcony.

Cheung went all the way up, to the roof.

Once on the edge of the roof he counted the balconies down- wards, until he was sure he had the right one. Then he tied one end of the nylon rope to a TV aerial support post and abseiled down to Sophie's balcony. He still felt like an emperor, a wild emperor of the north: invulnerable.

Using his knife he forced the balcony door open and stepped inside the flat. The lights were on and he stared about him in amazement at the opulence.

The size of the room was the first thing that impressed him. It was a large as the foyer of a big hotel. There was a huge chandelier hanging from an elaborately decorated ceiling. Around the walls were expensive looking paintings and tapestries. One of the paintings was of Sophie, in a ball gown, with a necklace of diamonds around her lovely throat. On the floor were Chinese silk rugs, covering highly-polished hardwood tiles. Much of the furniture was rosewood, with silk cushioned seats on the chairs, but an enormous leather suite dominated the far side of the room. Around the edge were various display cabinets, filled with china, marble and jade ornaments. On one or two small carved tables stood other objects: ceramic bowls, statuettes and heavy ash trays.

While Cheung stood engrossed in the scene around him a figure entered the room by the main door and gave a startled cry.

Cheung whipped round to see a man standing there, caught in an attitude of indecision.

'You're her father,' said Cheung, stepping forward. 'I am pleased to meet you, sir. Is Sophie here?'

At the mention of the name, the man seemed to collect his wits, and he drew himself up.

'What are you doing here? How did you get in?'

'My name is Lee Tam Cheung, sir,' said Cheung. 'I wish to marry your daughter.'

At that moment, Sophie herself came into the room, by another door, and gave out a little gasp when she saw Cheung.

They stood there, a loose group of three, for a few moments. Then the man found his voice again.

'What do you mean, daughter? I have no daughter. Sophie, do you know this boy?'

'He—he delivers the groceries sometimes,' said Sophie faintly. 'You must have seen him, darling, surely? He's the grocery boy, from the Welcome Shop, aren't you Cheung? Poor boy, he's a little touched in the head.'

Darling? Cheung was stunned by the word. Darling. It came to him then, in a rush. Sophie. She was twenty-six, not seventeen. And now that he was close to him, this man did not look so very old. He was overweight, unfit, but not more than forty. Sophie was not this man's daughter, she was his wife.

Cheung felt physically sick.

'I have to go,' he said.

'Yes, yes, go home to your mother, Cheung,' said Sophie quickly. 'Let him out, Michael.'

Something occurred to Cheung then, which made him feel hot and angry. Her words had stirred something unpleasant in his blood: something murky and unclean. His honour. His honour had been stained by this encounter. He needed to wipe out that stain before he could leave the flat. Otherwise she could laugh at him, for the rest of her life, and he would hear her in his dreams.

He reached out and snatched a statuette from a nearby table.

'I'm taking this,' he said, fiercely. 'It's what I came for—this.'

'You are not,' said the man. 'You . . . '

Cheung whipped out his knife and Sophie screamed.

'You get out of my way or I'll stab you,' snarled Cheung. 'Let me out of here. I've killed one man tonight—I can kill another just as easily. If you try to stop me the 14K gang will come for you. They'll pour acid on your precious Rolls Royce. They'll scar that sow over there until she won't be worth looking at—you understand me? I'm a chief in the 14K—we don't mess around, you understand me?'

The man started to say, 'Now look here . . . ' but stopped on meeting Cheung's burning eyes. He turned then and went through a hallway to the front door. He opened it, and the steel cage door beyond it, and held both of them wide for Cheung.

Cheung turned to Sophie and said, 'I know you—if you ever say my name again I'll kill you,' then he ran through the hallway and out of the flat. He did not bother with the lift, but took the fire escape stairs, four at a time, down to the ground floor. Cheung knew the watchman would have been warned by Sophie's husband, and he was standing by the glass doors.

'Out. Out of the way,' spat Cheung, brandishing his knife. 'Your life isn't worth what they pay you.'

The watchman, a small elderly man with a stoop, appeared to agree with him and stepped out of the way. Cheung ran to the doors, swept them open, and down the steps into the street.

The police would have been called too, but they would take a while to reach the block of flats.

Cheung hailed a taxi and took it to Kowloon City.

Once in the streets of Kowloon City, Cheung felt safe again, but he was depressed and still angry. He glanced at the green-stone object in his hand, under the still neon lights of the restaurants and shops. He was astonished to see that it was a jade representation of Sophie herself: he recognised her immediately. Some artist had faithfully captured her face and form in this small sculpture in his hand. It was her without any doubt.

The anger swept through him again. It was the real Sophie he had wanted, not a cold jade statuette. They were not the same thing, were they? He stroked the mottled green figurine. A beautiful work of art: perhaps even more perfect in form than Sophie herself? A perfected Sophie. Perhaps they weren't so different? They both had hearts of stone. And he had one of them. Maybe he had the finest one.

He wondered how valuable the statue was. It looked valuable. Cold, but valuable. Perhaps he had won after all? Perhaps he had got the best of what was Sophie and her husband was stuck with the worst of her? That felt good to him.

A jumbo jet roared low over the rooftops of the city, following the approach lights attached to the eves of the buildings. It seemed to miss the roof tiles by only a few feet as it thundered over, rattling doors and windows. A normal occurrence, since Kowloon City was in Kai Tak airport's flight path, it physically shook Cheung out of his mood.

He walked up to the swing doors of the Korean Bar and pushed them open, stepping inside. His friends were all there. They looked up and cheered, waving bottles of beer. Cheung's heart swelled inside him. He waved the figurine.

'A trophy,' he yelled. 'To honour our victory!'

They cheered again, wildly, and he walked among them, receiving the backslaps, feeling a prince.

THE RIVER-SAILOR'S WIFE

Actually, you do know all there is to know about life at twenty—or at least, all you're ever going to know. You just don't believe most of it until you experience it, or witness the experience in others. Certainly, I seem less aware of the world at forty-seven than I was at twenty. This is not nostalgia for a lost golden age: it was youth that was golden, not the time. I was vital then, to the whole scheme of things. Without me, the world would have squealed to a halt, seized and rusted. Everything was internal, to me, and I was not just an observer, as I am now. I was an enthusiastic participant.

Oh yes, the ego was so important then.

There is another important aspect about being seventeen. It is an age when you are at your most vulnerable, emotionally, yet ambiguously, at your strongest. You fall in love—love to the point of death—yet you recover amazingly swiftly. One day you are suicidal over a rejection, the next you have found someone else and the hurt disappears overnight. These days the wounds are not so deep, but they are slow to heal.

At seventeen I was in Singapore: a young British airman on my first posting abroad. Changi RAF Station. I was dazzled by the tinselled atmosphere of the new (to me) culture into which I had been tossed. Changi was not a closed station. There was an entire native village in the middle of it, with a double row of open-fronted shops and stalls lining the main street. There were also surrounding kampongs.

Singapore city was just twenty minutes away in a Mercedes 'flying taxi'—one that stopped for passengers, as would a bus. Sometimes we found ourselves sharing them with pigs and chickens on their way to market. In 1958 the journey cost just two dollars one way—about four shillings and sixpence. We would often pay an extra dollar, getting into separate taxis, for them to race. If a fare hailed down the car you were in, that was all in the game. Around Chinese New Year, we would throw firecrackers out of the window at the mah-jong players by wayside stalls. If they could have caught us, they would probably have killed us: the game was sacred to them.

I spent as little time at work, in the communications centre, as possible. We did shifts—two days on, three days off—so we had a lot of leisure time. Mostly, I walked the streets or rural paths around the city, looking at temples with their roofs covered in fantastical figures of men and beasts; strolling through Tiger Balm Gardens where an alien hell was depicted with three-dimensional models; walking along the wharves packed with overcrowded sampans; taking in the sights and smells of the food stalls along Bugis Street or at the bazaars which seemed to spring out of the ground with their colourful displays of textiles, brass and wood. God, it was all so wonderful. I loved it. The waves of Asiatic people with their waxpaper umbrellas, the heavy, damp heat like a constant sauna, the exotic lizards, birds, snakes, monkeys, that ran wild, the sudden wall of water that would descend at four o'clock on the dot during the monsoon season, the

choruses of bullfrogs, chit-chats and cicadas. I loved it all.
Even the mosquitoes that helped to feed my pet mantis,
which remained uncaged on my bedside locker, as faithful as
a Labrador dog.

I suppose part of my sentimental feelings for Singapore,
now, stem from the fact that I lost my virginity in a brothel
somewhere amongst the seething backstreets of Chinatown.

It was Christmas Eve. I had plenty of money and we—Bill
and I—had been to a swimming-pool party. There were girls
at the party, but untouchables: daughters of elder servicemen.
They could be 'fondled but not fucked'. In any case, at that
age, I was too shy of girls of my own race, creed and age. I
needed the distancing factors that bargirls provided. Bill, my
closest friend at that time, suggested that the two of us go
downtown to a brothel. With a stomach full of electric butter-
flies, I agreed.

Bill had already been to a whorehouse. It was one of the
first things he did on arrival in Singapore. I had been much
too frightened of catching something during those first three
months, but Bill had got away with it, so I saw no reason
to hold back any longer. I was prepared to risk my physical
health to satisfy a psychological need. As a virgin, I felt spiritually incomplete and was positive that what I lacked was the
experience of a sexual encounter; that once I had been with a
woman, the secrets of the universe would all be revealed to me
and I should never feel inadequate/bashful/unhappy/empty
again. The whole, broad canvas of the complete man would
be mine to possess, simply by fusing my flesh with that of
another human being. Such were the misunderstandings of a
seventeen-year-old. I had heard so much about the ecstasy of
an orgasm that I was convinced that at the point of complete
unification I would see everything clearly and become one
of the wise, with positive opinions on every subject. People
would realise, just by my face, that I was a man who knew.

We took a flying taxi from Changi village. There were several ways of obtaining a woman in Singapore. You could go to one of the twenty-five dance halls and pay for a string of dances with one of the hostesses on the understanding that you could spend the rest of the night with them. You could go to a bar and pick up a bargirl. Or you could get in a taxi and say, 'Jig-jig John,' and be taken to a brothel. It sounds sordid, doesn't it? It sounds crass. But it didn't seem like that then, to youth overwhelmed, drugged, by a way of life that captured our souls, our impressionable imaginations, with its atmosphere perfumed by the scent of camphorwood, by the fragrance of blossoms that only the Orient can produce. It seemed right. In our adolescent ignorance, we believed that the women did what they did because they wanted to.

The brothel was clean, if not wholesome. It smelled of joss sticks and perfume and was not in the least bit as intimidating as I had expected. I was shown to a room by an elderly, quietly spoken Chinese, who left me there on my own for a few minutes.

The room was whitewashed, with a large overhead fan turning slowly and clicking rhythmically, moving the warm air in gentle spirals down towards the clean-sheeted bed. There was a rush mat on the floor. No other furnishings were visible in the dim light.

As I stood, nervously awaiting the woman assigned to me, the curtain that served as a door moved, and a young Chinese girl entered. She was no older than I was—not beautiful, but certainly pretty, with a slim figure and small, neat hands and feet. She went, without a word, to the bed and placed a handtowel on its centre. Then she shrugged off her cheongsam and got on to the bed, her bottom on the towel. She beckoned to me, unsmiling, her hair like a river of jet flowing over the white pillow.

With a knot in my stomach I quickly undressed. Then I sat on the edge of the bed. She was the first woman I had ever seen without clothes on. I was not stirred to immediate arousal. I had time to reflect that there was very little difference (apart from the obvious) between our bodies. I was a slim youth, small in stature, and smooth-chested. She was delicately boned, with tiny breasts and a dry, silky skin. We were like two children. I noticed that she had shaved off all her body hair and looked entirely vulnerable, like a fragile seashell that had to be handled with extreme care.

I wanted her to like me. I wanted to tell her things: that I wouldn't hurt her; that she was the first girl I had ever been with; that I loved the texture of her skin; that her broad nose and black eyes were beautiful. I wanted us to be friends.

'What's your name?' I asked. 'Do you speak English?'

She stared at me, impassively.

'Lulu. You come to me now, please?'

She wanted to get it over with, get me over with, get me gone. I was depressed. I had paid twenty-five dollars for her body, yet I wanted her soul. I wanted her most priceless possession and I thought I could buy it with a handful of paper notes. I wanted her to like me. It was so important to get her to like me, to let me in, to share the secrets of her spirit with me.

I leaned towards her. She had oranges on her breath which mingled with the incense from the joss. The crisp sheet began to dampen beneath my palms as I supported my weight.

'My name is Tom,' I said, and she nodded.

'Please, you come now . . . '

The double entendre was lost on both of us. I lowered myself on top of her and after some fumbling, was able to enter her. After a few minutes it was over. I made no attempt to withdraw. I was disappointed. There had been no pyrotechnic display inside my head; no awesome revelations; no sudden influx of knowledge: merely an electric jolt in my loins which shuddered through my body, then relaxation and peace.

I stared down at the face, not an inch from my own, and she jerked her head aside.

'No kiss,' she said. 'Not to kiss.'

It was one of the rules. Bill had told me about the rules. I began to hate the rules.

I wanted to stay in her for a long time: feel her smooth skin against my own; share her body with her; share my body with her. The sheets were white and stiff beneath us, like those my grandmother used in her cottage at home.

But the act should have been better. I had given her my virginity and it meant nothing to her. It was nothing. I felt vaguely angry and it must have shown in my face, because she pushed at my chest with her thin arms.

'No hurt me,' she said.

I rolled away from her, shocked and puzzled.

'I don't want to hurt you,' I replied. 'I want . . . '

'Some men beat me—with the fist.'

Drunken louts. I was no drunk, no sadistic brute with a chip on my shoulder. There was not even a vestige of post-coital contempt, such as I have sometimes felt with other women since. I just wanted her to like me, to say to me shyly, 'Am I the first woman you have ever had? I could tell,' then hug me, possessively, as if it meant something to her.

But she was a prostitute, not the girl next door. I had paid for her body and that I had been given. I was entitled to nothing else. My rights had ceased with the jolt in my loins.

I began to get dressed as she fussed with a bowl of water on the far side of the bed. When I was ready to go, I said, 'Can I see you again? Will you see me again?'

Then she smiled—not a full smile, more a Mona Lisa stretching of the lips.

'You not butterfly? You like me for one woman?'

'Yes,' I replied, sincerely, feeling that at last I was getting somewhere. 'I just want to see you—no one else. I'm not interested in the others.'

I felt elated, quite out of proportion to the circumstances, as if I'd just asked the girl I loved to marry me and she had accepted. There was a fire in me now, burning happily. I was going to see her again. We were friends.

'You come here next week. Yes?' she said.

'What shall I say? Shall I ask for Lulu?'

'I be here,' she replied. 'You go now.'

I did as I was told. It occurred to me only later, much later, that minutes after I had left that room some boozed merchant seaman, or swaddy, belching and farting the fumes of Tiger Beer, breathing fried rice, lurched on to her delicate body and rammed her down into those starched cotton sheets with his heavy, sweaty bulk and pumped and grunted into that peach-coloured mound between her legs. Then after he was finished, another took his place. Then another. And yet another . . . The only thing that would change would be the white towel beneath her small buttocks. Some of them might be clean, wholesome men, but others would stink of dried vomit and stale alcohol—and all, all, including me, would be about as welcome to her as a bath of spiders. My poor Lulu.

In the taxi back to Changi, I could talk of nothing but Lulu, until Bill said, 'For Christ's sake, leave it out. You're a real prat sometimes.' He seemed angry at something, or someone, and stared moodily out into the dark night as the black shapes of the wayside palms flashed by us.

Before he left me for the night, he said, 'Tom, don't be a prick. They start some of these girls at thirteen—fourteen. Don't lose your head over a silly tart.'

But I refused to accept this. Lulu looked so fresh and young. I was almost tempted to dream that she had begun her work that night, and we had, unknowingly, helped each other to our first sexual union. I was full of false dreams in those days. They grew in me like flowers.

It was about 3.30 in the morning when we arrived back at Changi village. I went straight to Fred's for an egg banjo and fried rice. 'Fred' was a Chinese stall owner—one of dozens that lined the route from one end of the village to the other—and he had been given his nickname by Bill. Fred, like all the other stall owners, sold squid, eggs, rice, bread, coffee, twenty-four hours a day. They slept by their wares, amongst which there were a primus stove to cook on and a hurricane lamp to see by. They would rouse themselves from their slumbers to serve a single customer at five o'clock—or three—or two—any time. We took them completely for granted. We would arrive, singing and shouting, after a night in some bar and expect a dawn breakfast to be cooked without hesitation or a murmur of reproach. We were, completely and utterly, selfish. The kind of young men that now, in my forties, I detest with venom.

We, of course, could go back to our billets and sleep the day away, while Fred and his kind had to continue serving customers through the heat of the Singapore sun, and on into the night again.

Bill had picked out Fred's stall at random and bestowed his continual custom on the place. He had given the owner his nickname and had a sign painted at the workshops, which hung above the stall. Bill was something of a personality amongst us: a latter-day Beau Brummel, who originated trends. It was fashionable thereafter to eat at Fred's, rather than any of the other, similar stalls along the street. Fred rose in status and wealth, accordingly, though I think he was somewhat bewildered by his good fortune. I don't think he, or any of the other stall owners, really understood why young airmen queued for his food, which was no different from or superior to the rest.

It amused Bill to lift someone out of the dust and make him a local personality, at a whim. At that time, in that place, he had the power of a king. He could break Fred just as easily, by simply transferring his patronage; reduce him to one of the envious lookers-on. He had done such with a tailor; one of the many that struggled for our business. Bill was a clever, witty, good-looking, thoughtless young man, who found he could manipulate people, and did so with all the irresponsibility of a spoiled-brat monarch.

So it was to Fred's that I went, the night I lost my virginity, and I roused him from his rattan bed to cook me an egg banjo. Along the streets the hurricane lamps formed a line of light in the darkness. When the dawn came up, much later, it uncovered the beauties of a natural world of which England was but the hem of the skirt. The flared scarlet petticoats beneath a dark-green dress, decorated with emerald lizards and jewelled insects, gradually emerged from the grey. The lamps were extinguished by men with dirty, worn vests and barren faces. Faces un-visited by anything except care. Faces of prisoners serving life sentences.

The following week I visited the brothel again—and several times thereafter, until Lulu suggested that I go to a certain hut and spend my nights with her when I wished. All I had to do was pay the rent, buy the groceries and give her a little money for herself, all well within my means. I became, almost, a married man, except that I had none of the responsibilities.

Lulu was quiet, undemanding and completely devoted to my needs. I never once saw her get angry, though I often treated her with casual indifference. I took her utterly for granted, visiting her whenever I pleased and offering no explanation for long periods of absence. It may have appeared to an outside observer that she did not care, that I meant nothing to her, but I knew differently. Even a selfish young man recognises some of the signs.

In my mind's eye, I can still see her now, in the back of the tiny kitchen, her neat, economical movements ensuring that her presence caused me the least amount of irritation. I was confounded by this at the time and, to my small credit, felt a twinge of guilt.

'You're so quiet,' I said to her one day. 'And you hardly seem to move—yet you're always busy.'

'Not want to disturb you,' she replied.

Oh yes, I have lost sleep over my behaviour since, and not a minute too much. Now—now I feel a deep shame, even though I do not know that stupid youth who inhabited my body thirty years ago. But now is too late.

Once or twice I delighted Lulu by taking her to the pictures or to a dance, where she endured the baleful glares of other Chinese who did not approve of her escort. She bore them with calmness, uncomplaining. We went swimming on occasion, though for a reason unknown to me then she would stare out over the water with a wistful expression on her face and return to the hut with a sadness she could not disguise. It was after one of these trips that I discovered the baby.

She had been exhausted by her swim and was lying asleep on the bed. I remember being irritated by an insistent flying beetle that would not leave me alone and I rose from the bamboo chair on the veranda, intending to join her. Curled up, like a child, in her cotton trouser suit, she looked so peaceful I decided not to disturb her, but a wave of tenderness came over me and I could not help reaching down to stroke her cheek. She murmured something in her sleep and clutched at my hand, kissing the fingertips: something she had never done before.

I said, 'Lulu,' very softly.

She was instantly awake. She dropped my hand with a look of pain in her eyes. Then she jumped up and ran from the room. When I went to find her, she was sitting on the wooden steps to the hut, cradling a photograph, and crying.

I prised the print gently from her hand. It was of a small child, about three years of age. It suddenly dawned on me that she was not alone in the world. She had family. Why this had not occurred to me before, I don't know. Some uncon-

scious belief that prostitutes sprang from the dust, I suppose,
without connection to the rest of the human race.

'Your sister's child?' I asked, hopefully.

She lowered her head and snatched the photo from me.

'My baby.' She ran into the bedroom again, probably hoping
that I wouldn't follow her, but I did.

I went quite pale. I could see myself in the mirror by the
bed and the colour ran from my complexion, though I swear I
felt nothing inside.

'Your baby? Do you know the father?'

She raised her head and looked me directly in the eyes.

'The father my husband,' she said, fiercely.

Now I did feel something. I had been sleeping with this
woman for a year and I discovered that I knew nothing—absolutely nothing -about her past. I had talked about myself, but
I had asked not one single question about Lulu's life. I had
taken her as she was, without qualification or reference.

'Your husband,' I said, flatly.

'Yes.' The look was proud, haughty.

Slowly, I worked myself up into a state of rage. I was
totally incensed by the thought that there was another man
in this whore's life. Never mind all the others. Here was
someone—someone she had loved. Perhaps she still did? The
thought choked me. I could not speak, nor could I look at her.
I collected my clothes, dressed and left, indulging only in the
terrible, unjustified anger of a youth who had discovered that
his sweetheart was a normal woman and not a pet bird. She
had a husband. The thought made me sick. It did not matter
that after two years I would return to Britain and leave her to
whatever fate awaited her, without a twinge of remorse—as so
many young men did with their girls—it mattered only that
I had been fooled, duped, used. I wanted to kill her. I wanted
to break every bone in her body. I was insanely jealous of this
'husband'. He had given her a baby. She had not used that

infernal bowl of warm water after he had made love to her. I wanted to die.

I never went back to the hut again. Instead, I went on riotous evenings with Bill and his crowd, getting drunk, whoring for as little as three dollars a time in the most appalling places, running the very real risk of disease, and generally telling myself I was having a great time.

Bill congratulated me on a narrow escape.

'Let's face it,' he said, 'you were thinking of taking her back to the UK, weren't you?'

'I don't know,' I replied. dully.

'Come on, pal. I could see the signs. You almost became one of those prats that marry their whores and spend the rest of their lives regretting it.'

Would she have come with me? I thought about it often over the last six months I spent on the island and I believed I knew the answer.

One day Bill came into my billet as I was feeding my praying mantis. He staggered over to my bedside, drunk and dishevelled from a night on the town.

'Guess who I've just seen.' He grinned lopsidedly.

'Who?'

'Little Lulu-belle. She's back in the cathouse, doing her 'twenny-fi' buck' turns.' He put on a mock Chinese accent for the price. 'Been there ever since you left her.' He put his arm around my shoulder and I could smell the stale sweat wafting up from his armpit. 'An' I can tell you, pal,' he said in a conspiratorial whisper, 'she's just as good as ever. Personal observation.'

I shrugged off his arm and he moved back from me on seeing what was in my eyes.

'Well, fuck you,' he said. 'Who gives a shit anyway?'

Then he walked stiffly from the room. I continued feeding the mantis.

I did see her again, before I left Singapore.

I was sitting outside Fred's one evening, talking to him. His stall was no longer fashionable and he had gone back to contending with all the others, touting for business where he could. He said something that surprised me.

I cried, 'You have a family? But you spend all your time here.'

'Not choice. Must work, or family no eat. Many people— wife, mother, sister, chil'ren—all nee' food.'

That was a funny statement from someone who ran a food stall. Suddenly I saw what kind of life he had—and all the other stall owners -sitting by his stove twenty-four hours a day in order to keep his family alive. It was while we were talking that Lulu came along the road, with a young Chinese man of about twenty.

While I had been talking to Fred, I had been putting some thoughts together. What applied to Fred must also have applied to Lulu. She had a child to feed. The mother, too, also had to eat. Work in Singapore at that time was extremely scarce. If you didn't want to starve, you did what you could. Any job—any job—was better than nothing.

I thought at first they were going to pass by, without stopping, but then they turned towards me. I prepared myself for the onslaught of an enraged husband, wishing to exact revenge. I prepared myself for a vindictive attack by a woman I had abandoned to the whorehouse and its ugly performances. I was very, very frightened. The week before, an airman had been stabbed to death by angry Chinese because he had insulted them.

On the far side of the street, four old men were playing mah-jong.

I could hear the clicks of the tiles and the low murmur of voices. There was a stillness in the air that seemed to me to be the precursor of violence. I was soaked with sweat. I rose from my seat as they approached. Lulu stopped about a yard in front of me and held the man by the sleeve. She said something rapidly, in Hok Yen dialect. The young man nodded.

Then she said in English, 'Tom, this is my husband. He river-sailor -has come home. He put in jail, in Malaya, for long time. I send our money for him.'

I smiled, tentatively, and he returned the smile. 'Pleased to meet you,' I whispered, hoarsely. Lulu said, 'He no speak English.'

She turned and again spoke Hok Yen, then for my benefit translated the words, as if she were still speaking to him, though she looked directly into my eyes. 'Mr Tom has been very kind to me.' And then she smiled—a full-face smile.

I was stunned by the words, which had obviously been rehearsed. Kind? I had been a bastard. I had sent her back to that hole. Then they walked away, silent with one another. I stood there, awkwardly, as a burning sensation came to my eyes. I could not look at anyone, especially not Fred, who had heard all, seen all. I was so ashamed of the way I had treated her. Our money. She had called it our money—the money she had earned and kept until I had abandoned her. I stumbled away, hurried away, down to the beach where I could be alone.

Even now, whenever I think of that young woman, I have to find a place away from other people, in order to remember that even if she had loved me, as I believe she may have done, my unworthiness would have precluded any long-term relationship. Her capacity for self-sacrifice was beyond me and would have destroyed us, in the end, for I would not have handled it sensibly. I would have allowed her to indulge me beyond reason.

Outside my cottage, the moss grows thick on the path to the door. The winters seem to be getting longer.

TWICE-TOLD TALES

INSIDE THE WALLED CITY

They had been loud-hailing the place for days, and it certainly looked empty, but John said you can't knock down a building that size without being absolutely sure that some terrified Chinese child wasn't trapped in one of the myriad of rooms, or that an abandoned old lady wasn't caught in some blocked passageway, unable to find her way out. There had been elderly people who had set up home in the centre of this huge rotten cheese, and around whom the rest of the slum was raised over the years. Such people would have forgotten there was an outside world, let alone be able to find their way to it.

'You ready?' he asked me, and I nodded.

It was John Speakman's job as a Hong Kong Police inspector, to go into the empty shell of the giant slum to make sure everyone was out, so that the demolition could begin. He had a guide of course, and an armed escort of two locally born policemen, and was accompanied by a newspaper reporter— me. I'm a freelance whose articles appear mainly in the South China Morning Post.

You could say the Walled City was many dwellings, as many as seven thousand, but you would be equally right to call it a single structure. It consisted of one solid block of crudely built homes, all fused together. No thought or planning had gone into each tacked-on dwelling, beyond that of providing shelter for a family. The whole building covered the approximate area of a football stadium. There was no quadrangle at its centre, nor inner courtyard, no space within the ground it occupied. Every single piece of the ramshackle mass, apart from the occasional fetid airshaft, had been used to build, up to twelve stories high. Beneath the ground, and through every part of this monstrous shanty, ran a warren of tunnels and passageways. Above and within it, there were walkways, ladders, catwalks, streets and alleys, all wielded together as if some junk artist like the man who built the Watts Towers had decided to try his hand at architecture.

Once you got more than ten feet inside, there was no natural light. Those within used to have to send messages to those on the edges to find out if it was day or night, fine or wet. The homemade brick and plaster was apt to rot and crumble in the airless confines inside and had to be constantly patched and shored up. In a land of high temperatures and humidity, fungus grew thick on the walls and in the cracks the rats and cockroaches built their own colonies. The stink was unbelievable. When it was occupied, more than fifty thousand people existed within its walls.

John called his two local cops to his side, and we all slipped into the dark slit in the side of the Walled City, Sang Lau the guide going first. Two gweilos—whites—and three Chinese, entering the forbidden place, perhaps for the last time. Even Sang Lau, who knew the building as well as any, seemed anxious to get the job over and done with. The son of an illegal immigrant, he had been raised in this block of hovels, in the muck and darkness of its intestines. His stunted little body was evidence of that fact, and he had only volunteered to show us the way in exchange for a right to Hong Kong citizenship for members of his family still without Hong Kong citizenship. He and his immediate family had taken advantage of the amnesty that had served to empty the city of its inhabitants. They had come out, some of them half-blind through lack of light, some of them sick and crippled from the disease and bad air, and now Sang Lau had been asked to return for one last time. I guessed how he would be feeling: slightly nostalgic (for it was his birthplace), yet wanting to get it over with, so that the many other unsavoury remembrances might be razed along with the structure.

The passage inside was narrow, constantly twisting, turning, dipping, and climbing, apparently at random. Its walls ran with slick water and it smelled musty, with pockets of stale food stink, and worse. Then there were writhing coils of hose and cable that tangled our feet it we were not careful: plastic water pipes ran alongside wires that had once carried stolen electricity. When the rotten cables were live and water ran through the leaking hoses, these passages must have been death traps. Now and again the beam from the lamp in my helmet transfixed a pointed face, with whiskers and small eyes, then it would scuttle away, into the maze of tunnels.

Every so often, we paused at one of the many junctions or shafts, and one of the Chinese policemen, the stocky, square-faced one, would yell through a megaphone. The sound smacked dully into the walls, or echoed along corridors of plasterboard. The atmosphere was leaden, though strangely aware. This massive structure with all its holes, its pits and shafts, was like a beast at the end of its life, waiting for the final breath. It was a shell, but one that had been soaked in the feverish activity of fifty thousand souls. It was once a holy city, but it had been bled, sweated, urinated, and spat on not only by the poor and the destitute, but also by mobsters, hoodlums, renegades, felons, runaways, refugees, and fugitives, until no part of it remained consecrated. It pressed in on us on all sides, as if it wanted to crush us, but lacked the final strength needed to collapse itself. It was a brooding, moody place and terribly alien to a gweilo like myself. I could sense spirits clustering in the corners: spirits from a culture that no Westerner has ever fully understood. More than once, as I stumbled along behind the others, I said to myself, What am I doing here? This is no place for me, in this hole.

The stocky policeman seemed startled by his own voice, blaring from the megaphone: he visibly twitched every time he had to make his announcement. From his build I guessed his family originally came from the north, from somewhere around the Great Wall. His features and heavy torso were Mongol rather than Cantonese, the southerners having a tendency toward small, delicate statures and moon-shaped faces. He probably made a tough policeman out on the streets, where his build would be of use in knocking heads together, but in here his northern superstitions and obsessive fear of spirits made him a liability. Not for the first time I wondered at John Speakman's judgment in assessing human character.

After about an hour of walking, and sometimes crawling, along tunnels the size of a sewer pipe, John suggested we rest for a while.

I said, 'You're not going to eat sandwiches in here, are you?'

It was supposed to be a joke, but I was so tense, it came out quite flat, and John growled, 'No, of course not.'

We sat crossed-legged in circle, in what used to be an apartment: It was a hardboard box about ten-by-ten feet.

'Where are we?' I asked the torch-lit faces. 'I mean in relation to the outside.' The reply could have been 'the bowels of the earth' and I would have believed it. It was gloomy, damp, fetid, and reeked of prawn paste, which has an odour reminiscent of dredged sludge.

Sang Lau replied, 'Somewhere near east corner. We move soon, into middle.'

His reply made me uneasy.

'Somewhere near? Don't you know exactly?'

John snapped, 'Don't be silly, Peter. How can he know exactly? The important thing is he knows the way out. This isn't an exercise in specific location.'

'Right,' I said, giving him a mock salute, and he tipped his peaked cap back on his head, a sure sign he was annoyed. If he'd been standing, I don't doubt his hands would have been on his hips in the classic 'gweilo giving orders' stance.

John hadn't been altogether happy about taking a 'civilian' along, despite the fact that I was a close friend. He had a very poor opinion of those who did not wear a uniform of some kind. According to his philosophy, the human race was split into two: There were the protectors (police, army, medical profession, firemen, et al.) and those who needed protection (the rest of the population). Since I apparently came under the second category, I needed looking after. John was one of those crusty bachelors you find in the last outposts of faded empires: a living reminder of the beginning of the century. Sheena, my wife, called him 'the fossil,' even to his face. I think they both regarded it as a term of endearment.

However, he said he wanted to do me a favour, since he knew that my job was getting tough. Things were getting tight in the freelance business, especially since Australia had just woken up to the fact that Hong Kong, a thriving place of business where money was to be made hand over fist, was right on its doorstep. The British and American expatriates equalled each other for the top slot, numerically speaking, but Aussie professionals were beginning to enter, if not in droves, in small herds. With them they brought their own parasites, the free lancers, and for the first time I had a lot of competition. It meant I had to consolidate friendships and use contacts that had previously been mostly friendships and use contacts that had previously been mostly social.

Sheena and I were going through a bit of a rough time too, and one thing she would not put up with was a tame writer who earned less than a poorly paid local clerk. I could sense the words 'proper job' hanging in the air, waiting to condense.

Even the darkness in there seemed to have substance. I could see the other young policeman, the thin, sharp Cantonese youth, was uncomfortable too. He kept looking up, into the blackness, smiling nervously. He and his companion cop whispered to each other, and I heard 'Bruce Lee' mentioned just before they fell into silence again, their grins fixed. Perhaps they were trying to use the memory of the fabled martial-arts actor to bolster their courage? Possibly the only one of us who was completely oblivious, or perhaps indifferent, to the spiritual ambiance of the place was John himself. He was too thick-skinned, too much the old warrior expat, to be affected by spooky atmospheres, I thought he might reassure his men though, since we both knew that when Chinese smiled under circumstances such as these, it meant they were hiding either acute embarrassment or abject terror. They had nothing to be embarrassed about, so I was left with only one assumption.

John, however, chose to ignore their fears.

'Right, let's go,' he said, climbing to his feet.

We continued along the passageways, stumbling after Sang Lau, whose power over us was absolute in this place, since without him we would certainly be lost. It was possible that a search party might find us, but then again, we could wander the interior of this vast wormery for weeks without finding or being found.

A subtle change seemed to come over the place. Its resistance seemed to have evaporated, and it was almost as if it were gently drawing us on. The tunnels were getting wider. more accessible, and there were fewer obstacles to negotiate.

I have an active imagination, especially in places of darkness, notorious places that are steeped in recent histories of blood and founded on terror. Far from making me feel better, this alteration in the atmosphere made my stomach knot, but what could I say to John? I wanted to go back? I had no choice but to follow where his guide led us, and hope for an early opportunity to duck out if we saw daylight at any time.

Although I am sensitive to such phrases, I'm not usually a coward. Old churches and ancient houses bother me, but I normally shrug and put up with any feeling of spiritual discomfort. Here, however, the oppressive atmosphere was so threatening and the feeling of dread so strong, I wanted to run from the building and to hell with the article and the money I needed so much. The closer we got to the centre, the more acute became my emotional stress, until I wondered whether I was going to hyperventilate. Finally, I shouted, 'John!'

He swung round with an irritated 'What is it?'

'I've—I've got to go back . . .'

One of the policemen grabbed my arm in the dark, and squeezed it. I believed it to be a sign of encouragement. He too wanted to turn round, but he was more terrified of his boss than of any ghost. From the strength of the grip I guessed the owner of the fingers was the Mongol.

'Impossible,' John snapped. 'What's the matter with you?'

'A pain,' I said. 'I have a pain in my chest.'

He pushed past the other men and pulled me roughly to one side.

'I knew I shouldn't have brought you. I only did it for Sheena—she seemed to think there was still something left in you. Now pull yourself together. I know what's the matter with you, you're getting the jitters. It's claustrophobia, nothing else. Fight it, man. You're scaring my boys with your stupid funk.'

'I have a pain,' I repeated, but he wasn't buying it.

'Crap. Sheena would be disgusted with you. God knows what she ever saw in you in the first place.'

For a moment all fear was driven out of me by an intense fury that flooded my veins. How dare this thick-skinned, arrogant cop assume knowledge of my wife's regard for me! It was true that her feelings were not now what they had been in the beginning, but she had once fully loved me, and only a rottenness bred by superficial life in the colony had eaten away that love. The mannequins, the people with plaster faces, had served to corrode us. Sheena had once been a happy woman, full of energy, enthusiasms, colour. Now she was pinched and bitter, as I was myself: made so by the shallow gweilos we consorted with and had become ourselves. Money, affairs and bugger-thy-neighbour were the priorities in life.

'You leave Sheena's name out of this,' I said, my voice catching with the anger that stuck in my throat. 'What the hell do you know about our beginnings?'

Speakman merely gave me a look of contempt and took up his position in the front once more, with the hunchbacked Lau indicating which way he should go when we came to one of the many junctions and crossroads. Occasionally, the thin one, who now had the megaphone, would call out in Cantonese, the sound quickly swallowed by the denseness of the structure around us. Added to my anxiety problem was now a feeling of misery. I had shown my inner nature to a man who was increasingly becoming detestable to me. Something was nagging at the edge of my brain too, which gradually ate its way inward, toward an area of comprehension.

God knows what she ever saw in you in the first place.

When it came, the full implication of these words stunned me. At first I was too taken aback to do anything more than keep turning the idea over in my mind, in an obsessive way, until it drove out any other thought. I kept going over his words, trying to find another way of interpreting them, but came up with the same answer every time.

Finally, I could keep quiet no longer. I had to get it out. It was beginning to fester. I stopped in my tracks, and despite the presence of the other men, shouted, 'You bastard, Speakman, you're having an affair with her, aren't you?'

He turned and regarded me, silently.

'You bastard,' I said again. I could hardly get it out, it was choking me. 'You're supposed to be a friend.'

There was utter contempt in his voice.

'I was never your friend.'

'You wanted me to know, didn't you? You wanted to tell me in here.'

He knew that in this place I would be less than confident of myself. The advantages were all with him. I was out of my environment and less able to handle things than he was. In the past few months he had been in here several times, was more familiar with the darkness and the tight, airless zones of the Walled City's interior. We were in an underworld that terrified me and left him unperturbed.

'You men go on,' he ordered the others, not taking his eyes off me. 'We'll follow in a moment.'

They did as they were told. John Speakman was not a man to be brooked by his Asiatic subordinates. When they were out of earshot, he said, 'Yes, Sheena and I had some time together.'

In the light of my helmet lamp I saw his lips twitch, and I wanted to smash him in the mouth.

'Had? You mean it's over?'

'Not completely. But there's still you. You're in the way. Sheena, being the woman she is, still retains some sort of loyalty toward you. Can't see it myself, but there it is.'

'We'll sort this out later,' I said, 'between the three of us.'

I made a move to get past him, but he blocked the way. Then a second, more shocking realisation hit me, and again I was not ready for it. He must have seen it in my face, because his lips tightened this time.

I said calmly now, 'You're going to lose me in here, aren't you? Sheena said she wouldn't leave me, and you're going to make sure I stay behind.'

'Your imagination is running away with you again,' he snapped back. 'Try to be a little more level-headed, old chap.'

'I am being level-headed.'

His hands were on his hips now, in the gweilo stance I knew so well. Once of them rested on the butt of his revolver. Being a policeman, he of course carried a gun, which I did not. There was little point in my trying force anyway. He was a good four inches taller than I and weighed two stone more, most of it muscle. We stood there, confronting one another. Then we heard that terrible scream that turned my guts to milk.

The ear-piercing cry was followed by a scrabbling sound, and eventually one of the two policeman appeared in the light of our lamps.

'Sir, come quick,' he gasped. 'The guide.'

Our quarrel put aside for the moment, we hurried along the tunnel to where the other policeman stood. In front of him, perhaps five yards away, was the guide. His helmet light was out, and he seemed to be standing on tiptoe for some reason, arms hanging loosely by his sides. John stepped forward, and I found myself going with him. He might have wanted me out of the way, but I was going to stick closely to him.

What I saw in the light of our lamps made me retch and step backward quickly.

It would seem that a beam had swung down from the ceiling, as the guide had passed beneath it. This had smashed his helmet lamp. Had that been all, the guide might have got away with a broken nose, or black eye, but it was not. In the end of the beam, now holding him off his feet, was a curved nail-spike. It had gone through his right eye, and was no doubt deeply imbedded in the poor man's brain. He dangled from this support loosely, blood running down the side of his nose and dripping onto his white tennis shoes.

'Jesus Christ!' I said at last. It wasn't a profanity, a blasphemy. It was a prayer. I prayed for us, who were now lost in a dark, hostile world, and I prayed for Sang Lau. Poor little Sang Lau. Just when he had begun to make it in life, just when he had escaped the Walled City, the bricks and mortar and timber had reached out petulantly for its former child and brained it. Sang Lau had been one of the quiet millions who struggle out of the mire, who evolve from terrible beginnings to a place in the world of light. All in vain, apparently.

John Speakman lifted the man away from the instrument that had impaled his brain, and laid the body on the floor. He went through the formality of feeling for a pulse, and then shook his head. To give him his due, his voice remained remarkably firm, as if he were still in control of things.

'We'll have to carry him out,' he said to his two men.

'Take one end each.'

There was a reluctant shuffling of feet, as the men moved forward to do as they were told. The smaller of the two was trembling so badly he dropped the legs straight away, and had to retrieve them quickly under Speakman's glare.

I said, 'And I suppose you know which way to go?'

'We're near the heart of the place, old chap. It doesn't really matter in which direction we go, as long as we keep going straight.'

That, I knew, was easier said than done. When passageways curve and turn, run into each other, go up and down, meet new forks and crossroads and junctions with choices, how the hell do you keep in a straight line? I said nothing for once. I didn't want the two policemen to panic. If we were to get out, we had to stay calm. And those on the outside wouldn't leave us here. They would send in a search party, once nightfall came.

Nightfall.

I suppressed a chill as we moved into the heart of the beast.

Seven months ago Britain agreed with China that Hong Kong would return to its landlord country in 1997. It was then at last decided to clean up and clean out the Walled City, to pull it down and re-house the inhabitants. There were plans to build a park on the ground then covered by this ancient city within a city, for the use of the occupants of the surrounding tenement buildings.

It stood in the middle of Kowloon on the mainland. Once upon a time there was a wall around it, when it was the home of the Manchus, but Japanese invaders robbed it of its ancient stones to build elsewhere. The area on which it stood was still known as the Walled City. When the Manchus were there, they used it as a fort against the British. Then the British were leased the peninsula, and it became an enclave for China's officials, whose duty it was to report on gweilo activities in the area to Peking. Finally, it became an architectural nightmare, a giant slum. An area not recognised by the British, who refused to police it, and abandoned by Peking, it was a lawless labyrinth, sometimes called the Forbidden Place. It was here that unlicensed doctors and dentists practiced, and every kind of vice flourished. It was ruled by gangs of youths, the Triads, who covered its inner walls with blood. It is a place of death, the home of ten thousand ghosts.

For the next two hours we struggled through the rank smelling tunnels, crawling over filth and across piles of trash, until we were all exhausted. I had cuts on my knees, and my hair felt teeming with insects. I knew there were spiders, possibly even snakes, in these passageways. There were certainly lice, horseflies, mosquitoes and a dozen other nasty biters. Not only that, but there seemed to be projections everywhere: sharp bits of metal, cables hanging like vines form the ceiling and rusty nails. The little Cantonese policeman had trodden on a nail, which had completely pierced his foot. He was now limping and whining in a small voice. He knew that if he did not get treatment soon, blood poisoning would be the least of his troubles. I felt sorry for the young man, who in the normal run of things probably dealt with the tide of human affairs very competently within his range of duties. He was an official of the law in the most densely populated area of the world, not I had seen his type deal cleanly and (more often than not) peacefully with potentially ugly situations daily. In here, however, he was over his head. The situation could not be handled by efficient traffic signals or negotiation, or even prudent use of a weapon. There was something about this man that was familiar. There were scars on his face: shiny patches that might have been the result of plastic surgery. I tried to recall where I had seen the Cantonese policeman before, but my mind was soggy with recent events.

We took turns carrying the body of the guide. Once I had touched him and got over my squeamishness, that part of it didn't bother me too much. What did was the weight of the corpse. I never believed a dead man could be so heavy. After ten minutes my arms were nearly coming out of their sockets. I began by carrying the legs, and quickly decided the man at the head, carrying the torso, had the best part of the deal. I suggested a change round, which was effected, only to find that the other end of the man was twice as heavy. I began to hate him, this leaden corpse.

After four hours I had had enough.

'I'm not humping him around anymore,' I stated bluntly to the cop who was trying to take my wife from me. 'You want him outside, you carry him by yourselves. You're the bloody boss man. It's your damn show.'

'I see,' John said. 'Laying down some ground rules, are we?'

'Shove it up your arse,' I replied. 'I've had you up to here. I can't prove, you planned to dump me in here, but I know, pal, and when we get out of this place, you and I are going to have a little talk.'

'If we get out,' he muttered.

He was sitting away from me, in the darkness, where my lamplight couldn't reach him. I could not see his expression.

'If?'

'Exactly,' he sighed. 'We don't seem to be getting very far, do we? It's almost as if this place were trying to keep us. I swear it's turning us in on ourselves. We should have reached the outside long ago.'

'But they'll send someone in after us,' I said.

And one of the policemen added, 'Yes. Someone come.'

'Fraid not. No one knows we're here.' It came out almost as if he were pleased with himself. I saw now that I had been right. It had been his intention to drop me off in the middle of this godforsaken building, knowing I would never find my own way out. I wondered only briefly what he planned to do with the two men and the guide. I don't doubt they could be bribed. The Hong Kong Police Force has at times been notorious for its corruption. Maybe they were chosen because they could be bought.

'How long have we got?' I asked, trying to stick to practical issues.

'About five more hours. Then the demolition starts. They begin knocking it down at six a.m.'

Just then, the smaller of the Chinese made a horrific gargling sound, and we all shone our lights on him instinctively. At first I couldn't understand what was wrong with him, though I could see he was convulsing. He was in a sitting position, and his body kept jerking and flopping. John Speakman bent over him, then straightened, saying,

'Christ, not another one . . .'

'Six-inch nail. It's gone in behind his ear. How the hell? I don't understand how he managed to lean all the way back on it.'

'Unless the nail came out of the wood?' I said.

'What are you saying?'

'I don't know. All I know is two men have been injured in accidents that seem too freakish to believe. What do you think? Why can't we get out of this place? Shit, it's only the area of a football stadium. We've been in here hours.'

The other policeman was looking at his colleague with wide, disbelieving eyes. He grabbed John Speakman by the collar, blurting, 'We go now. We go outside now,' and then a babble of that tonal language, some of which John might have understood. I certainly didn't.

Speakman peeled the man's stubby fingers from his collar and turned away from him, toward the dead cop, as if the incident had not taken place. 'He was a good policeman,' he said. 'Jimmy Wong. You know he saved a boy from a fire last year? Dragged the child out with his teeth, hauling the body along the floor and down the stairs because his hands were burned too badly to clutch the kid. You remember. You covered the story.'

I remembered him now. Jimmy Wong. The governor had presented him with a medal. He had saluted proudly, with heavily bandaged hands. Today he was not a hero. Today he was a number. The second victim.

John Speakman said, 'Goodbye, Jimmy.'

Then he ignored him, saying to me, 'We can't carry both bodies out. We'll have to leave them. I . . . ' but I heard no more. There was a quick tearing sound, and I was suddenly falling. My heart dropped out of me. I landed heavily on my back. Something entered between my shoulder blades, something sharp and painful, and I had to struggle hard to get free. When I managed to get to my feet and reached down and felt along the floor, I touched a slim projection, probably a large nail. It was sticky with my blood. A voice from above said, 'Are you all right?'

'I—I think so. A nail . . . '

'What?'

My light had gone out, and I was feeling disorientated. I must have fallen about fourteen feet, judging from the distance of the lamps above me. I reached down my back with my hand. It felt wet and warm, but apart from the pain I wasn't gasping for air or anything. Obviously, it had missed my lungs and other vital organs, or I would be squirming in the dust, coughing my guts up.

I heard John say, 'We'll try to reach you,' and then the voice and the lights drifted away.

'No!' I shouted. 'Don't leave me! Give me your arm.' I reached upward. 'Help me up!'

But my hand remained empty. They had gone, leaving the blackness behind them. I lay still for a long time, afraid to move. There were nails everywhere. My heart was racing. I was sure that I was going to die. The Walled City had us in its grip, and we were not going to get out. Once, it had been teeming with life, but we had robbed it of its soul, the people had crowded within its walls. Now even the shell was threatened with destruction. And we were the men responsible. We represented the authority who had ordered its death, and it was determined to take us with it. Nothing likes to die alone. Nothing wants to leave this world without, at the very least, obtaining satisfaction in the way of revenge. The ancient black heart of the Walled City of the Manchus, surrounded by the body it had been given by later outcasts from society, had enough life left in it to slaughter these five puny mortals from the other side, the lawful side. It had tasted gweilo blood, and it would have more.

My wound was beginning to ache, and I climbed stiffly and carefully to my feet. I felt slowly along the walls, taking each step cautiously. Things scuttled over my feet, whispered over my face, but I ignored them. A sudden move and I would find myself impaled on some projection. The stink of death was in the stale air, filling my nostrils. It was trying to drive fear into me. The only way I was going to survive was by remaining calm. Once I panicked, it would all be over. I had the feeling that the building could kill me at any time, but I was savouring the moment, allowing it to be my mistake. It wanted me to dive headlong into insanity, it wanted to experience my terror, then it would deliver the coup de grace.

I moved this way along the tunnels for about an hour: Neither of us, it seemed, was short of patience. The Walled City had seen centuries, so what was an hour or two? The legacy of death left by the Manchus and the Triads existed without reference to time. Ancient evils and modern iniquity had joined forces against the foreigner, the gweilo, and the malodorous darkness smiled at any attempt to thwart its intention to suck the life from my body.

At one point my forward foot did not touch the ground. There was a space, a hole, in front of me.

'Nice try,' I whispered, 'but not yet.'

As I prepared to edge around it, hoping for a small ledge or something, I felt ahead of me, and touched the thing. It was dangling over the hole, like plumb-line weight. I pushed it, and it swung slowly.

By leaning over and feeling carefully, I ascertained it to be the remaining local policeman, the muscled northerner. I knew him by his Sam Browne shoulder strap. I felt up by the corpse's throat and found the skin bulging over some tight electrical cords. The building had hanged him.

Used to death now, I gripped the corpse around the waist and used it as a swing to get myself across the gap. The cords held, and I touched ground. A second later, the body must have dropped, because I heard a crash below.

I continued my journey through the endless tunnels, my throat very parched now. I was thirsty as hell. Eventually, I could stand it no longer and licked some of the moisture that ran down the walls. It tasted like wine. At one point I tongued up a cockroach, cracked it between my teeth, and spit it out in disgust. Really, I no longer cared. All I wanted to do was get out alive. I didn't even care whether John and Sheena told me to go away. I would be happy to do so. There wasn't much left, in any case. Anything I had felt had shriveled away during this ordeal. I just wanted to live. Nothing more, nothing less.

At one point a stake or something plunged downward from the roof and passed through several floors, missing me by an inch. I think I actually laughed. A little while later, I found an airshaft with a rope hanging in it. Trusting that the building would not let me fall, I climbed down this narrow chimney to get to the bottom. I had some idea that if I could reach ground level, I might find a way to get through the walls. Some of them were no thicker than cardboard.

After reaching the ground safely, I began to feel my way along the corridors and alleys, until I saw a light. I gasped with relief, thinking at first it was daylight, but had to swallow a certain amount of disappointment in finding it was only a helmet with its lamp still on. The owner was nowhere to be seen. I guessed it was John's: he was the only one left, apart from me.

Not long after this, I heard John Speakman's voice for the last time. It seemed to come from very far below me, in the depths of the underground passages that worm-holed beneath the Walled City. It was a faint pathetic cry for help. Immediately following this distant shout was the sound of falling masonry. And then, silence. I shuddered, involuntarily, guessing what had happened. The building had lured him into its underworld, its maze below the earth, and had then blocked the exits. John Speakman had been buried alive, immured by the city that held him in contempt.

Now there was only me.

I moved through an inner darkness, the beam of the remaining helmet lamp having faded to dim glow. I was Theseus in the Labyrinth, except that I had no Ariadne to help me find the way through it. I stumbled through long tunnels where the air was so thick and damp I might have been in a steam bath. I crawled along passages no taller or wider than a cupboard under a kitchen sink, shared them with spiders and rats and came out the other end choking on dust, spitting out cobwebs. I knocked my way through walls so thin and rotten a single blow with my fist was enough to hole them. I climbed over fallen girders, rubble and piles of filthy rags, collecting unwanted passengers and abrasions on the way.

And all the while I knew the building was laughing at me.

It was leading me round in circles, playing with me like a rat in a maze. I could hear it moving, creaking and shifting as it readjusted itself, changed its inner structure to keep me from finding an outside wall. Once, I trod on something soft. It could have been a hand—John's hand—quickly withdrawn. Or it might have been a creature of the Walled City, a rat or a snake. Whatever it was, it had been live.

There were times when I became so despondent I wanted to lie down and just fade into death, the way a primitive tribesman will give up all hope and turn his face to the wall. There were times when I became angry, and screeched at the structure that had me trapped in its belly, remonstrating with it until my voice was hoarse. Sometimes I was driven to useless violence and picked up the nearest object to smash at my tormentor, even if my actions brought the place down around my ears.

Once, I even whispered to the darkness:

'I'll be your slave. Tell me what to do—any evil thing—and

I'll do it. If you let me go, I promise to follow your wishes. Tell me what to do . . . '

And still it laughed at me, until I knew I was going insane.

Finally, I began singing to myself, not to keep up my spirits like brave men are supposed to, but because I was beginning to slip into that crazy world that rejects reality in favour of fantasy. I thought I was home, in my own house, making coffee. I found myself going through the actions of putting on the kettle, and preparing the coffee, milk and sugar, humming a pleasant tune to myself all the while. One part of me recognised that domestic scene was make-believe, but the other was convinced that I could not possibly be trapped by a malevolent entity and about to die in the dark corridors of its multi-sectioned shell.

Then something happened, to jerk me into sanity.

The sequence of events covering the next few minutes or so are lost to me. Only by concentrating very hard and surmising can I recall what might have happened. Certainly, I believe I remember those first few moments, when a sound deafened me, and the whole building rocked and trembled as if in an earthquake. Then I think I fell to the floor and had the presence of mind to jam the helmet on my head. There followed a second (what I now know to be) explosion. Pieces of building rained around me: bricks were striking my shoulders and bouncing off my hard hat. I think the only reason none of them injured me badly was because the builders, being poor, had used the cheapest materials they could find. These were bricks fashioned out of crushed coke, which are luckily light and airy.

A hole appeared, through which I could see blinding daylight. I was on my feet in an instant, and racing toward it. Nails appeared out of the woodwork, up from the floor, and ripped and tore at my flesh like sharp fangs. Metal posts crashed across my path, struck me on my limbs. I was attacked from all sides by chunks of masonry and debris, until I was bruised and raw, bleeding from dozens of cuts and penetrations.

When I reached the hole in the wall, I threw myself at it, and landed outside the dust. There, the demolition people saw me, and one risked his life to dash forward and pull me clear of the collapsing building. I was then rushed to hospital. I was found to have a broken arm and multiple lacerations, some of them quite deep.

Mostly, I don't remember what happened at the end. I'm going by what I've been told, and what flashes on and off in my nightmares, and using these have pieced together the above account of my escape from the Walled City. It seems as though it might be reasonably accurate.

I have not, of course, told the true story of what happened inside those walls, except in this account, which will go into a safe place until after my death. Such a tale would only have people clucking their tongues and saying, 'It's the shock, you know—the trauma of such an experience,' and sending for the psychiatrist. I tried to tell Sheena once, but I could see that it was disturbing her, so I mumbled something about, 'Of course, I can see that one's imagination can work overtime in a place like that,' and never mentioned it to her again.

I did manage to tell the demolition crew about John. I told them he might still be alive, under all that rubble. They stopped their operations immediately and sent in search parties, but though they found the bodies of the guide and policemen, John was never seen again. The search parties all managed to get out safely, which has me wondering whether perhaps there is something wrong with my head—except that I have the wounds, and there are the corpses of my travelling companions. I don't know. I can only say now what I think happened. I told the police (and stuck rigidly to my story) that I was separated from the others before any deaths occurred. How was I to explain two deaths by sharp instruments, and a subsequent hanging? I let them try to figure it out. All I told them was that I heard John's final cry, and that was the truth. I don't even care whether or not they believe me. I'm outside that damn hellhole, and that's all that concerns me.

And Sheena? It is seven months since the incident. And it was only yesterday that I confronted and accused her or having an affair with John, and she looked so shocked and distressed and denied it so vehemently that I have to admit I believe that nothing of the kind happened between them. I was about to tell her that John had admitted to it, but had second thoughts. I mean, had he? Maybe I had filled in the gaps with my own jealous fears? To tell you the truth, I can't honestly remember, and the guilt is going to be hard to live with. You see, when they asked me for the location of John's cry for help, I indicated a spot . . . well, I think I told them to dig—I said . . . anyway, they didn't find him, which wasn't surprising, since I . . . well, perhaps this is not the place for full confessions.

John is still under there somewhere, God help him. I have the awful feeling that the underground ruins of the Walled City might keep him alive in some way, with rejected water, and food in the form of rats and cockroaches. A starving man will eat dirt, if it fills his stomach. Perhaps he is still below, in some pocket created by that underworld? Such a slow, terrible torture, keeping a man barely alive in his own grave, would be consistent with that devious, nefarious entity I know as the Walled City of the Manchus.

Some nights when I am feeling especially brave, I go to the park and listen—listen for small cries from a sub-terranean prison—listen for the faint pleas for help from an oubliette far below the ground.

Sometimes I think I hear them.

THE HUNGRY GHOSTS

Hong Kong at the end of August is at its hottest time of the year and the humidity is such that normally good stiff paper turns limp and damp, and forgotten clothes form beds for fungi at the bottom of drawers. Residents of Kowloon Tong and the more airless districts make excuses to visit Hong Kong Island, so that they take the Star Ferry across a cool stretch of water. British gweilos complain wearily to each other about the human condition in those same self-satisfied tones they used back home on cold, wet and windy days.

Perhaps it is because August is a sultry, steamy month which tries both the body and spirit, that Yen Lo, the keeper of the underworld, allows the ghosts out of his domain for twenty-four hours, to visit their relatives. Perhaps Yen Lo believes that his ghosts will find it so unpleasant along the crowded Nathan Road, or in the thick of the masses at Temple Market, that they will be anxious to return to the more acceptable climate of the underworld at the end of the day. Maybe Yen Lo has no need to spend his time chasing runaways the following day, since his charges are no doubt happy to be back home where at least their difficulties remain arid.

Yen Lo's day is celebrated amongst the local population as the Festival of the Hungry Ghosts, and to placate the roving spirits fires are lit in open spaces, and food is left on offer.

At such festive times roadside Cantonese operas blossom in the evening hours, for the entertainment of both the living and the dead.

Richard Tang and his wife Sara drove home from one of these performances in Tsimshatsui, to their new tenth-floor flat on Diamond Hill. They were Christians but they still, like the gweilo Christians did with their own pagan festivals, observed many customs and traditions of their ancestors. During the drive they spoke little to each other, immersed in their own particular thoughts. The journey was slow and tedious, as always on the roads of a city which housed six million people. As they travelled along they studiously avoided looking at the roadside fires, which was difficult since there were so many of them.

When they arrived back at their apartment, Richard drove the Mercedes into his personal space under the building and they took the elevator to their floor. Once inside their rooms Sara made some tea and they sat on the balcony watching the aircraft float over the rooftops in and out of Kai Tak, still saying nothing, each still locked into their own private remi- niscences. Occasionally one of them would try to glance at the other without being observed doing so. There were problems between them and a barrier had formed like a wall of glass. They could see each other, like a stranger on the far side, but there was no spiritual contact. Each acknowledged that it was not the other's fault, that any blame was mutual,

But still there remained this spectral obstacle between them.

Finally, Richard said to Sara, 'Shall we leave some food for the ghosts? What do you think?'

'We usually do,' she replied. 'Why behave any differently this year?' She turned to him, the rattan chair squeaking with her movements. 'I don't think we have very much in the larder. Shall I make something? Some cakes?'

Richard suddenly became animated.

'Why not? And I'll do some sweetmeats. How about that?'

She exclaimed, 'You, cook?'

'Of course!' He puffed out his chest. 'A man can do anything, if he puts his soul into it.'

So they went into the kitchen and set about their individual tasks with an energy that had the air conditioning units working overtime. As they prepared the dishes, incredibly, they chatted to one another.

Unknown to the two adults, their children Tim and Susie had been eavesdropping on the conversation. While the parents were busy in the kitchen, and flour was like vapour in the air, the youngsters hid behind the hall cupboard and discussed these events in whispers with some excitement. Their mother and father were doing something, together, at long last. It was a cause for celebration in itself. For six months the adults had hardly spoken to each other. Since moving to their new apartment they had communicated in grunts when they had to, but preferred to maintain silence most of the time. It was as if words were subject to the heavy humid conditions of the weather and the effort of producing them too wearisome. Perhaps at last conversation was becoming less of a strain, less of a torture, and some semblance of normality was returning to the household.

Soon there was an aromatic atmosphere to the apartment. Sara always said that cooking odours were fragrances, rather than smells, and tonight the two children understood what their mother meant. Had they not already eaten their fill at their grandmother's not two hours earlier, where they had swallowed sweet-and-sour pork, egg fried rice, Singapore noodles, chilli prawns, glutinous rice, and other dishes, with abandon, the fragrance issuing from the kitchen would have them smacking their lips in anticipation. They were almost sorry, once the cakes and sweetmeats were cooling on wire trays, that they had been so greedy at Grandma's apartment. Had they known what was in store, they agreed that they could have sneaked into the kitchen during the night and sampled the gifts left for the ghosts. Those who have left home will know that there are few things in the world to equal a mother's cakes, and the results of a father's cooking are always interesting, if nothing else.

Sara arranged the cakes on a china plate of floral design, while Richard chose a stoneware dish, plain on the inside but having an exterior pattern, a fishing boat battling against fast-flowing seas. Chinese believe artistic arrangements to be just as important as the taste of the food, and much thought goes into the overall shape of the presentation. Once this was done, the adults retired for the night.

Out amongst the misty crags of Lion Rock, amongst the boulders of Poh Ping Chau, over the natural stone arch known as Hopeless Buttress, the phantoms of the dead roamed at will. They had but a few more hours of freedom, before Yen Lo gathered them in and herded them back to their places in the underworld. They looked down on the tall buildings below, where the religious observances having been completed, paper representations of the gods of hell had been set on fire. Other spectres wandered through the streets, or walked the water-fronts of Aberdeen Harbour, where the junks and houseboats jostled each other for dirty wavespace. In the most densely populated area of all, the Walled City, a giant slum housing some fifty thousand people, the ghosts scrambled up ladders, ran along walkways, through alleys and streets that never saw natural light, wondering if they were indeed still in hell and had not been allowed their annual holiday at all.

The Festival of the Hungry Ghosts was in full swing.

When the two adults were in bed, the children crept back to the kitchen and hid between the refrigerator and the wall where a dark shadow always dwelt, even when the lamp was on. They had the feeling that something was going to happen during the night and they wanted to be there to witness it.

Sure enough, half an hour later a figure in a white flowing gown entered the kitchen. In the near darkness it paused by the work surface and, after a few moments, began eating sweetmeats from one of the two dishes. The children could hear chewing and the smacking of lips and they nudged one another in the darkness of their hiding place. Only when all the sweetmeats had been devoured, did the white figure leave, floating through the kitchen doorway and down the hall.

An hour after this event a second shape crept through the doorway of the kitchen, felt along the top of the work surface and found the plate of cakes. These were eaten even faster than the sweetmeats. Susie and Tim had to suppress giggles during this feast and pinched each other to stop from laughing out loud.

Eventually, all was still in the household.

The following morning Richard Tang was sitting at the breakfast table when Sara brought in the tea. He looked up from reading his newspaper and took the tray from his wife so that she could sit down opposite. For a while they said nothing to each other and merely busied themselves with pouring and stirring, and any small task the table had to offer.

Finally Richard looked at his wife with a tight wan smile on his face.

'I see Susie ate the cakes you left for her,' he said. 'She must have enjoyed them, especially from that plate. It used to be her favourite, you remember.'

Sara nodded and her lips formed a smile similar to the one on her husband's face.

'And Tim obviously enjoyed your sweetmeats. The boat on the dish must have reminded him of the times you two went fishing together.'

Externally, the porcelain smiles remained intact, but inside each adult fine cracks spread over their souls like the hairline fissures on a glazed Tsung urn. Their spirits threatened to craze and shatter within, but as if each knew of the other's feelings, they reached across the table, touched fingertips, and saved one another.

When Richard could trust himself to speak again, he said, 'It was you that ate the sweetmeats, wasn't it?'

Sara nodded. 'And you, the cakes. That was very thoughtful of you. What a pity we can't keep up the pretence. The children are gone and nothing can bring them back—but still, it was kind of you, my husband.'

'My wife.'

They touched again, lightly, aware of the two empty chairs on either side of the table, one beside mother, one beside father. They could have talked about the children and the happy times before that terrible fire in their other flat, six months previously. They could have said things like, 'When the children were alive . . . ' But neither parent was ready for such a large step. After all, the children had only been dead six months, and wounds like that take years, even decades, to close.

At least the Festival of the Hungry Ghosts was over and there would be no more roadside fires to rekindle terrible memories for another year.

Outside, a humid August heat brought hell to the streets.

MEMORIES OF THE FLYING BALL BIKE SHOP

The old Chinese gentleman was sitting cross-legged in the shadow of an alley. He was smoking a long bamboo pipe, which he cradled in the crook of his elbow. I had noticed him as we climbed the temple steps, and the image stayed with me as we wandered through the Buddhist-Tao shrine to Wong Tai Sin, a shepherd boy who had seen visions.

It was so hot the flagstones pulsed beneath our feet, but despite that David was impressed with the temple. We waded through the red-and-gold litter which covered the forecourt, the dead joss sticks cracking underfoot. Cantonese worshippers were present in their hundreds, murmuring orisons, rattling their cans of fortune sticks. Wong Tai Sin is no showcase for tourists, but a working temple in the middle of a high rise public housing estate. Bamboo poles covered in freshly washed clothes, overhung the ornate roof, and dripped upon its emerald tiles.

The air was heavy with incense dense enough to drug the crickets into silence. We ambled up and down stone staircases, admiring carvings the significance of which was lost in gener-

| 173 |

ations of western nescience and gazed self-consciously at the worshippers on their knees as they shook their fortune sticks and prayed for lucky numbers to fall to the flagstones.

We left the temple with our ignorance almost intact.

The old man was still there, incongruous amongst the other clean shaven Hong Kong men, with their carefully-acquired sophistication, hurrying by his squatting form.

He had a wispy Manchu beard, long grey locks, and dark eyes set in a pomelo-skin face. A sleeveless vest hung from bony shoulders, and canvas trousers covered legs that terminated in an enormous pair of bare feet. The bamboo pipe he was smoking was about fifty centimetres long, three centimetres in diameter, with a large watercooled bowl at one end, and a stem the size of a drinking straw at the other. He had the stem in his lipless mouth, inhaling the smoke.

There was a fruit stall owner, a man I had spoken to on occasion, on the pavement nearby. I told David to wait by the taxi stand and went to the vendor. We usually spoke to each other in a mixture of Cantonese and English, neither of us being fluent in the foreign language. He was fascinated by my red hair, inherited from my Scottish highland ancestors.

'Jo san,' I said, greeting him, 'leung goh ping gwoh, m'goi.'

I had to shout a to make myself heard above the incredibly loud clattering coming from behind him, where sat three thin men and a stout lady, slamming down mah jong tiles as if trying to drive them through the Formica table top.

He nodded, wrapped two apples in a piece of newspaper, and asked me for two dollars.

Paying him, I said, 'That man, smoking. Opium?'

He looked where I was pointing, smiled, and shook his head vigorously.

'Not smoke opium. No, no. Sik yin enemy.'

I stared at the old gentleman, puffing earnestly away, seeming to suck down the shadows of the alley along with the smoke.

'Sik yin dik yan-aa?' I said, wanting to make sure I had heard him properly. 'Smoke enemy?'

'Hai. Magic smoke-pipe,' he grinned. 'Magic, you know? Very old sik yin-pipe.'

Gradually I learned that the aged smoker had written down the name of a man he hated, on 'dragon' paper, had torn it to shreds, and was inhaling it with his tobacco. Once he had smoked the name of his enemy, had the hated foe inside him, he would come to know the man.

The idea was of course, that when you knew the hated enemy—and by know, the Chinese mean to understand completely—you could predict any moves he might make against you. You would have a psychological advantage over him, be able to forestall his attacks, form countermoves against him. His strategy, his tactics, would be yours to thwart. He would be able to do nothing which you would not foresee.

'I think . . . ' I began saying, but David interrupted me with a shout of 'I've got a taxi, come on!', so I bid the stall owner a hasty goodbye, and ran for the waiting vehicle. We leapt out into the fierce flow of Hong Kong traffic, and I put the incident aside until I had more time to think about it.

That evening, over dinner at the Great Shanghai Restaurant in Tsimshatsui, I complained bitterly to David about John Chang.

'He's making my life here a misery,' I said. 'I find myself battling with a man who seems to despise me.'

David was a photographer who had worked with me on my old Birmingham paper. He had since moved into the big time, with one of the nationals in London, while I had run away to a Hong Kong English language newspaper, after an affaire had suffered a greenstick fracture which was obviously never going to heal.

David fiddled with his chopsticks, holding them too low down the shafts to get any sort of control over them. He chased an elusive peppered prawn around the dish. It could have still been alive, the way it evaded the pincers.

'You always get people like that, on any paper, Sean, you know that. Politicians, roughriders, ambitious bastards, you can't escape them just by coming east. Some people get their kicks out of stomping on their subordinates. What is he, anyway? Senior Editor?'

David finally speared the prawn with a single chopstick and looked around him defiantly at the Cantonese diners before popping it into his mouth.

'He's got a lot of power. He could get me thrown out, just like that.'

'Well, suck up to the bastard. They like that sort of thing, don't they? The Chinese? Especially from European gweilos like you. Take him out to lunch, tell him he's a great guy and you're proud to be working with him—no, for him. Tell him the Far East is wonderful, you love Hong Kong, you want to make good here, make your home here. Tell the bastard anything, if it gets him off your back. Forget all that shit about crawling. That's for school kids who think that there's some kind of virtue in swimming against the tide. You've got to make a go of it, and this bloke, what's his name? Chang? If he's making your life hell, then neutralise the sod. Not many people can resist flattery, even when they recognise what it is—hookers use it all the time—'you big strong man, you make fantastic lovey, I never have man like you before'. Codswallop. You know it, they know it, but it still makes you feel good, doesn't it? Speaking of hookers, when are you going to take me down the Wanch . . . ?'

He was talking about Wan Chai, the red light district, which I knew I would have to point him towards one evening of his holiday. David liked his sex casual and stringless, despite all the evil drums in such a lifestyle these days. I needed emotion with my love making, not cheap scent and garlic breath.

I lay in bed that night, thinking about what David had said. Maybe the fault did lie with me? Maybe I was putting out the wrong signals and John Chang thought I did not like him, had not liked him from our first meeting? Some men had sensitive antennae, picked up these vibrations before the signaller knew himself what messages he intended to transmit.

No, I was sure that wasn't it. I had gone out of my way to be friendly with John Chang. I had arrived in Hong Kong, eager to get to know the local people, and had seen John Chang as a person to whom I would have liked to get close. But from the beginning he had come down hard on me, on my work, on everything I did. I had been singled out for victimisation and he piled adverse criticism on my head whenever he got the chance.

However, I was willing to admit that I was not the easiest of employees to get along with, from a social point of view.

John Chang had a happy marriage. I had never met his wife, but she phoned him at the office quite often, and the tone and manner of the conversation indicated a strong loving relationship. This caused me to be envious of him. I once dreamed of having such a relationship with Nickie, and had failed to make it work. I still loved her, of course, and on days I missed her most I was testy and irritable with everyone, including John Chang.

I fell asleep thinking that perhaps I was more than partly to blame for John Chang's attitude towards me. I vowed to try to improve things, once my vacation was over and I was back at work.

There was a cricket making insistent noises, somewhere in the bedroom. It took several sleep-drugged minutes for me to realise that it was the phone chirruping. David? Had he gone down the Wanch and got himself into trouble?

'Hello, Sean Fraser . . . '

'Fraser?' John Chang's clipped accent. 'Get down to the office. We need you on a story.'

I sat up in bed.

'I'm on vacation. I've got a guest, here dammit!'

'Sorry, can't help that. Tim Lee's gone sick. He was covering the Governor's annual speech. You'll have to do it.'

The line went dead. He had replaced the receiver.

I slammed the phone down and seethed for a few minutes. before getting out of bed to have a shower and get dressed. David was still asleep on the living-room couch when I went through to the kitchen. I woke him and told him what had happened, apologised, and said I would see him that evening.

'Don't worry about me, mate. I can sort myself out. It's that bastard of a boss you want to sort out.'

Once I had covered the usual bland yearly speech presented by the British Governor of Hong Kong—written by a committee into a meaningless string of words—John Chang wanted me to visit a fireman who lived in the Lok Fu district. The man had been partially blinded six weeks previously while fighting a fire in Chung King Mansions, a notorious giant slum where holidaying backpackers found relatively cheap accommodation in an impossibly expensive city.

'It's five o'clock,' I protested to Chang, 'and I have a guest to look after.'

He regarded me stone faced.

'You're a reporter. You don't work office hours.'

'I'm on bloody holiday.'

'That's tough. You cover this, then you're on vacation—unless I need you again. If you want to work for someone else, that's fine too. Understand me?' He stared hard at me, probably hoping I would throw his job in his face. I was not about to do that.

I said coldly, 'I understand.'

I rang David and said I would be home about nine o'clock. I advised him to go out and eat, because I was going to grab some fast food on my way to Lok Fu. He seemed happy enough, and told me not to worry, but that wasn't the point. The point was that I was close to strangling John Chang with my bare hands.

I saw the young fireman. He seemed philosophical about his accident, though to me his disability pension seemed incredibly small. His wife was working as a bank clerk and now he could look after their two infants, instead of sending them to the grandparents for the weekdays. He could still see a little, and as he pointed out, government apartments, like most private apartments in Hong Kong, were so small it had only taken him a short while to get a mental picture of his home.

During the interview the fireman pressed brandies upon me, as is the custom amongst the Hong Kong Chinese. By the time I left him, I was quietly drunk. I caught a taxi. The driver took me through Wong Tai Sin, and I passed the temple David and I had visited the previous evening. On impulse I told the driver to stop and paid him off.

The old man was still there, at the opening to the alley. He was sitting on a small stool, staring dispassionately at passersby with his rheumy eyes. The pipe was lying on a piece of dirty newspaper, just behind him. I stumbled over to him, trying to hide my state of inebriation.

I pointed to the pipe.

'Ngoh, sik yin-aa?' I said, asking to smoke it.

Cantonese is a tonal language, the same words meaning many different things, and by the way he looked at me I knew I had got my tones wrong. I had probably said something like 'Me fat brickhead' or something even more incomprehensible.

'M'maai,' he said emphatically in Cantonese, thinking I wanted to by the pipe and informing that it was not for sale.

I persisted, and by degrees, got him to understand that I only wanted to smoke it. I told him I had an enemy, a man I hated. I said I wished 'to know' this man, and would pay him for the use of his magic pipe. He smiled at me, his face a tight mass of contour lines.

'Yi sap man,' he agreed, asking me for twenty dollars. It was a very small sum for gaining power over the man that was making my life a misery.

I tore off a margin piece of newspaper and wrote JOHN CHANG on it, but the old man brushed this aside. He produced a thin strip of red-and-gold paper covered on one side with Chinese characters and indicated that I should write the name on the back of it. When I had done so, he tore it into tiny pieces. I could see the muscles working in wrists as thin as broom handles, as his longnailed fingers worked first at this, then at tamping down the paper shreds and tobacco in the pipe bowl.

He handed the musty-smelling instrument to me and I hesitated. It looked filthy. Did I really want that thing in my mouth? I had visions of the stem crawling with tuberculosis bacilli from the spittle of a thousand previous smokers. But then there was a flame at the bowl, and I was sucking away, finding the tobacco surprisingly smooth.

I could see the dark smoke rising from the rubbish burning cauldrons of Wong Tai Sin Temple, and as I puffed away on the ancient bamboo pipe, an intense feeling of well-being crept over me. I began to suspect the tobacco. Was it indeed free of opium? Had I been conned, by the fruit seller and the old man both? Maybe the old man was the fruit stall owner's father? It didn't seem to matter. I liked the pair of them. They were wonderful people. Even John Chang seemed a nice man, at that moment in time.

When the holiday was over, David left Hong Kong, and I returned to work. John Chang was in a foul mood the morning I arrived, and was screaming at young girl for spilling a few drops of coffee on the floor. A woman reporter caught my eyes and made a face which said, 'Stay out of his way if you can.'

The warning came too late.

'You,' snapped John Chang, as I passed him. 'That fireman story was bloody useless. You didn't capture the personal side at all.'

'I thought I did,' I said, stiffly.

'What you think is of no interest to me. I asked you to concentrate on the man and his family, and you bring in all that rubbish about government pensions.'

'I thought it needed saying.'

He gave me a look of disgust and waved me away as if I were some coolie that was irritating, but not worth chastising further. I felt my blood rise and I took a step towards him, but Sally, the woman reporter, grabbed my arm. She held me there until John Chang had left the room.

I turned, the fury dissipating, and said, 'Thanks.'

She gave me a little smile.

'You would only be giving him the excuse he needs,' she said in her soft Asiatic accent. Peter Smith, another reporter, said, 'Too bloody right, mate. Don't give him the satisfaction.'

'He looked as if he could have killed that girl,' I said to Sally, a little later. 'All over a few spots of coffee.'

'It was her perfume. For some reason that brand drives him crazy. I used to wear it myself, but not anymore. Not since I realised what it does to his temper . . . '

Understand the one you hate.

I had to admit my temporary drunken hopes for a magical insight into John Chang had failed. There was no magic on the modern streets of Hong Kong. An antique pipe, nicotined a dirty yellow, stained black with tobacco juice, dottle clinging to the bowl, was nothing more than what it was—a lump of wood. Had I really believed it would help me?

I guess a desperate man will believe anything, even that he will someday manage to forget a woman he loves: will wake up one morning free of her image, the sound of her voice in his head gone, her smell removed from his olfactory memory. Memory sometimes works to its own secret rules and is not always subject to the will of its owner.

Memories can be cruel servants.

I began to have strange dreams, even while awake, of a woman I did not know. She was small, slim and dark, with a familiar voice. We were very intimate with one another. I pictured her in a kitchen, her hands flying around a wok, producing aromas that drove my gastric juices crazy. I saw her brown eyes, peering at into mine from behind candles like white bars, over a dining-room table made of Chinese rosewood. There was love in those eyes. We drank a wine which was familiar to my brain but not to my tongue. She chattered to me, pleasantly, in Cantonese. I understood every word she said.

These pictures, images, dreams, began to frighten me a little, not because they were unpleasant, but because they felt comfortable. They worried me with their cosiness. I wondered whether they were some kind of replacement for the memories that I was attempting to unload: the result of a compensatory mental illness. Perhaps I was trying to fill emotional gaps with strange fantasies of a Chinese woman.

I began to look for her in the street.

There were other, more disconcerting thoughts, which meant very little to me. Scenes, cameos, flashes of familiar happenings that meant nothing to me emotionally. I pictured myself going into stores and shops I did not recognise, for articles I had never even considered buying. There was an ambivalence to my feelings during these scenes. I saw myself buying an antique porcelain bowl, the design of which I instinctively and intensely disliked. Yet I purchased it with loving care and a knowledge of ceramics I had not previously been aware of possessing. In another scene, I went into a bakery and bought some Chinese moon cakes, a highly-sweetened, dense foodstuff which most gweilos avoid, and I was no exception.

I was sure I was going quite mad.

John Chang kept me busy, hating him. He did not let up on me for one moment during the sweltering summer months, when the wealthy fled to cooler climes and school teachers blessed the long vacations they got during the season when Hell relocated to the Hong Kong streets.

During this humid period the Chinese lady with the loving eyes continued to haunt me. I would languish at my desk after work, reluctant to leave the air conditioned building, picturing myself making love with this woman in a bed with satin sheets, surrounded by unfamiliar furniture. It seemed right. Everything about it seemed right, except when I questioned it with some other part of my mind, the part firmly based in the logic that said, you do not know this woman. It was true. I had never met anyone like her, yet she looked at me as if I were hers, and some unquestioning area of my mind, less concerned with what I knew, and content to be satisfied with what I felt, told me yes, this had happened, this was a proper interpretation of my experiences.

I began to read about schizophrenia, wondering whether I was one of those people who have more than one personality, but the books that I read did not seem to match what was happening to me. I baulked when it came to seeing a therapist. I was afraid there was something quite seriously wrong with me.

In October, some people organised a junk trip to Lamma Island, the waterfront of which is lined with excellent fish restaurants. Sally asked me if I was going and I said I might as well. Most of the newspaper's employees would be there, and a few of the employers as well. The weather had turned pleasantly hot, had left the dehumanizing summer humidity behind in September. It promised to be a good evening.

There were rumours that John Chang would be going, but that did not deter me. I wondered if I could get drunk enough to tell him what I thought of him.

I was one of the last to jump aboard the junk, which then pulled out into the busy harbour. I stared at the millions of lights off to port: Causeway Bay, Wan Chai and Central, resplendent during the dark hours. A beer was thrust into my hand. I drank it from the can and looked around me. Sally was there. She waved. Peter Smith stood in animated conversation with another of our colleagues, his legs astride to combat the rolling motion of the craft in the choppy harbour waters. Then I noticed John Chang, sour-faced, standing by the rail.

Beside him was a lady I had never seen before, not in the flesh, but a woman with whom I had made love, in my head, a thousand times. My heart began to race and I felt myself going hot and cold, alternately, wondering whether I should try to hide somewhere until the evening was over. If she sees me, I thought, she's bound to recognise me as the one . . .

Then I pulled myself up short. One what? What had I done to her? Nothing. Not a blessed thing. So where did these pictures come from, that had invaded my head? The best way to find out was to talk to her. I tried to catch her eyes, hoping she would come over to me without bringing John Chang.

Eventually I captured her attention and she looked startled. Did she know me after all? Was I indeed living some kind of Jekyll and Hyde existence? It was only after a few minutes that I understood she was not staring into my face at all: it was my red hair that had her attention. Then she realised she was being rude and averted her gaze, but Chang had caught us looking at each other and motioned for her to cross the deck

with him. Before I could turn away, he was standing in front
of me, gesturing towards the woman at his side.

'I don't believe you've met my wife, have you Fraser?'

She spoke in gentle tones, admonishing him.

'John, Mr Fraser must have a first name?'

He looked a little disconcerted.

'Yes, of course,' he said stiffly. 'Sean. Sean Fraser. Scottish
I think.'

'My ancestors were,' I blurted, 'but we've lived south of the
border for two generations. The red hair, you know, is proof of
my Celtic origins. I'm still a Scot, in spirit.'

I shook her hand, acutely embarrassed by the fact that I
knew what she looked like naked, lying on the bed, waiting
for me to press myself against her. John Chang's wife. There
were two small brown moles under her left breast. There were
stretch marks around her abdomen.

I felt the silkiness of her palm, knowing that soft touch.
I remembered the time she had whispered urgent nonsense
into my ear, the first time our orgasms had coincided exactly,
a miracle of biology which had left us breathless for several
minutes afterwards, when we had both laughed with the utter
joy of the occasion.

Staring into her eyes, I knew that if there was a memory of
such happenings, they did not include me. What I saw there
was a terrible sadness, held in check by a great strength. Alice
Chang was one of those splendid people who find a natural
balance within themselves. When a negative aspect of life
causes them to lose equilibrium, a positive one rises from
within their spirit, to meet it, cancel it out.

'I'm very pleased to meet you, Alice,' I said.

'Oh, you know my name.' She laughed. 'I thought John
tried to keep me a secret. Do you know this is the first time he
has allowed me to meet his colleagues?'

I looked quickly at John Chang, and then said, 'I'm afraid

I've heard him speaking to you on the phone. The office has good acoustics. I don't eavesdrop intentionally.'

'I'm sure you don't,' she said, and then he steered her away, towards one of the directors, leaving me sweating, holding onto the rail for support. Not because of the rocking motion of the boat, but because my legs felt weak.

The following weekend I took a boat trip to Lantau Island and sat at a beach restaurant, staring at the sea and sand. I needed a peaceful place to think. Hong Kong's national anthem, the music of road drills, pile drivers, traffic, buzz saws, metal grinders et al was not conducive to reflective thought.

There were evergreens along the shoreline of Silvermine Bay, decorated with hundreds of tattered kites. The children used the beach to fly their toys, which eventually got caught in the branches of the large conifers, and remained there. The brightly-coloured paper diamonds gave the firs the appearance of Christmas trees. Around the trunks of the kite-snatchers were dozens of bicycles, chained to each other for security, left there by adolescents now sprawled on the sands.

I had managed to engineer one more chat with Alice Chang, before the end of that evening on Lamma, and spoke about the antique porcelain bowl, describing it. I had to lie to her, telling her that John had spoken to me about it, seemed proud to be its owner.

'Oh, yes. He loves ceramics you know. It's his one expensive hobby.'

I knew now I was experiencing John Chang's memories.

It was nothing to do with me. I had not made love to Alice Chang, but I carried John Chang's memories of such occasions, those that he wished to recall, and some he did not. It was a disturbing ordeal. There was a grim recollection of being hit a glancing blow by a truck, when he was small, and another when he was falsely accused of stealing from his school friends. I was gradually getting 'to know' my Chinese boss and there were some dark areas in there which terrified me. I woke up at night, sweating, wondering where the fear was coming from, what was causing the desire to scream.

The night after the junk trip, I had spoken to Sally.

'How many kids has John Chang got?' I asked her casually.

She shook her head.

'None, so far as I know. Why do you ask?'

'Oh, no reason. I met his wife, last night. I thought she mentioned something about a child, but I couldn't be sure. I suppose I must have been mistaken.'

Sally said, 'I'm positive you are.'

I drank steadily, as I tried to puzzle through my jumbled memories of his early marriage, and my eyes kept being drawn towards the bicycles, chained to the tree trunks. I struggled with a black beast of a memory, which was utterly reluctant to emerge from a hole it had dug itself.

A bicycle.

This was the key, but something prevented me from opening the lock. There was the idea that a bicycle was a detested thing, a deadly, ugly machine that should be outlawed, banned from use. People who sell bicycles should be prosecuted, imprisoned, hung by the neck . . .

That was very strong, very strong.

One of the kids from the beach came and unlocked her bike, climbed into the saddle, and rode away along the path. I experienced a forceful desire to scream at her, tell her to get off, return the machine to the salesman.

Where?

A shop sign popped into my head, which read: THE FLYING BALL CYCLE CO.

Then that dark cloud extended itself from the back of my brain, blacking out anything that might have followed.

* * *

Back at the flat I received a surprise telephone call from England. From Nickie. She asked me how I was. Did I like the Far East? Yes, she was fine. She was seeing one or two people (she didn't call them men) and things were absolutely fine.

Her voice was recognisably thin and tight, even over the phone. There was great anger there, pressing against her desire to sound casual. I noticed that it was 3 o'clock in the morning, her time, and I guessed she had been unable to sleep, obsessed with relentlessly reviewing the bitter times, furious with herself for failing to retaliate strongly, when something hurtful had been said, wishing she could raise the subject again, but this time be the one to wield the knife, cut the deepest.

I knew how she felt, having gone through the same cycle, many nights. We had both fired words, intended to wound, but we both remembered only being hit.

I told her I was having some trouble with one of my bosses. She sympathised coldly, but what she had really called about was the fact that I still had two of her favourite poetry books. She would like them back again, please, the Hughes and the Rilke.

Oh, those, yes, but three o'clock in the morning?—she really must want them badly, I said. I told her I remembered seeing them, just before leaving England for Hong Kong, but could not put my hand on them at this time. Could she call again later, when I had done some more unpacking?

No, she couldn't. I had been in Hong Kong for nearly a year. Hadn't I unpacked my things yet?

Her words became more shrill as the anger seeped through like a gas, altering the pitch of her voice.

When I did manage to unpack, could I please post them back to her? Yes, she was aware they were only paperbacks and could be replaced, but she didn't see why she should buy new copies when she already owned some—goodbye.

The emptiness that filled the room, after she had put down the phone, would have held galaxies.

I tried not to hate her, but I couldn't help it. She was there, I was here. Thousands of miles apart.

I picked up the Rilke, from the bedside table, open at Orpheus. Eurydice. Hermes. It was pencil marked in the margins, with her comments on the text. It was her handwriting I had been reading, not Rilke's poem. The flourishes were part of her, of the woman I had loved, and I had been sentimentalising, as well as studying them for some small insight into her soul. I wanted to understand her, the secret of her self, in order to discover why. Why had it gone wrong?

The terrible ache in me could not be filled by love, so I filled it with hate instead. I wanted to kill her, for leaving me, for causing me so much emotional agony. I wanted to love her. I wanted her to love me. I hated her.

On Monday afternoon, I cornered Peter Smith. I recalled that he used to cover cycling stories for the paper. At one time his speech had been full of jargon—accushift drivetrains, Dia-Compe XCU brakes, oversized headsets, Shimano derailleurs. The language of the initiated, for the enthusiasts.

'You're a bike fanatic,' I said. 'You cycle in New Territories, don't you?'

'Not so much now,' he patted a growing paunch, 'but I used to. Why, you looking for a sport to keep you fit?'

'No, I came across this guy who kept raving about the Flying Ball Bike Shop. Know it?'

Smith laughed.

'My boy, that shop is a legend amongst cyclists. You can write to the owner of the Flying Ball from any corner of the earth, and he'll airmail the part you need and tell you to pay him when you eventually pass through Hong Kong.'

'Why Flying Ball? Is that some kind of cog or wheel bearing invented specifically for push bikes?'

Smith shook his head.

'I asked the owner once. He told me the shop had been named by his grandfather, and he forgot to ask the old man what it meant. The secret's gone with grandpa's polished bones to a hillside grave overlooking water. Part of the legend now.'

'Where is it? The shop, I mean.'

'Tung Choi Street, in the heart of Mong Kok,' he said, 'now buzz off, I've got a column to write.'

I went back to my desk. A few moments later I experienced a sharp memory pang and looked up to see the office girl placing a polystyrene cup of steaming brown liquid on my desk top. She smiled and nodded, moving on to Sally's desk. I could smell her perfume. It was the same one she had been wearing the day John Chang had bawled at her.

It was twilight when I reached Tung Choi Street. Mong Kok is in the Guinness Book of Records as the most densely populated area on the face of the earth. It is teeming with life, overspilling, like an ants' nest in a time of danger. It is run down, sleazy, but energetic, effervescent. Decaying tenements with weed-ridden walls overhang garage sized factory-shops where men in dirty vests hammer out metal parts for everything and anything: stove pipes, watering cans, kitchen utensils, car exhausts, rat cages, butter pats, fish tanks, containers, and so on. What you can't buy ready-made to fit, you can have knocked up within minutes.

Over the course of the day the factory-shops vomit their wares slowly, out, across the greasy pavement, into the road. The vendors of fruit and iced drinks fill in the spaces between. Through this jungle of metal, wood and plastic plough the taxis and trucks, while the pedestrians manage as best they can, to hop over, climb, circumnavigate. Business is conducted to a cacophony caused by hammers, drills, saws, car horns. It can have a rhythm if you have a broad musical tolerance and allow it flexibility.

THE FLYING BALL CYCLE CO.

I found the shop after two minutes walking.

I stood on the opposite side of the road, the two-way flow of life between me and this unimposing little bike shop, and I remembered. It hit me with a force that almost had me reeling backwards, into the arms of the shopkeeper amongst whose goods I was standing. The dark area lifted from my brain and the tragedy was like an awful light, shining through to my consciousness. The emotional pain revealed by this bright-ness, so long covered and now unveiled, was appalling.

And this was not my agony, but his.

I turned and stumbled away from the scene, making for the nearest telephone. When I found one I dialled John Chang's home number. It had all come together the moment I laid eyes on the Flying Ball: the hate John Chang bore towards me; the unexplained stretch marks on Alice Chang's abdomen; the blankness in his eyes, the sadness in hers.

'Mrs Chang? This is Sean Fraser. We met on the junk—yes, the other night. I wonder if you could ask John to meet me, in the coffee shop by Star Ferry? Yes, that's the one. Can you say it's very important? It's about your son, Michael . . . Yes, I know, I know, but I have to talk to him just the same. Thanks.'

I put down the receiver and hailed a taxi.

I was on my second cup of coffee when he arrived. He looked ashen and for once his facade of grim self-assur-ance was missing. I ordered him a cup of coffee and when it arrived, put some brandy in it from a half-bottle I had bought on the way. He stared at the drink, his lean face grey, his lips colourless.

'What's all this about?' he said. The words were delivered belligerently, but there was an underlying anxiousness to the tone. 'Why did you ask me to come here, Fraser?'

He hadn't touched his coffee, and I pushed it towards him.

'I know about Michael,' I said.

His eyes registered some pain.

'I know how he died.'

'What business is it of yours?' he said in a low voice. 'How dare you? You're interfering in my family affairs. You leave my family alone.'

'I'm not interested in your family. I'm interested in the way you treat me. Since I've been in Hong Kong you've made my life hell. I didn't bring your family into the office, you did. You're punishing me for something you won't even allow yourself to think about. You've blocked it out and the guilt you feel is causing you to hurt other people, especially red-headed gweilos.

'I've been the target for your suppressed anger, your bottled grief, for as long as I can stand. It's got to stop, John. I'm not responsible for Michael's death, and you know it, really. I just happen to be a European with red hair. I wasn't even in Hong Kong when that driver took your son's life . . . '

'Shut up!' he shouted, causing heads to turn and look, then turn back again quickly. His face was blotched now, with fury, and he was gripping the cup of coffee as if he intended to hurl it into my face.

'This is what happened, John,' I said quietly, ignoring his outburst. 'It was Christmas, and being a Christian, you celebrated the birth of Christ in the way that gweilo Christians do. You bought presents for your wife and twelve-year-old son. You gave your wife some perfume, a brand you won't allow her to use now because it reminds you of that terrible time, and you asked your son what he would like most in the world . . . '

There were tears coming down John Chang's face now, and he stumbled to his feet and went through the door. I left ten dollars on the table and followed him. He was standing against the harbour wall, looking down into the water, still crying. I moved up, next to him.

'He said he wanted a bicycle, didn't he, John? One of those new mountain bikes, with eighteen, twenty gears. You took Michael down to Mong Kok, to the Flying Ball Bike Shop, and you bought him what he wanted because you were a loving father, and you wanted to please him. He then begged to be allowed to ride it home, but you were concerned, you said no, repeatedly, until he burst into tears—and finally, you relented.

'You said he could ride it home, if he was very, very careful, and you followed behind him in the car.'

I paused for a moment and put my arm around his shoulders.

'The car that overtook you, halfway home, was driven by a red-headed foreigner, a gweilo, and he hit Michael as he swerved in front of you to avoid an oncoming truck. The bike itself was run over. It crumpled, like paper, and lay obscenely twisted beside your son's body. You stopped, but the other driver didn't. He sped away while you cradled Michael's limp body in your arms, screaming for an ambulance, a doctor.

'They never caught the hit-and-run driver, and you've never forgiven yourself. You still want him, don't you, that murdering red-headed gweilo, the man that killed your son? You want to punish him, desperately, and maybe some of that terrible guilt you feel might go away.'

He turned his tear-streaked face towards me, looked into my eyes, seeking a comfort I couldn't really give him.

I said gently, 'That wasn't me, John. You know it wasn't me.'

'I know,' he said. 'I know, I know. I'm so sorry.'

He fell forward, into my arms, and we hugged each other, for a brief while. Then we became embarrassed simultaneously, and let go. He went back to leaning on the wall, but though the pain was still evident, his sobbing had ceased.

Finally he turned asked the obvious question: how did I know so much detail, about Michael's death? It had happened many years ago.

Rather than go into the business with the pipe, I told him I had been to Wong Tai Sin, to a clairvoyant, and the man had looked into John's past for me.

'It cost me a lot of money,' I said, to make it sound more authentic. If there's one thing that Hongkongers believe in, it's the authority money has to make the impossible possible. John Chang did not laugh at this explanation or call me a liar. A little brush with the West does not wipe out five thousand years of Chinese belief in the supernatural.

Then he went home, to his wife, leaving me to stare at the waters of the fragrant harbour and think about my own feelings of love and hate. Understand the man you hate. How can you hate a man you understand? I began to realise what the old man with his magic pipe was selling. Not power over one's enemy. Love. That's what he had for sale. His was a place where you could look at hate, understand it enough to be able to turn it into love.

I knew something else. Now that I had confronted John, now that we understood one another, the memories of his past would cease to bother me. The pipe had done its work.

The following week, one evening when a rain as fine as Irish drizzle had come and gone, leaving a fresh scent to the air, I took a taxi to Wong Tai Sin Temple. The old man was still there, sitting at the entrance to the alley, his pipe by his side.

I went up to him and gave him twenty dollars, and he smiled and silently handed me the pipe and a piece of red-and-gold paper decorated with Chinese characters.

On the back of the paper I wrote the name of a person I loved and hated—NICHOLA BLACKWOOD—and tore it into tiny pieces hoping that distance was no barrier to magic.

THE DRAGON SLAYER

Only a handful of years ago, in the British Crown Colony of Hong Kong, people still believed in dragons. Indeed, the name of the district called 'Kowloon' means 'Nine Dragons' and was taken from the range of hills which separates this part of the peninsula from the New Territories in the north. Of course, European gweilos scoffed at such beliefs, since they had known for many centuries that dragons were mythical creatures which had existed only in the minds of men. Foremost amongst those who looked with contempt upon such archaic convictions were the officers of the Hong Kong police force. One of the younger officers was in charge of the top section of Kowloon, just under a hill known as Lion Rock.

The young man's name was John Witherstone and he was a keen, ambitious policeman. He was blond, tanned and had a fine set of white teeth that set off his smile very well. His superiors thought he would go far and this made him slightly arrogant towards his subordinates and colleagues. Though he was not universally liked, and knew this, he was not terribly concerned. He expected to make a few enemies on his climb up the career ladder and as long as he was popular in the right quarter he was not too worried. Once he had more power, it would not matter if he was highly regarded amongst the other gweilos or not.

Gweilo is the term given to people of European origin by the Chinese. It means ' ghost people'. When the British first heard of this nickname they had been given, far from being insulted, they were amused and began using it to describe themselves. There was even a football team called The Gweilos from Hong Kong Island. John Witherstone did not like being called a gweilo, but then he had very little sense of humour. His colleagues called him 'stoneface', though not in his hearing, because he had a fierce temper.

One day, up in the hills of the New Territories, a tribe of farmers known as the Hakka People came across a dragon sleeping in one of their orchards. They immediately got together and asked each other what was to be done.

'If we wake the dragon, he might burn down our orchard,' said one farmer. 'And possibly eat a few people afterwards,'said another. 'On the other hand,' said a third, 'we can't leave him where he is because we have to harvest the fruit very soon.'

They decided to try to wake the dragon, but in order to placate it they placed gifts all around its sleeping form. There were baskets of oranges wrapped in gold paper and pears wrapped in silver. There were red and gold paper banners, these being the lucky colours, planted in the earth. Colourful kites adorned the trees and wind chimes made from seashells hung from the branches, tinkling musically in the breezes. Red lanterns with gold fringes had lighted candles glowing from their hearts, the smell of incense perfumed the air. Beautiful pyramids of painted eggs were placed at the four corners of the orchard.

When all was ready the villagers created a great cacophony of sound, clashing huge brass cymbals together and beating giant kettle drums with wooden spoons. Primitive instruments like one-stringed violins wailed around the hillside, gongs sounded and bull-roarers bellowed. Ancient bronze trumpets, not used for a thousand years, blared their dirty-sounding notes. Bamboo wind-instruments moaned and groaned, and hollow gourds sent mooning notes into the rocks and around the terraces.

The Hakka People played their instruments on tip-toe, ready at a moment's notice to run like the wind once the dragon woke. The dragon hardly stirred. The players stopped after three hours, exhausted, with chapped lips, numb fingers and ears that rang with bells like those in high mountain temples.

One very old lady, whose face was a map of wrinkles hidden by the black fringe that Hakka People wear around the brims of their hats, had this solution to offer.

'We need a demon to drive out this dragon from our orchard. What we need is a gweilo with great authority, who will come here and tell the dragon to leave.'

This advice was accepted with much nodding of heads and murmuring of tongues. A group of three farmers was despatched to Kowloon to request the assistance of the most important gweilo in the area, the police officer John Witherstone. Reluctant to miss the chance of having a procession, the rest of the village marched behind their spokesmen, waving bold flags and singing brave songs.

August in Hong Kong is the worst month for humidity and heat. John Witherstone was sitting in his office in his starched khaki uniform sweltering under a slowly moving ceiling fan. He was dreaming of icebergs and snowy wastes and thinking of the long cool drink awaiting him at his club after duty finished. While he was immersed in such thoughts, one of his Cantonese policemen, Peter Li, knocked on his open door.

'Step inside,' said Witherstone curtly.

'Sir,' said Constable Li, 'there is a group of Hakka farmers to see you, from the New Territories. They seem very upset.'

'Can't the desk sergeant deal with it?' said Witherstone, not bothering to keep the impatience out of his voice.

'Sir, they make a special request to see you. They say they must talk to an important man.'

John Witherstone felt mildly flattered.

'Oh, very well, show them in, and stay to interpret for me, constable.'

'Yes, sir.'

Hats in hands, the trio of farmers was ushered into the small office and stood smiling nervously before the great man. One of them had been elected to speak and he explained their problem and requested the assistance of the mighty officer in driving away the dragon from the orchard. John Witherstone listened in silence as his constable translated this message into English. Finally, he rapped his stick on the desk top.

'Isn't this just a little ridiculous, constable?' he asked of Peter Li.

'Sir?'

'This dragon business. I mean, surely these people don't still believe in mythical beasts in this day and age. Good God, this is the twentieth century, not the Middle Ages.

Peter Li smiled and said, 'These are simple people, sir. Their beliefs are still strong in these matters. Of course, your constables do not believe in such things—we are civilized men of the world—but these farmers . . . some of them have never been more than ten miles from their village. The world passes them by without leaving them a good education.'

'Hmmmmm.' John Witherstone regarded his desk top and then the shy faces of the farmers. 'And sending a sergeant and a couple of men to investigate this dragon will not satisfy them?'

'No, no, sir. Certainly not,'said Peter Li hastily. 'It must be someone of great importance.'

John Witherstone weighed up the advantages and the disadvantages of proceeding with the request. On the one hand it would be hot and dusty up in the New Territories, but there was countryside there, hills and valleys and stretches of water. Such scenery would make a change from the streets of Kowloon. Then he had to decide whether his superiors would consider him a fool for following up such a request. It would not do to lower his stature in the eyes of those responsible for promoting him.

He picked up his phone.

'Wait outside,' he waved his hand at the Chinese. 'I'll give you my decision in a moment.'

Peter Li led them out.

A call to his immediate boss gave John Witherstone all the justification he needed to make the trip up into the New Territories.

'Find out what it's all about, John, will you? I mean, what seems like damn tomfoolery to us is taken seriously by the Hakka. We don't want to upset them and it's good for our image, to be seen to be taking a firm interest in the local culture. You'll probably find a dead monkey up there or something. Make the most of the situation. We need to be seen to be doing 'good works' on occasion.'

'Yes, sir.'

Witherstone put down the receiver and shouted to Peter Li, who stood in the doorway once again.

'I'm going up to investigate,' he told the constable. 'You and another man come with me.'

'Me, sir?' said Peter, turning a little pale.

'Yes, you sir. Come on man, get your skates on, we haven't got all day. Order me a Land Rover from the car pool.'

So up into the New Territories they went: two unhappy policemen, three relieved farmers and one grim gweilo.

When they arrived, the police were led up to the bottom terraces of the orchard. The villagers said that they were convinced that the dragon was Jek Lai, one of the smaller but ferocious brothers of the great Jek Mai. John Witherstone said he would see, once he and his constables got to the top of the terraces, where the dragon was sleeping.

With the two Cantonese policemen clutching their rifles, John Witherstone led the way up through the orchard. There, at the top, he came across a remarkable sight. There was a reptile of some kind, stretched between two fruit trees. It had a long body covered in scales, but its head was a monstrous size. There were two horns protruding from its brow and its skin was covered in colourful patterns which John Witherstone recognised after a few moments. Its eyes were wide and staring. The creature had obviously just woken up and it began to move.

One of the policemen gave out a startled cry and immediately retreated back down the hill, despite an order to remain. The other, Peter Li, stood his ground, but his legs were shaking and once he had looked on the form of the dragon, he refused to do so again, averting his eyes.

Contemptuously, John Witherstone took the rifle from the hands of his constable, levelled it at the beast, and shot it between the eyes. It writhed on the ground for several minutes before finally succumbing to the inevitability of death. Peter Li was then ordered to collect brushwood and build a pyre, on which John Witherstone burned the body of the dragon. When the villagers came up, the charred remains of Jek Lai were there for them to see and they were both shocked and horrified.

Peter Li translated their fears to John Witherstone.

'While they are pleased that you have destroyed the dragon, they fear for you, sir. You were not expected to kill the creature—merely drive it away. Now you will be hunted down by other dragons. They are calling you the 'dragon slayer' and are admiring of your great prowess as a powerful mortal. Your name will be made famous, and stand amongst the names of heroes who have slain dragons in the past. . .'

John Withers tone waved his hand. 'It was nothing,' he said.

Privately, once he got back to his desk, he telephoned his boss once again.

'It was only a snake, a big python that had half-swallowed a young cow,' he told his superior. 'The cow's horns were sticking through the skin, giving it a kind of ugly, distorted appearance. I must admit I was a bit startled until I'd had a better look. One of my policemen did a bunk straight away. Can't say I blame the beggar, though I'll have to put him on report.'

'Your fame has preceded you,' said his boss. They're already calling you the 'dragon slayer' on the island. One of my boys has just been in to tell me how the great white hunter slew the beast.' His boss laughed. 'You're a local folk hero. This won't do you any harm, John. I shouldn't be surprised if you don't make a little on the side out of this.'

True enough, the next morning the gifts began to arrive from all corners of Hong Kong. Officially, officers in the colony's police force are not permitted to receive gifts, which might be regarded as bribes, but Witherstone declined to send them back. After all, some of them were very valuable items—gold watches and jade jewellery—and there was no harm in becoming rich on the way up the ladder to success.

It was almost six months later when another group of Chinese came down from the New Territories to ask for the assistance of the Dragon Slayer once again. One of the villagers had been eaten and the dragon had disappeared into a large cave in the side of a mountain. The people were fearful that the dragon would reappear and wanted John Wither-stone to match his legendary skills against the beast. Since his earlier success, John Witherstone had been bragging about his prowess with the gun.

'I slew the dragon Jek Lai,' he continually told new recruits, and they pursed their lips because they knew the four winds will always carry a boast to the ears of one's foes.

With his tongue in his cheek, the gweilo set forth again, this time without his two policemen. He was shown the cave entrance and then the local people retreated to what they regarded as a safe distance, at the foot of the mountain. There was the sound of distant thunder in the air and the gweilo looked up in search of dark cloud, but the sky was clear. He was glad, because he did not want to be trapped inside the cave if it rained hard and swelled any underground streams which crossed his path.

John Witherstone had taken the precaution of bringing with him a torch. He also had his revolver, which he considered adequate for the task. No doubt there was some kind of creature in the cave which would require shooting, and he could think of nothing dangerous enough in the area that could not be disposed of with a hand gun. The tigers had long since gone. It was probably another snake, or some mangy cur that was half mad. The thing to be wary of was a hound with rabies, but he was a good shot with a pistol so he need only be careful of being taken by surprise.

He entered the cave expecting it to be quite shallow, like most of those in the district. However, it became obvious that it went beyond the normal length as his torchlight probed the darkness and found no rear. After a while he came to a fork and decided to begin laying a trail, so that he did not get lost. Like the Ancient Greek hero Theseus, who had to find his way out of the labyrinth which held the Minotaur, John Witherstone used a ball of thread. He tied one end to a rock and unravelled it as he went through the left-hand tunnel. There was a faint smell of sulphur in the atmosphere of the cave, but this did not worry him at all.

Instead of narrowing, the tunnel began to get wider and John Witherstone could hear running water in the distance. He had already had to negotiate one or two pits in his path, had climbed a rock chimney and was on his way through a passageway full of stalagmites and stalactites. He was beginning to consider turning around, since it seemed doubtful now that he was going to catch up with the animal that had gone into the cave, wherever it was. All he need tell the farmers when he got out, was that he had slain the dragon and they had no more need to worry. Of course, if the creature went out again and hurt someone else, his credibility would suffer enormously and his reputation would not be worth a hoot. So he had wanted to be sure that the animal was not going to reappear.

Just as he was considering following his line of thread back to the entrance, he felt a warm breeze on his cheek. There had to be an exit ahead, for the air to be getting into the tunnel. He had already seen one or two living creatures, snakes and bats, which indicated that the outside world was not too far away.

Sure enough, as he turned the next corner, he found himself in a huge cavern with a high ceiling. It was dimly lit by cracks of sunlight. When he had climbed the rock chimney he must have been going upwards, alongside the wall of the mountain. There were fissures in the rock face, which let the daylight in. Water trickled through the limestone on the far side of the cavern.

Suddenly, there was a movement somewhere in the cavern, and the chamber echoed eerily with the sound of stones dropping from a ledge. John Witherstone flicked his torch backwards and forwards over the floor, rapidly, in an effort to find what had caused the noise. The torchlight revealed many distorted and frightening shapes, but these were the result of water erosion and the build-up of calcium deposits on the limestone. There were cathedral-like flutings rising from the bedrock and sinister columns with hollow faces. From the distant ceiling hung giant stalactites that looked at any moment as if they would fall and bury their points in the ground beneath.

'Nothing here,' murmured John Witherstone, to reassure himself. 'Must have been the water or something.'

Then, as his sight became used to the natural light, he saw a huge form on a ledge on the far side of the cavern. He strained his vision to define its shape. It seemed narrow at both ends (one end more than the other) and wide of girth in the middle. Once he had some points of reference, he calculated its length at around a hundred metres. Two large red-rimmed eyes regarded him balefully from above a set of hissing nostrils. In the dimness he could see what looked like the wings of a giant bat, situated about two-thirds of the way along the body, towards the head. The wings fluttered as he stared, giving out a leathery rustle. On the end of the one muscled, scaly leg he could see, was a terrible three-toed foot with claws like the blades of ancient scythes. A row of triangular spikes ran from the creature's terrible head to the tip of its tail, which ended in a thorn-shaped point not unlike that of a scorpion's sting, except that it was the size of a man's arm.

'What . . . ?' cried John Witherstone, but the rest of his sentence was swallowed up by a thunderous roar. The great jaws opened to reveal a thousand daggers, and the beast spoke.

Its language was as old as the dust in the heart of the cave and not understood by the gweilo police officer, but there were those further down the mountain who heard it, and knew what it meant. They understood that terrible retribution had at last caught up with the slayer of dragons, and if they had been asked for a translation of the sounds that came through the fissures in the rock and rolled down the mountain scree, they would have said, without hesitation that these were the words they heard:

'The wind tells me that you slew my brother Jek Lai.'

THE CAVE PAINTING

We had hoped to reach the cave by noon.

The long drive across the Gibson Desert had made us testy and irritable. Somewhere along the gravel road chips of stone had shattered the windscreen of the Honda turning it into glass hail which the wind blew into the car. Janet was cut a little around the cheeks and Mace, who had been driving, had specks of blood like a rash of measles over his whole face. I was in the back seat and consequently escaped unhurt.

Once the screen had gone the car filled with choking red dust and the air conditioner ceased to function with any degree of efficiency. We soon got the full force of the Australian desert sun, somewhere in the region of fifty, and began to bake inside our cake tin on wheels. The lung-grabbing blast of air coming through the hole was hot and full of grit. By the time we saw the rock, Mace had gone into the sulks, and Janet stated she was ready to strangle anyone who tried to treat our situation with flippancy. This remark had followed an attempt by me to treat the episode lightly.

'I hate people trying to cheer me up,' she grumbled.

'I'm British,' I said, my tone almost apologetic, 'we always make jokes when the chips are down.'

She gave me another blood-and-dust glare, I suppose wondering whether my mention of the word 'chips' was alluding to the gravel that had been the cause of our present condition. Her left arm was draped along the back of Mace's seat, her fingers lightly touching his shoulder. Long black hair tumbling down to her dirty white blouse and obscured most of her face as she turned to face front again and presumably stare into the billowing red dust, rolling ahead of us like the bow wave from a marine landing craft.

I studied Mace in the rear view mirror. There was no indication from his expression that he was aware of the touch of those slim fingers. I wished they were on my shoulder, not his. When Janet and I had begun our ten month tour of Australia, we had been lovers as well as good friends. Things happen on the road though, and now we were, as they say, just good friends.

It would be more accurate to say I was 'just good friend'. For my part, I still had much stronger feelings. I still wanted her, emotionally and physically, as a lover again. God, my guts ached for the touch of those fingers. She had become supremely beautiful, wondrously fascinating since we had parted. What was once taken for granted was now unattainable and the fact that I had once had it all—love, intimate companionship, sex—made the craving that much worse. I wanted it back. I still loved her, but I didn't dare let her know it. She would have sent me away. So I maintained this minor war with her, taking ground, giving ground, remaining interested and, hopefully, interesting.

Mace was a second generation Japanese-Australian we met on our travels. We stopped for him because he had a backpack and was obviously travelling on the cheap. Leaning in through Janet's window he told us he'd just passed his medical exams and was celebrating by going on walkabout. I didn't like the way he was looking into Janet's eyes, or the way she was returning that look, so I replied that if he was on walkabout he wouldn't need a lift in our car.

'It's just an expression,' he told me, with a pained look. 'It just means I've got no set destination, not that I've got to do the whole thing on foot.'

'Don't mind him.' Janet said, dismissing me with a flick of her head, 'he's a pom.'

Janet is English too, but since we'd stopped sleeping together she was about as approachable as a Martian. We were still going through what she called our 'period of adjustment', which to her meant getting rid of all those uncomfortable pieces of emotion that still surfaced during unguarded moments. As soon as she recognised one of these flimsy remnants of past love, she dealt with it ruthlessly in some way unknown to me. Her expression hardened and she suddenly became very brisk and businesslike in whatever she had been doing when the unwelcome feeling struck. How did she do it? If she had let me on the secret I would have gladly employed the same technique. Instead, found myself anticipating such moments, looking for them, and (I suppose) enjoying the hurt they brought with them. Such pain is better than a nothing at all.

This tall doctor with his Melbourne drawl very soon slipped into my place inside her sleeping bag. I couldn't believe how quickly it happened and the pain was then no longer pleasurable. Janet had once told me she had to be in love with a man to sleep with him. Yet here was the first unattached guy she had met since falling out with me, and he took over as smoothly as if he had been ordained my replacement. He had come to my tent late one evening, about a month ago.

'I want you to know I intend going to bed with Janet. She's in agreement with this. Do you have any objections?'

Mace was a gentleman. He wanted what he saw, and intended to have it, but felt the need to declare war before he bombed Pearl Harbour, so that there could be no accusations of sneak treachery later.

'If you've already got her permission,' I tried to keep the emotion out of my voice, 'what do you need mine for? I'm not in any position to object anyway.'

'You were lovers-'

'Right. Past tense. Your turn now.'

The worst of it was, I had actually grown to like Mace. From that point on I hated his guts. I was sure I hated both of them and I only stayed because . . . because . . . hell, I don't know why I stayed. Maybe I thought it wouldn't last, that Janet and I would drop back in together again, the way it had been before. There were these fantasies in my head, of her coming to my tent one night, weeping and saying it was no good, she couldn't do without me. Or looking into my face suddenly, in the campfire light, and no words being necessary, just putting our arms around each other, and Mace getting the message, walking away into the night with his pack without even saying goodbye.

Once, when Mace was off somewhere collecting wood, she turned to me and said, 'Why didn't you object?'

'Object?'

'When Mace came to you that night.'

I became a very angry then.

'I don't know how to play these games,' I said. 'I'm a prac- tical man. I like to know the rules first.'

She smiled, not unfriendly.

'Practical man? You're a dyed in the wool romantic, Jimmy, and you know it.'

And thereafter I was plagued by the thought that she had been testing the waters that night, to see if I still loved her, and I'd failed to recognise it. Should I have leapt on Mace and beaten him senseless? (Since Mace was a head taller than me, it would probably have been a very different result). Or perhaps I should have said in a very dignified tone that I objected very much, because I was still in love with her? I don't know. The skills necessary, the nuances of a three-cornered affaire, were beyond me. When it came to playing the game I was hopeless, my head spun with possibilities, none of which seemed right for me. I ended up being flat and pathetic.

Janet was right about one thing, I was a terrible romantic. There were even times when I convinced myself that although they slept in the same tent, they weren't doing anything, that Mace was still waiting for her to say yes.

So I had had a month of being the outsider, the observer. I thanked the lord that Janet was not one of those women who like canoodling in public, so I didn't have to watch them kissing and cuddling and whispering into each other's ears. The light touch on the shoulder was bad enough. Just that small show of affection was enough to turn on the flow of acid in my stomach. I suppose I still couldn't understand how she could do this thing to me: fall for the first man she saw on the road. I could go a lifetime and not find someone to replace her.

The rocky outcrop appeared to rush towards us, yet remain unreachable. It seemed we had been driving towards it forever. Overhead the sky was a hard brittle blue, without a cloud. I could see no signs of life, either in the air, or out on the desert.

There's a lot of space on the Australian continent and we'd been using it well. We'd been keeping away from towns and the radio in the car had died on us, so we had little news of the outside world. The trading posts we stopped at for goods and petrol were run by thin men with faces like burned lizards: taciturn men who could spit twenty feet, but apart from that hardly opened their mouths. I had asked the last one if the civilized world was all right.

'Who the hell cares?' he snapped.

He had been one of those crusty frontiersmen who feel the place is getting crowded when someone moves into a neighbouring valley. There were several like him and they never looked unhappy to see us go, even though we were probably the only people they saw all month.

I stared out of dustcovered side window at the passing desert. I found the apparent stillness, the facelessness of the wilderness, disconcerting. Nothing appeared to have moved since it was all part of the great Gondwanaland. In Europe we expressed fears about the way the human race was reshaping the world, but out here the landscape mocked us for being ineffectual and fleeting. It had a spiritual presence that was undeniable.

To me, the desert felt like a deity, all knowing, all powerful. I wondered if anyone had ever prayed to the desert, revered it in the way that animists worship single trees and rocks. The Aborigines? As I stared out over the wasteland, I indulged in one of those banal daydreams, where Janet and I were all that remained of the human race. A desert island, an Adam and Eve, a begin-again dream. Everyone has one of these melliferous fantasies at one time or another. They're hackneyed, it's true, but then love itself is a cliché, the emotional patterns eternally repetitive.

The desire behind this well-used vision was strong enough. I suppose I prayed, to the desert, in those few moments.

Let it happen. Let it happen.

Janet's voice brought me sharply out of my reverie.

'What's the name of the place again,' I heard her yell, trying to make herself heard over the tyre and engine noise.

'Wallabenga Cave,' Mace shouted.

The hill which housed the cave had been suggested by Mace as an alternative to visiting Ayer's Rock . . . 'Everybody goes to Ayer's Rock. Let's try for something different—whaddya say? There's some wall paintings in Wallabenga—a special one, I heard, not like the rest of them . . . '

So we had driven out into the head-flattening heat of the Gibson, to brave the kraits and spiders, under a sun whose rays could probably light paper, into dust that found every crease, every fissure of our bodies. On top of that, Mace had only three tapes for the car's cassette, all of them by MIDNIGHT OIL. I had to listen to Dust and Diesel six times a day. I used to like it.

We finally reached the rock, a sandstone crag like a natural giant cathedral, standing proud of the desert. Bas-relief formations bulged from an otherwise smooth face. There was something faintly familiar about these projections, as if they had been carved at one time into forms representing human features, or perhaps the heads of animals. The whole crag looked as if it had been chiselled from a mountain somewhere else, then tossed out into the Gibson, where its contours had been worked by itinerant craftsmen. I had to admit that it's red colour and projections made it look magnificent under the afternoon sun, like the burning palace of some desert king. It had the same feel about it as Petra, except that there was no city carved out of this conglomerate, only the merest suggestion of architecture running like wet paint down the walls of the cliff.

Mace switched off the car engine and then untied the handkerchief he had used as a dust filter. It left a whitish mark around his mouth in contrast to the rest of his engrimed face. He pulled a pack onto his right shoulder by one strap.

I said, 'Are you taking that in the cave with you?'

'Thought it would be a good idea,' he replied. 'We might want to sleep in there, just for tonight. Then we can set out in the cool tomorrow, early.'

'Good thinking,' said Janet, grabbing her own pack.

No one ever consulted me, asked me what I thought of an idea. Once the other two had accepted something from each other, I was expected to go along, like a family pet. I wanted to argue, but I didn't. Mace was right anyway, the cave would be better than a tent or the car. I was waiting, longing for him to say something stupid, so I could tear into him and let out a little pressure, but he never did.

I took my time getting my own pack, until Janet yelled, 'Jimmy, are you coming, or what?'

She had her hands on her hips, as if she were scolding a three-year-old. I stared back, noticing that she was getting a little chubby around the middle.

'You can't lay down the law with a tummy like that,' I said. 'You ought to lay off the boiled sweets.'

She glanced down at herself, but instead of the distressed expression I was expecting, she looked up again with soft eyes. That fond look startled me for a moment. Then she disappeared into the cave entrance.

I ran after the pair of them. They were waiting for me just inside. Mace had a flashlight and he switched it on.

'The guide book says we have to keep going until we come to a cavern. We can't get lost because there's only one tunnel.'

He set off and Janet and I followed behind, in single file. After long while I realised that while the book might have been right about there being no turn-offs, it hadn't mentioned the length of the cave. We seemed to be walking for decades—or stumbling might be a better description—until finally I could detect a strong odour of something burning.

'What's that smell?' I said, using the opportunity to touch Janet's shoulder .

'Oil,' replied Mace. 'There's an old Abo who lives in here.

He burns oil lamps for light. They call him the 'guardian of the painting' or something.'

'Aboriginal tribesman,' I stressed.

Janet said, 'Don't be so prim. You think he's worried what we call him? Anyway, Mace has spent three summers with

Aborigines. He's got friends amongst them, so I guess he can call them what he thinks is right.'

My own reply was cut short as we entered a world glowing with yellow light. We had reached the central cavern. The three of us stepped into a great natural hall, with fluted columns on either side, and magnificent scalloped rock curtains hanging from the ceiling. There were lamps in many of the recesses, some balanced on rounded stalagmites. Our footsteps echoed as we crossed a floor worn smooth by running water. It was strange how all around this hill was a desert, while within it there was water in plenty. In the far right-hand corner of the cavern was a pool some twenty metres in diameter. We went to this and washed ourselves, getting rid of the dust and stale sweat, before exploring further.

Mace had spoken of a side chamber, which we found after a short search, inside which sat the old man who had been given the task of caretaker by his tribe. The walls and ceiling of this offshoot cavern were amazing. Not several normal-sized paintings as I had expected, but a single work covering all the available space within the large chamber, even the floor. It was dazzling, not with colour for the usual ochres and stains had been used, but with intricate detail. A desert scene, with rocks, mountains, waterholes and strange elongated figures, neither man nor beast, who seemed to be on a slow laborious trek across the hot sand-and-stone world of the picture. The scope of the work took my breath away. Such a painting must have taken decades to complete, and by people with such an eye for perspective that when you stared into the chamber you could have been looking down on a vast landscape from a cloud. Yet each individual stone, soak or patch of sand was evident with all its tiny markings, as if you were holding it in your hand and studying it closely. One moment I got the giddy feeling of being suspended, even flying, above a ruddled countryside worked over in places with orpiment; yet the next second I was peering at a small desert bloom from just inches away, its petals seeming to close against the fierceness of the sun.

'Wow, this is really something!' I said. 'This was worth the drive.'

'You're not kidding,' cried Janet. 'Does the old man speak English, Mace?'

'Try him,' said the Australian.

The wizened round face of the dark-skinned man beamed at us. He was squatting on his haunches. There were no shoes on his feet, the skin of which looked tougher than any leather. He was wearing a red-chequered shirt, stuffed into an ancient pair of slacks.

'Speak a small bit, boss,' he said, showing us a tiny space between his thumb and forefinger, and he grinned.

Janet squatted down to his level, but stayed in the entrance, careful not to tread on the painting.

'What is this?' she indicated the picture with a wave of both arms.

'Him one world, boss,' he replied. 'This what happen outside, see? Him hare-wallabies come and put'em here, tell us what's what.'

Mace said, 'The hare-wallaby people. They're a mythological race from the Dreamtime. He's saying they did the painting.'

I interrupted.

'I've heard that the educated Aborigines object to the word Dreamtime. They say it's not accurate. It's supposed to be their Genesis, isn't it?'

'Yeah, when the world was formed by their forefathers, tribes like the carpet-snake men and hare-wallaby people—strange hybrid creatures—and the songs were made which they use as maps to find water. The animal-people were instrumental in shaping the earth, giving it form. Abo's will point out striations on rocks where they say ancient battles were fought, and lumps of stone that are dead ancestors.'

Then Mace spoke to the old man in his own tongue, and the old man replied.

'What's he saying?' asked Janet.

Mace said, 'Just what he said before, that this painting represents the world, but I was curious. The book says that the meaning of the picture changes. It's dynamic, not static. The content remains the same of course, no one alters the painting in any way, but the interpretation varies according to what's happening in the outside world.'

I asked the inevitable question.

'How does he know what's going on outside? I mean, we're in the middle of nowhere . . .'

'Middle is right,' replied Mace. 'This chamber is supposed to be the centre of the earth. Outside this room everything is mutable, subject to time and tide, decay, growth. In here things are always the same.'

'I still don't understand,' said Janet. 'How can it reflect the outside world if it doesn't change itself?'

Mace was patient with us.

'It has to be interpreted. The changes aren't evident to us, but they are to the painting's guardian. This is a sacred trust, handed down from a tribal elder to his successor. At this time only this one man can read the picture and tell us what it means.'

'But how does he know?' I insisted.

'He sees it in the picture,' remarked Mace, losing patience at last. 'What do you want me to say? I don't understand the mystique of this thing. If I did, I would be him. I only know what the book tells us.'

He spoke again to the old man, who replied with a smile.

'What?' cried Janet, obviously unhappy that she couldn't be directly privy to the meaning of the conversation. 'Tell me!'

'I just asked him how it is with the world,' laughed Mace.

'And what did he say?' said Janet.

'Fine, I suppose.'

'What do you mean, you suppose?'

Mace shrugged. 'The picture's full of calmness. Yes, I think that's the closest meaning of the words he used, 'there is a calmness over the earth'.'

Although I didn't mention it at the time, the old man might have meant 'stillness' I suppose: a stillness over the world. The state that is said to exist immediately before a holocaust or the fulfilment of an apocalypse. Expectation.

We decided we would sleep in the cave that night, so we went out and got the rest of the gear from the car. I took a look at the night sky while I was out there. It was all right. It seemed fine. Not that I knew much about the bottom of the globe. There were unrecognisable constellations embedded in the darkness: my familiarity with the heavens ended at the equator. This wasn't my sky, it belonged to the south lands. I could find the Southern Cross, but there my knowledge ended. The Polynesians used this sky like a dynamic chart, to navigate by, following star paths as they moved up individually from below the horizon and crossed the heavens. They could interpret the oceans too, the swells, the currents, even water temperatures, gaining navigational insights from them. I knew this for a fact. Western seamen, with their finely-drawn paper charts and shiny sextants, had challenged Polynesians to navigational runs from one island to another, and had lost.

So who was I to challenge this old man, who said he could read the world in a painting? We opened a can of beans and I took him some. He ate them with relish.

We slept uneasily that night, not for any reason but that it was an unusual bedroom. I could hear beetles, or lizards, or something, scuttling in amongst the stones, going down to the water to drink. The old man kept the lamps going too, so there was no sense of night or day. It induced insomnia in all of us. I played a game with Mace.

'What if you were to go to a planet,' I said, 'where every-thing was the opposite. Where night was actually day, and day was night. Exactly the opposite from what we have now. A place where black men were white, and white men were black. A negative world. Would you know it? If it was the exact opposite to this world, then it would be the same. Left-handed people using their right hands to do things, and vice versa. It would be the same.'

'No, but it would feel different, because it would be different. You'd have a kind of deja vu sensation, only not that, just a sense that something's wrong. Like when you look out of a mirror at yourself from the glass, and you think, 'I can't tell us apart, we look exactly the same, yet he's the real one, not me . . . I'm just two-dimensional quicksilver.'

'When you look out from a mirror? Boy you are one wacky . . . '

'Go to sleep you two,' interrupted Janet, 'before mamma deals a few heavy hands.'

And we did manage it then, sleeping well into the day, if it was day.

We trooped over to the old man after we'd had breakfast and asked him to interpret the picture for us. He started in by showing us where the sun was, and the mountains and seas, until Mace said, yes all that was very interesting, but what was happening out there, anything special? The old man smiled and said, nothing was happening, and Mace took this to mean nothing had changed, but there's a difference. Nothing's changed means that things are going on the way they normally do, whereas nothing's happening might mean that, but it could also be interpreted as meaning absolutely nothing is happening out there.

We knew it was midday outside, so we didn't bother leaving the cavern. It would be hot, dusty and no place for delicate skin. So we opened a pack of cards and played poker for match-sticks, then read our books, then when all was tranquil and I was deeply engrossed in my novel, Janet rolled over on her sleeping bag and said in a quiet voice that she wasn't getting fat on boiled sweets, she was having a baby.

'WHAT?' cried Mace.

I studied his expression as it went through various emotions, from horror to delight and back again, finally to settle on something between these two extremes. I couldn't see Janet's face. I just wanted to kill them both. I felt like I had a rock jammed in my windpipe.

'I'm going to be a father,' Mace cried at last.

And Janet said in the same quiet voice, 'No, I don't think so.'

Everyone was silent after that and I listened to the dust settling on the floor of the cavern and the microbes battling it out in my body, before I said, 'Me?'

She looked up and nodded.

'I missed one before we met Mace.'

'And you didn't say anything?'

'I wasn't sure, I've missed before, and anyway we weren't talking at the time. Are you angry?'

I didn't even think about it.

'No. No, not really, as long as I get to have something to do with him . . . her—whatever. What are you going to do now? I mean, about us?'

She rolled onto her back.

'I don't know. I'll have to think about it.'

Mace said acidly, 'Well do let us know when you've made up your mind, sweetheart.'

But she had already started crying by then, and we both rushed to comfort her at once and it got all confused, arms and arms, and bodies, and legs, until the three of us lay there in a knot, no one willing to let go, least of all me. All I knew was that I was being hugged and it felt good. I was going to be a father! The whole world had changed its face in a split second. One moment I'd been at the bottom of a deep pit, with no hope of ever getting out. I'd been solitary, bitter, sent out into the wilderness and close to despair. Suddenly, I was back in the garden, with people touching me, hugging me. And I was going to have a child by the woman I loved. Just like that, without me doing anything but waiting patiently. I could've waited a million years, without anything happening, but I didn't have to. One second the world was a dark lonely place, the next a place full of light and laughter. Just like that. Just like that.

We stayed wrapped around each other for quite a while, until we heard voices coming from the cave and then we untangled ourselves only just in time. A middle-aged couple came into the cavern, blinking, and staring around them with their mouths open. Mace started giggling, and Janet and I followed, until we were all snorting and snuffling, trying to stifle our laughter in case the couple thought we were making fun of them, which we weren't.

The woman, tall and slim in a floppy hat, went in to see the old man. The male half of the pair, also hatted, came over to us.

'Sky's looking kinda red out there,' he said.

'Red?' Mace repeated.

'Yeah. Sort of. Think we're in for a storm?'

Mace said, 'I don't know. The book doesn't say anything about inclement weather at this time of the year. We're tourists too. That is, I'm from Melbourne but this is my first time out here in the desert.'

'Well, the sky looks kinda funny,' said the man, glancing towards the picture chamber. 'We're pretty far out, here. I wouldn't want to get stuck in a dust storm or anything. I'm from the U.S.—Mississippi. Place called Flatten. You wouldn't have heard of it, I s'pose?'

We shook our heads.

'No. Anyway, name's Carter, like Jimmy only I'm called John. My wife's, Sarah.' He smiled and nodded in her direction. 'I'd better see what's doin'.'

I said, 'My name's Jimmy. Together we make an ex-president.'

He smiled. 'I don't think so,' he said.

As we watched him making his way over the uneven floor a ripple went through the ground. It felt like the skin of the world had just shivered. The American tottered, almost lost his balance. I found myself gripping at the wavy stone floor with my fingernails. I had a sense of falling for a moment, as if the earth were slipping away from underneath me. When I turned to look at Janet she had a frightened expression on her face.

'What was that?' she whispered.

'Felt like an earth movement,' said Mace.

'An earthquake? Here?' I said.

We all waited for a follow-up. John Carter was standing, looking at his feet, as if he expected something more too.

After a while nothing had happened and we all began to relax. Sarah Carter came out of the picture chamber. She had a short conversation with her husband, who immediately left the cavern. I went to see the old man's painting, thinking if it reflected the outside world it must give a clue to the reason for the earth movement. It didn't. The figures were in the same positions that I'd seen before. I heaved a sigh of relief, then immediately felt very silly. What had I been expecting? That the old man had modified the painting, altered it while we slept. Or that it really was a mirror image of the outside world?

I pointed to a little group of brown-skinned people.

'Walkabout?' I suggested.

The old man shook his head.

'Him run, boss. Him hide.'

I stared hard at the primitive two-dimensional beings. When I stepped a little closer, looking down on the figures, concentrated on them, I admitted to myself there was the possibility of fast movement, of haste. It was a matter of viewpoint. One of those tricks of perception, like staring at an Escher print and accepting that water can flow uphill. Or better still, a line drawing of a square figure. One moment it looks solid, but if you concentrate on a different perspective, it becomes hollow.

'Hide? What do they want to hide from?' I said at last.

'Nothin', boss. Him hide from the nothin'.'

'The nothing? Was that just the way it came out in pidgin, or did it mean that 'nothing' was a frightening non-thing? A thing that was not a thing. A 'no thing.' A negative some-thing. Hell, an athletically obsessive mind like mine can do somersaults with such thoughts.

I returned to the others, but kept the old man's words to myself. I wasn't sure what they meant anyway, and Mace might have made a meal out my unease. Sarah Carter was speaking to Janet, who now looked as if she'd forgotten the tremor and was listening and chatting with an animated expression on her face. Maybe we had just had too much of each other, the three of us, and had become too internalised? Fresh company was making all the difference, putting our feet back on the ground. We talked for a good hour after that, until every one of us was taking surreptitious glances at the tunnel, waiting for Carter to make an appearance.

John Carter never came back.

Finally, Sarah Carter said, 'I'd better go out and see what's the matter. Will you look after my things?' She gave Janet a rather heavy-looking crocodile skin handbag and a Pentax camera. 'I'll be back in a while. John's probably looking for the drink. I put it under the front seats to keep it out of the sun.'

She left the cavern.

Sarah Carter never came back.

'What's happening?' asked Janet, after a couple of hours had gone by. 'Even if he'd had a heart attack or something, she would've come back for us. And what about her things?'

I said, 'The old man thinks there's something going on out there. He said everyone was running and hiding from something.'

Janet said,'You're scaring me, Jimmy.'

Mace got up and went to the side chamber. He stayed there quite a while, talking to the old man. When he came back he looked a little shaken.

'Well?' I said.

He glanced down at Janet, who said, 'Don't mind me. I'm all right now. I want to know what he said.'

Mace squatted beside us and his words were like a line from a fairy tale. They sent a chill down my back and had my skin tingling unpleasantly, the way it had done when I was told my father had died.

The same faint buzzing in my brain, too.

'He told me that there's no world out there.'

Janet said in a choked voice.

'What do you mean, no world?'

Mace looked a little angry.

'I don't know, I'm just telling you what he said. The world's gone—at least, the world as we knew it. It's changed. It's not our world anymore.'

'Crap,' I said, and laughed. 'Come on, folks. Lighten up a little. This place is spooking us. Screw him and his picture. He probably wants us to stay here and feed him.'

It was true we had been giving the old man scraps.

Janet said a little wildly, 'I'm not going out there until I know it's safe. Those people didn't come back. This bag must be worth, I don't know, it's a Gucci for Christsakes. And the camera. I don't want to put my baby at risk . . . '

So that was it. The baby. It was probably her hormones causing the hysteria. Mace and I exchanged significant male looks. The protector surfaced in both of us.

'One of us will check first,' Mace said, soothingly. 'I know what you're thinking. That maybe they tested a bomb or something, in the Gibson. We'll have a look. I mean, if the air's not clean, we'll know.'

'The world,' she snapped. 'The whole world.'

Mace laughed.

'Look, to the Aborigines the 'whole world' is Australia. That is their world. One of us will check . . . '

'You go, Mace. I want Jimmy to stay here. I want the father of my child here.'

Mace's face darkened. His eyes narrowed and he ran a hand through his long black hair. I took his arm and led him aside.

'Look, she's just a bit overwrought. We've been in here too long. Go out and have a quick look, then come back in and get us. I think we should drive to a town straight away, find a few people and get our heads back to normal.'

He sighed. 'Yeah, you're right, Jimmy. We're cracking up in here. I won't be a minute.'

He strode towards the tunnel.

Mace never came back.

We lay in each other's arms that night, if it was night. I kept telling her that Mace had gone off in a huff, driven away, and was cooling down somewhere, feeling guilty.

'I don't think he'll abandon us, not completely. He's just punishing us for something.'

'He's punishing me,' she said.

After that we fell asleep.

When I woke I went to the old man. He grinned at me. I said, 'Those people in the picture . . . ' but he interrupted with, 'Not people, boss,' and when I went right up to a group of them, got down to their level by kneeling on the floor, I realised only then that they might not be human. You see what you want to see, just like when you revise a document full of errors, but miss the obvious ones time and time again. Your eyes send the expected messages to your brain. In fact, when I got right down to it, studied their outlines very closely, they were really quite weird, though the flat style of the painting had made them little more than dark shadows against the white landscape.

'The world changed?' I asked.

He nodded. 'All gone, boss.'

'The whole world? Or just Australia?'

'All things change, boss. Him different place now. Me and you, we're not here, not properly see?'

I shook my head.

'No, I don't see. How the hell did it change, just like that?' and I snapped my fingers.

'S'how things happen, boss. One time this, one time that.'

'Was it a bomb? A war? What then?'

He shook his head and smiled, the texture of his skin looking like a dry river bed.

'No bombs. Nothin' like that. Dreamtime come again. New world, see.'

'The world's re-formed? What the hell are you grinning at? Aren't you scared? What about the hare-wallabies, or the carpet-snake people? Are they here? Aren't you worried about it?'

'Old man, boss,' he said apologetically. 'Gonna die soon, see.'

I left him there and went back to Janet.

'What did he tell you?' she asked.

I made a sudden decision.

'He said it was okay to go outside now.'

'Are you sure?'

I forced a smile. I was thinking that there had to be a reason for all this, and the only one I could think of was that

I had prayed to the landscape, to the ancient dust and rocks, to wipe out everyone but Janet and I. And when I got it into those terras, I didn't feel guilty, I just felt stupid. It was ridiculous. I would have needed an ego a mile high to believe that anything out of my mouth could make the slightest difference to the world as a whole. Who did I think I was? No, the world was the same place we had left it. There was just something funny going on out there, that was all. Something a bit weird but with an explanation behind it. Everything has a rationale, doesn't it? Sure it does. Absolutely. The world reduced to nothing and then the landscape gardeners being sent in, creatures whose purpose it was to shape it again? How could I bring all that about with a single prayer? There must have been millions of prayers like it, gone before, to no effect. It was stupid. It was ridiculous.

There was something at the back of my brain that nagged at me a little, a cliché that began, 'The final straw . . . ', but I suppressed it under the heavy weight of logic I had accumulated in my short lifetime.

I said, 'Of course I'm sure. It's all right, really. We'll just walk out of here. I don't believe in all that crap anyway. I don't know what happened to Mr and Mrs Carter, but Mace is probably on his way back to us right at this minute, with a new windscreen as his excuse. I don't want to stay in here, Janet. Let's go outside and wait for him there?'

With that speech I convinced both her and myself that this whole unhealthy scene was the product of overactive imaginations. The old man had had us dancing to some strange tune. He was playing with us for reasons of his own, using his damn painting to put the fear of God in us. Well, I wasn't having any more of that. We were getting out of the cavern and back to sanity. I had a family to take care of.

'Let's go,' I said, but before I could pull Janet to her feet, we heard voices coming from the tunnel.

'There!' I said, triumphantly. 'It's probably the Carters.'

I walked over to the tunnel and peered down it, waiting for them to come into the light. Janet followed me, staying at my shoulder. I felt an enormous sense of relief washing through me and it was then that I realised I had believed, subconsciously, in the old man's words. He had been quietly persuasive: a powerful personality in a passive way. Well, we had been delivered from the nightmare. A nightmare that never really was. A return to the Dreamtime? It seemed so silly now, now that those voices were on their way.

I listened hard.

They didn't sound like American accents. They sounded foreign: a language I couldn't recognise.

When they turned the corner, coming into the light I could see it wasn't the Carters. It wasn't anybody. Although I had seen silhouettes like them, just a short while ago, I actually didn't know what they were.

All I know is that as soon as we saw them we knew the truth, even though we didn't want to know it, because sometimes that kind of truth can stop your heart dead in the middle of a beat, and you're out of it all for good. Then again, sometimes it doesn't. Sometimes your heart races on through, survives that initial mindnumbing shock, and leaves you still alive and aware—and that's even worse.

ISLAND WITH THE STINK OF GHOSTS

The Chinese jetty clans, who ruled the waterfronts along Penang's Georgetown harbour, fostered the myth that their hawkers had been responsible for its formation. It was said that chicken fat, glutinous rice, fishheads, hokkien noodles, prawn shells, and other waste matter, had gathered together in a stretch of still water between the currents and had formed the foundation of the floating island. Sargasso had rooted itself in the rich oils and savoury spices, on top of which gathered soil from the mainland. A rainforest had grown from its earth.

The island was about three miles off the Malaysian coast and was held precariously in place by the fronds of seaweed rooted in the ocean floor. No one, not even the ancient Wan Hooi, who ran a clan curry mee stall on the Larong Salamat, could remember the time when the island had not been there. Wan Hooi was the oldest hawker on Penang, but it was pointed out that he had only been around for a hundred years. The clans had been using the harbour as a waste bin for more than a thousand.

Whenever there was an onshore breeze, a sickly, perfumed odour wafted over from the island. This smell, according to both Malays and Chinese, was the stink of ghosts rotting—or to be more accurate, the odour of decaying souls. The body, when it decomposes, has a foul smell. Therefore, it seemed logical that a putrefying soul should have a sweet, cloying scent. The island was the burial ground for malefactors and murderers, whose punishment after death was for the corrupt soul to remain with the body, and rot within it.

These beliefs had little to do with religion, but came from a deeply rooted local superstition, such as is found in any region: a myth from earlier, darker minds, when reason and evidence were less important than fear.

Fishermen gave the island a wide berth, and only the old grave-digger, Lo Lim Hok, set foot upon the place.

Ralph Leeman, an Englishman in his late twenties, was one of those who witnessed the event on a hot, sultry June evening, when the island broke loose from its natural mooring. Not that there was any drama, for there was no sound and little fuss. The island simply detached itself from its anchoring reeds and began drifting down the Malacca Straits, which run between Indonesia and Malaysia. Possibly heavy rains in Thailand, to the north, had been responsible for a strong swell. This had resulted in a momentary change in the direction of the main current, the East Monsoon Drift, which put pressure on the island. That was Leeman's theory.

Leeman was on secondment to the Malaysian Harbour Authority from the British Coastal Service. Alone in the observation tower, he had been studying the erratic behaviour of a large motor launch when he suddenly became aware that the island was moving. He watched it for a few moments, as it passed a distant marker buoy.

'Good God! Stinker's on the move.'

He immediately made a call to his superior.

Sumi Pulau, the harbourmaster, arrived at the tower thirty minutes later, having fought his way through the Georgetown traffic. He studied the island through binoculars and expressed his amazement and concern. His English, like that of many educated Malays, was extremely good.

'Directly in the shipping lane. We'll have to do something about it immediately. It'll be dark soon. Got any suggestions?'

Leeman had already been considering the problem and gave his opinion.

'We could attach tugboats to it and tow it to the mainland, but given the nature of the island—the fact that it's a grave-yard—I'm not sure the coastal villages would want it on their doorstep.'

Pulau nodded.

'Yes, and in any case, I'm not sure tugs would do it. Might take something bigger. That's a pretty sizeable piece of land out there.'

'My second thought was that we could blow it out of the water with high explosives—but I'm worried about the jetties and the stilt-houses. An explosion might create a flood wave.'

'Not to mention the fact that we would have corpses washing up on the tourist beaches

'So,' continued Leeman, eager to impress, 'I suggest we just let it float down the Straits. We put a boat in front and behind, to warn other craft of the shipping hazard. I've been judging its speed, using the marker buoys, and by my reckoning the island should reach Singapore in thirteen days. Then it can be towed into open water and disposed of . . . '

The harbourmaster looked thoughtful.

' . . . and I have a final suggestion,' said Leeman.

'Which is?'

'That we put a caretaker on the island, to place and maintain lights, fore and aft. This man could keep in radio contact with the accompanying boats and inform them of any problems.

The sort of thing I envisage is the island running aground on a sandbank—which might solve all our worries—or breaking up in a storm. That sort of thing.'

Pulau scratched his head thoughtfully.

'I like it all except the caretaker. I'm not sure it's necessary to have someone actually on the island. It would have to be you, you know. I wouldn't get any of my men near the place. The island with the stink of ghosts—they would die of fright.'

'I realise that. Of course, I would volunteer. It would be an additional safety factor.'

The harbourmaster smiled at Leeman.

'You're not afraid of ghosts, I take it?'

'Not in the least.' Which was not entirely true. The thought of spending thirteen nights in a graveyard was mildly discomfiting, but only that. The physical dangers? Well, that part of it might be rewarding.

'Right.' said Pulau. suddenly becoming decisive. 'that's how we'll play it. I'll call the Minister. You get back to your lodgings and pack what you think you'll need and I'll arrange it. Tent and provisions?'

'And gaslights.'

'Of course . . . You really aren't concerned about the supernatural side of it?'

'No.'

Leeman looked at the dark mass, moving slowly through the water in the distance. Despite his disbelief, it looked eerie and forbidding. A fishing canoe, one of those traditional craft with modern outboard engines thrusting it obscenely across the water, cut away sharply from the island's path.

'What did they do—most of them? Those people buried on the island? It seems a harsh judgement on the dead,' he murmured.

'Drug runners,' replied Pulau. 'You know how we feel about them, here in Malaysia.'

A shadow crossed Leeman's mind, painfully. He remembered that drug trafficking carried a mandatory death sentence in Malaysia, for those convicted of the crime. It was, perhaps, one of the reasons why he had chosen to do his secondment in this part of the world.

'I see,' he said, quietly.

Pulau regarded him with a quizzical expression.

'Does it make any difference? To you, I mean.'

Leeman thought about his younger brother, Pete. Of course it made a difference. The cycle of thoughts which he continually had to fight, to break out of, began whirling in his head. Not again, he thought. Please. Why are there so many reminders? Why can't I be left alone?

It made a hell of a difference.

'No,' he said. 'I just wondered, that was all.'

On the way to the boarding house, in Lebuh Campbell, he told himself how much he liked it on Penang, in the Far East. He enjoyed the expatriate life, with its accompanying indulgence in a completely different culture. He was an advocate of an older way of life, with values he felt the modern world had wrongly placed aside. In the Far East, you could get closer to such values. They gave one a sense of historical continuity: a connection with the past. He could enjoy it more, if only . . . if only he could throw off the mistakes of the immediate past. But they clung to his mind like leeches, sucking it dry . . . He had said sorry many, many times, but there were no ears to hear, no one to listen . . . He had run to the Far East in order to get away from the leeches, but that had not been far enough. Here he was, running again, to a small, floating island that had detached itself from the world.

At first he was too busy to allow the sweet fragrance of the island to disturb him. He had to place the Calor gas lamps at either end of the rainforest, involving a mile-long walk along the shore. Then there was the business of setting up camp (something Pete would have enjoyed): erecting the tent, unpacking provisions, starting a fire and, finally, using the radio transceiver. He reported to the accompanying craft that all was well and he was preparing to bed down for the night.

Once these duties had been accomplished, he had more time to consider his environment.

There were the usual jungle noises that he had often heard on Penang. There were cicadas which gave out sounds like factory whistles; frogs that bellowed like megaphones; and birds that ran up and down scales as if they were taking some form of musical training.

There were also other sounds: the breeze in the palms and the rippling of water through the thick weed on which the island was based.

Then there was that smell.

It was by no means a disagreeable perfume and reminded him of incense, but it seemed so dense as to stain the air with its presence. Perhaps the cause lay in some unusual plant? Then again, it might have come from the thick sargasso which supported the soil and rainforest? That explanation seemed much more likely.

He took a torch and went to the edge of the island, to peer down into the shallows. There was no beach. Instead, a soil bank dropped sharply into the sea, beneath the surface of which he could see the myriad vines of sargasso, knotted together to form a mass of spongy weed. It was alive with sea creatures, mostly eels.

Leeman backed away, a little disconcerted. He was revolted, not by the creatures themselves, but by their numbers. It almost seemed as if the island were a live thing, crawling with tentacles. This, coupled with the thought that there was a great depth of ocean beneath him—a strange sensation until he managed to convince himself that the island was only a raft: a craft fashioned by nature instead of man—made him tread lightly for a while. Once he had got used to the idea that it was in effect nothing more than a platform of weed, a natural Kon Tiki, carried along by the current, he managed to keep his imagination under control.

He slept very little that first night, the smell overpowering his desire for rest. He rose, once or twice, to watch the lights drift by on the mainland, and gained some comfort from those of the accompanying craft.

When morning came, sweltering but happily blessed with bright sunlight, he was able to explore his surroundings without the intrusion of irrational fears of rotting souls. The rainforest, half a mile wide, was much like any other he had seen on Penang. It was dense, its undergrowth and canopy formed of a thousand different plants of which he knew few by name. He recognised the frangipani trees, of course, regarded by the Chinese as unlucky, and tamarind, and various types of palm. He knew there would be snakes amongst the vines, and large spiders quivering on the under-sides of waxy leaves, but these did not bother him overmuch. He had sprayed the area around the tent with paraffin, which would keep any wildlife away. Pete would have been terrified of them, of course, but then Pete was not with him.

He managed to busy himself with small tasks that occu-pied his mind to a degree, but there was no ignoring the smell. He recalled Pulau's statement, about the graves containing the bodies of drug runners, and felt sick at heart as the guilt washed through him. He kept telling himself that he was in no way to blame. He had not known what the launches were carrying; still did not know. He guessed their cargo consisted of contraband of some kind, but surely not narcotics? It could have been anything. Booze? Cigarettes? But did he honestly believe that people smuggled such things into Britain anymore? The real money was in heroin and cocaine. Organised crime syndicates did not bother with tobacco and alcohol. And they had been organised. Oh, yes. His payments had arrived, on the dot, every month. A plain brown envelope full of crisp banknotes. Very efficient, he thought bitterly. And all he had to do was turn a blind eye.

He began weeping, softly, as he stoked his fire.

'The bastards,' he said. 'The bloody, fucking bastards. They killed my baby brother . . . '

The island's peculiar cloying scent became an irritant over the next day or two. It was like a spirit in constant attendance and it bothered him a lot. He thought about the graves and wondered about their number. Were they unmarked, or were there headstones? Perhaps his tent was sited directly over a murderer's corpse, its putrefied flesh and corroding soul exuding opposing, distinctive odours? He dismissed the idea. The layer of soil was too thin near the shore. He could see the white stains of the saltwater, seeping through the grass.

He studied these white patches with loathing. They were threatening, simply because they were reminders of white powder. They demanded his attention, and once they had it, initiated that terrible cycle of thoughts which had his mind reeling. How swiftly nature turned from friend, to enemy . . .

'How long have I been here?' he asked the boat.

'Five days,' came the reply.

Another eight to go. The mosquitoes were biting well. (He preferred to think of them as biting, rather than sticking their needle mouths into his skin. That was too much like being injected, with a hypodermic . . .) It meant he had to spend time with his body, inspecting it, ministering to its minor problems.

He began doing all tasks with elaborate precision: making rituals of them, taking pains to perfect methods. Pete used to like rituals. When they were children, sharing a bedroom, he used to make fun of Pete, who would fold his clothes in just the same way, every night. It was supposed to keep away the bogeymen. Pete had liked high church, too, because of its mystical rituals. Then later—not so much later—those other rituals: the strings of powder—chasing the dragon. He should have seen all this in Pete, earlier. Done something to . . . to divert the course.

'Seven days.'

Sometimes he found himself staring at the forest that hid the graves that breathed the scent of the dead. He discovered something which he decided no other living person had yet noticed: that shadows were not all of the same thickness. There were those that lay black and heavy, rarely moving. There were those, slightly thinner, that changed position and shape lethargically. Then there were the younger shadows, like smoky movements on the grass.

He found he had power over the shadows. Those he did not like, he removed with his machete. He gave birth to new shadows, using mats of woven palm leaves. Screens and shields were placed around the camp area, so that they cast their dark shades on the ugly white stains, neutralising them. The artist in him helped to create a territory in which the reminders were few.

Then it rained, battering down his palmthatch shields. The new, unprotected shadows drained away in rivulets.

He passed his reports at the specified times, but avoided social discourse. The reason, if he asked himself at all, was that disembodied voices from the outside world tended to emphasise his solitude, rather than provide relief from it.

He found the heat of the day extremely oppressive, and often fell asleep in his tent during the afternoon, to wake in a pool of sweat as the evening approached. Though he had plenty of drinking water, he lost so much body fluid in the airless atmosphere of the tent that he began to develop dehydration headaches.

'Nine days.'

It rained heavily for the third time since he had arrived on the island. The fire was difficult to light. He used many matches, and when he looked down at their spent forms, he saw with surprise that they made a word. He did not like the word, was angry with it, and kicked it out of any understanding. After his rebellion, night and day they took it on themselves to confuse him. They lost their sense of rhythm, their timing. He would lift the tent flap to find darkness where he expected light. Or the other way round. Such happenings only served to erode further his trust in the world. There were other problems. He had ceased to breathe air. There was none on the island. He breathed only the perfume that had replaced it. The fragrance was corrosive, staining him internally. He tried making masks to filter out its impurities, but there was no mesh fine enough to prevent the sickly odour from entering his lungs.

'Ten days.'

How stupid he had been! He had allowed the island to feed his guilt, keep the cycle of thoughts turning until he was physically sick, until he was so locked into himself that only a major event, like a rainstorm, could break him out. He now dismissed such ideas as weak and foolish. It was up to him to resist, not succumb, to the island's pressures. He was the master of the island. He told it this fact, in no uncertain terms.

On the twelfth night they called him, waking him from a muzzy sleep to say that the lights at the rear of the island had failed. He took a torch and trudged along the coastline, to relight the gas. On the return journey, he stumbled off the path, into the jungle, and found himself on a well-worn track. He followed it to a central clearing, where gravestones sprouted from the tall grass. The scent was overpowering here, in the glade. He turned, to leave the place quickly.

At the edge of the clearing he stumbled over an ovoid object. He shone his torch on it. It was a durian. Since arriving on the island, he had deliberately avoided eating any of its produce, though rambutan grew in abundance. The durian at his feet had split on impact with the ground and lay open. Leeman had developed a taste, almost a craving, for this addictive fruit, which the locals regarded as a delicacy. It had a sweet flavour, but highly offensive smell. Someone had once described it as like eating honey in a public toilet.

In his half-asleep state he picked up a piece of the durian and sniffed the white flesh. For a moment the perfume of the island was swamped by the foul but pleasant stink of the durian. Without thinking, he took a bite and swallowed. It tasted good.

He realised, almost instantly, what he had done. The green dragon had seduced him. He stared around him, in horror, at the graves which the roots of the durian tree must surely have penetrated, feeding there. The pressure built in his head, until he felt his skull was splitting. A numbness overcame his legs and he lost his balance, falling to the ground, where he lay trembling violently. He heard himself shouting, 'Oh, God . . .' over and over again. He had tried to ride the back of the green dragon, and had lost control. It had carried him to savage days and cruel nights, working insidiously from within him.

He crawled back to camp on his hands and knees and, once there, fell into a deep sleep. His dreams were sour.

They came for him the following morning: Singapore was in sight. He felt drugged and heavy-headed, as though he had spent some time in a smoke-filled room. Sympathetic hands helped him to the boat.

'What about the island?' he asked, as they sailed away.

'There's a dredger ready, to tow it out into open waters,' a sailor replied.

Then someone asked him, 'Are you all right? You look ill— are you sick?'

He did not feel sick, and shook his head.

'I found it hard to sleep.' They would understand that.

'I'm OK now—now that it's over. That place could send you mad—was it only thirteen days? It seemed much longer.'

'You don't look crazy.' 'The sailor smiled. 'Just exhausted.'

He tried to smile back.

'Yes—tired, that's all. I seem to have done nothing but slept, but I'm still tired. It gets to be a habit, when you're on your own.'

'I'm glad it wasn't me. I hate being lonely.'

On the journey across the water, he cleared his lungs, breathing deeply. Familiar odours were beginning to reach him, from the harbour. The smell of garbage around the sampans; of cooking from the hawker stalls; of decaying fruit. To Leeman, they were clean smells.

The cycle of thoughts, the arguments that had raged continuously in his brain, had ceased. He had reached a dreadful conclusion. He was no better than those men in the island's graves. In fact he was worse. He had been responsible, even if indirectly, for the death of his own brother. While he had been collecting payments for allowing certain launches to go unreported, past his observation tower on an English rivermouth, Pete had been dying of an overdose of heroin. He had not even known his brother was an addict: that was how much he had cared.

Not wanting to return on the boat, he booked into a hotel in Singapore town, close to the harbour. Once in his room, he undressed and threw the shirt and shorts into the waste bin. Then he showered himself, carefully, soaping his skin. He did this several times. As he shaved, his breath misted the mirror, so that his eyes were hidden from him.

Later, he went down to the bar and drank down two straight whiskies that hardly touched his throat. Although he would have preferred to keep his own company, an American began to talk to him, and he found himself responding. After several more drinks, he told the man about the ghosts of the island and the sweet stink of their souls.

'Embalming fluid,' said the American. 'Take it from me—I've smelt the stuff. It carries. Boy, does it carry. My brother-in-law was an undertaker . . .'

'I expect you're right,' said Leeman.

When he was sufficiently drunk, he went out and began to walk the streets. He needed a little more comfort than the American could offer. He wanted arms around him and a soft voice, talking nonsense. There is nothing more comforting than empty talk, when you want to keep your head clear.

He found a young woman, outside a bar, and bought her a few drinks before she took him home to bed. She chattered the whole while, even as she stripped, about her relations, about the difficulties of making ends meet, about the meanness of her landlord. He let her words wash over him, without interrupting.

Then, while they were making love, she told him that he was good. He was very, very good. He looked good, he tasted good, he smelled good . . .

Leeman threw her out of the bed, savagely, and screamed abuse at her. The frightened girl grabbed her sarong and ran out into the night. He dressed quickly, and left.

He walked the streets. He thought about the island's air and the fruits of its earth. It was in him, in his system. He could not scour it from him with words. It had breathed its breath into his murderer's lungs. It had tricked him into ingesting its offspring.

He found another bar and, while he was being served a drink, asked the young Chinese waiter to smell his skin. The boy hurried away, without a backward glance. Leeman stared after him bleakly, then studied the sweat on his forearm, coming through his pores.

He brought the back of his hand up to his face—slowly—convinced that time was his terrible enemy, that time was in league with corruption, leaving nothing in its wake but the faint odour of hell's flowers.

LOVE CHILD

The steam train came to a halt with a great deal of respiratory noise. Burnett stepped from the first-class compartment on to the platform at Kuala Lumpur totally unprepared for architecture that was more suited to an Eastern temple than a railway station in the 1950s. Had there been a reclining Thai buddha beneath one of the arabesque archways, or a jade eye in the centre of the main cupola, it would not have been out of place. That was what Burnett loved about the East: the cultural surprises it continually produced from its bulging pockets.

The third-class passengers from the open trucks were beginning to swarm over the platform, carrying trussed chickens and cardboard luggage fastened with string. He motioned for porters to retrieve his own luggage from the train, taking only one item himself: his Smithfield twelve-bore in its cowhide case.

Burnett took a tri-shaw to the Stamford Hotel, through street crowds that periodically closed in upon the transport until the clangour of bells and taxi horns cleaved the way for another few yards. In K.L. the pedestrians compose a single, large, amorphic lifeform that moves like an amoeba, pulsating under the hot sun. Wares were constantly thrust into Burnett's face during the frequent pauses for clearance. He ignored the traders, staring steadfastly at a point in the sky just above the horizon, as if this were his destination and nothing must be allowed to turn his attention from it, not for one second. He knew that a single word, even a sharp 'No', was all the key they required to gain access to the pockets of his white suit. If he spoke or altered his gaze he would find himself with a pineapple or a carving he did not require. His problem was, he was weak. He pitied them their poverty, and they, being poor and desperate, could sense that lack of strength in his character. 'Please,' they would say, once they had his eyes. 'My children need food.' And guilt would guide his hand to his wallet. They knew him through his aspect and his demeanour. But there were too many of them. He could not feed them all. They would leave him as destitute as themselves. It was an impossible situation. So he avoided their faces, all of them, and fought a desperate battle within himself. In Singapore he was known as 'Old Stoneface'. but the expatriates who thought they knew him were less aware of his real feelings than the Malayan strangers who whispered their entreaties to him now.

Stamford Hotel was situated at the top of a rise, and the trishaw man had to stand on the pedals in order to force the vehicle up the slope. Burnett fingered his pigskin luggage on the seat beside him, having transferred his guilt to concern over its weight and bulk. The Chinese grunted and heaved as he forced the pedals down, sweat trickling under the holes in his ragged vest. He looked emaciated; but then they all did, these morose little men of the Orient, with their stick-thin legs poking from khaki shorts three sizes too large for them.

At the hotel Burnett over-tipped the man and watched him touting for business as a middle-aged Japanese matron with the bearing of an empress came down the marble steps from the main entrance. Then a porter was there, reaching for the pigskin suitcases, and Burnett transferred his attention, and, once again, his sympathy.

His first-floor room was cool, having a high ceiling with two large fans whirling gently at half speed. After removing his jacket and placing it carefully on a hanger, Burnett made a local telephone call. Then he made a second call to room service, for a jug of ice-water. The porter had offered to unpack the suitcases but Burnett had declined; he did not like anyone touching the clothes he was going to wear. While he waited for the ice-water he removed a bottle of Scotch from his hand luggage. There followed a moment's reflection. There was something about this whole business which was very disturbing. Not his adultery and the subsequent result—that was physical. No, there was something else: an unpleasant sensation of not being in control, of being drawn, as it were, to this place. Yes, he had made the decision to come himself, but were there other influences beyond the obvious . . . ? God, this is idiotic, he thought. I'm master of my own destiny.

Kam Jalan arrived fractionally after the water but raised his hand at the offer of a drink.

'No thank you, sir,' he said in a respectful tone. 'It is against my religion to touch alcohol.'

Burnett regarded the Indo-Malay steadily. What religion was he? Hindu? Buddhist?

'Fine,' he said, swilling the ice cubes around his glass. 'I got your wire.'

Kam Jalan nodded deferentially. 'Yes, sir, but there is a small problem. It seems she is no longer in Kuala Lumpur.'

Burnett was sitting on the edge of his bed. He leaned forward and pointed to a green wicker chair. Kam Jalan sat down, but stiffly, with his backbone as straight as a pole. The hairless skin was taut across his skull, and an over-active thyroid gland made his eyes protrude, revealing the whole of the iris. Until a year ago he had been the housing agent for the British Council, Burnett's employers, but he had since retired and moved to Kuala Lumpur. It seemed to Burnett that the old man had lost some of his previous regard for him. Kam Jalan's manner was distant—almost unfriendly.

Burnett asked, 'But she is pregnant?' He paused, wondering how much of himself he needed to show to his former employee. 'You see,' he said at last, 'my wife . . . we are unable to have children of our own.'

Kam Jalan cleared his throat. His hands played nervously with a small cap that he wore to protect his baldness from the sun.

'I must respectfully ask you, sir, whether the girl will be well treated.'

'I beg your pardon?'

'The girl, Siana Nath.'

Burnett was about to rebuke the old man, was on the point of correcting his manners, when something stopped him. He sat for a moment wondering whether a lie would be acceptable, even if it were an obvious untruth. Sometimes they just wanted to avoid the responsibility, these people. A flying beetle hit the overhead fan and ricocheted across the room like a bullet. It struck the wall and landed upside down by Burnett's toe, kicking its legs and buzzing furiously. Burnett moved his feet. Kam Jalan reached out and turned the beetle right side up. He then looked up expectantly.

* * *

'I'm not in love with her,' said Burnett quickly. 'That must be obvious. But she will be provided for . . . Is that acceptable?'

Kam Jalan nodded. 'It is as I thought. In that case I will take you to the village.' He pointed to the beetle, now skittering across the tiles. 'He will recover soon and before long fly into the blades again. How many times he does it will make no difference. There is no learning in a beetle.'

A silence descended between them now. Burnett took one or two sips of whisky but found he was not enjoying it under the placid gaze of his companion. Then he realized the man had something more to say. Something important. He waited attentively.

'Do you intend,' said Kam Jalan slowly, 'to adopt the child?' His staring eyes were disconcerting, and Burnett looked away as he digested this unexpected question. Outwardly, he knew, he looked calm. Inside there was a maelstrom of emotions.

A shadow passed over Burnett's soul. He dismissed it, almost instantly.

'Certainly. The child is mine.' He paused. 'How many months?'

'I am told eight.'

Burnett nodded, almost with relief. 'The child is mine.'

'Good,' said Kam Jalan.

Burnett stood up and walked towards the window.

'Not good, Jalan. Not good at all. You see, I come from a family . . . not wealthy, but very respectable. Do you understand?' He turned to receive an answering nod, then his attention was on the bright redness of the flamboyant trees that cushioned the balcony from beneath and around. 'They would not approve of . . . such a child. Fortunately my wife is a very understanding woman. Of course, she did not endorse the liaison, but that's over. She is willing ., . no, she is desirous of raising the child. We realize, too, that Siana Nath will want to visit, to see the baby from time to rime—I understand that.

Money does not quench a mother's natural yearning for her child. But there will be complications . . . '

Kam Jalan nodded again. 'Yes,' he said, 'she will have the same problem. This is why she ran away from Singapore— then from Kuala Lumpur. The village where she has gone is not her home. Merely the home of a sympathetic friend.'

Burnett was completely taken aback. That he would be unacceptable . . . the thought had not even crossed his mind. He hoped his surprise had not been recognized for what it was. Without turning around, he said, 'We shall have to live in Singapore, probably for the rest of our lives.'

'That is a long time. Things change.'

'Not in my world. But don't let me give you the idea that this life doesn't appeal to me. I love it.' He paused, then added, 'Very much. I am a born colonial, you see.' He did not add that the attraction was in the relatively small number of expatriates and exiles. He felt secure amongst a small band of people. It was like being in a little English village, without the disadvantages of geographical isola-tion. He was part of a community, an island of whites, in a sea of natives.

Kam Jalan coughed politely. Burnett reluctantly turned away from the cloud of blossom before his eyes and said, 'Will tomorrow at six o'clock be too early to start?'

'No, sir. That will be fine. Shall I hire a Land-Rover? It will be necessary to have four-wheel drive. The monsoons . . . '

'Jalan, thank you. I do appreciate this.'

'You are very welcome, sir.'

Kam Jalan gave an abrupt bow before opening the door.

That night, under the mosquito net, Burnett listened to the whining of his small enemies and the scuttle of cockroaches across the floor. I suppose, he thought, people like Jalan would be angry if I killed a mosquito. And how they could believe a soul was trapped inside such a disgusting creature as a cockroach was beyond him. Primitives! He fell asleep with the jungles of Rousseau crawling into his bed, the loathsome waxy leaves finding out his mouth and ears and nose.

From the moment he entered the rainforest Burnett had the feeling that he was being watched.

Had the real rain forest been less frightening it would not have surprised Burnett. The following morning, however, his nightmare became tangible, and for the first time in his life he compromised his fears. Nothing would have induced him to step from the Land-Rover into the thick undergrowth on the side of the track. There were eyes . . . creatures, everywhere, half-hidden by the leaves and tall ferns.

Silently, knowingly, it seemed, they watched him travel through their domain. He was uncomfortable in the extreme. The feeling of gross insecurity mingled with that strange sense of being manipulated. Had he come of his own free will? Of course he had, he decided. This mood would soon pass. He looked upwards, as the trees closed in overhead and he recalled stories of things that fell from branches.

Burnett gripped his shotgun until his fingers began to hurt.

At the end of the track, some seven miles into the forest, the sky suddenly opened up before them and they were in the kampong, the Malay village. He was safe, relatively safe, for a time. Children, and one or two women, came running up to the vehicle shouting and laughing, but soon a lean man with a regal bearing appeared and called them away. Kam Jalan climbed from the Land-Rover and went to hold a long conversation with him. Burnett kept his eyes moving over the scene. He was uneasy in these alien surroundings.

One of the tributaries of the Panang River flowed by the kampong, and Burnett stared into its grey waters from his perch on the Land-Rover. Finally, Kam Jalan finished speaking

with the Headman and returned to the vehicle. His wrinkled
forehead gleamed as he looked into Burnett's face.

'I am afraid, sir, that there is some bad news.'

'She's gone?'

Kam Jalan shook his head. 'Much, much worse. I am sorry
to say she has died.' He gestured at the growth behind them.
'There are many illnesses one can catch in this place. The
doctor tried to save her and failed. It is a sad thing. They
buried her last week.'

The girl was dead. That was not such a terrible thing if one
considered it inevitable. He was not unfeeling, but early death
was a common occurrence amongst the natives.

'The doctor . . . did he save the child?'

Kam Jalan seemed to hesitate, just for an instant, then
he shook his head again. 'He is not the doctor you think. A
native. He uses magic, not medicine.'

'A witchdoctor?'

Kam Jalan seemed confused. 'Not for witches, sir, for people.
But the magic is bad. It comes from evil spirits.'

Burnett felt hollow inside. All this way. And now this. The
child was dead. He was an ordinary man again.

'I see.' Black magic. They had tried to save her life with
the help of the devil. Kam Jalan was obviously thinking of
the same thing, for he muttered in a disturbed tone: 'It is not
religious.'

'I'm afraid it is,' said Burnett, 'but not the sort of religion
you and I practise. Well, we'd better get back to K.L.'

'The Headman has asked that we stay. He is anxious that
you avail yourself of his hospitality.' Kam Jalan's voice was
apologetic.

Burnett frowned. 'For how long?'

'One or two days.'

'Impossible,' said Burnett. 'I have to get back to Singapore.'

'He was insistent, sir, that you stay. You are the father of the

unborn child. It is a decent thing to do, to pay your respects.
Their law is very strict on such things.'

'Tribal laws, surely?' said Burnett stiffly. Suddenly the
atmosphere of the village had become very oppressive. He felt
entangled and helpless. Something was not right.

'But for them it is important. There is to be a ceremony.
They would be very angry if we left before that.'

Burnett thought, uncomfortably, of the local murders he had
read about in the Straits Times. Bodies mutilated by knives. Every
one of these natives carried a parang, the Malayan equivalent of
a machete. Then there was this black magic business. Even some
of the expatriates, those who had lived in the jungle, would not
state, emphatically, that it was so much bunk, and none of them
ever laughed about it. Burnett remembered tales of men who
vomited live fish, or spiders, or snakes, until they collapsed and
died, simply because they had upset a local sorcerer.

'We'll stay, then,' he said. 'But just until the ceremony is
over. Then we leave.'

'Yes, Mr Burnett. The Headman has asked that we stay at
his house. He does not sleep in an ataphut like the others, but
in a solid wooden structure. It is a great honour.'

'Well, I'd rather we weren't so honoured, but I don't want
to appear ill-mannered or unfriendly.'

Burnett inspected the village, accompanied by the solemn
Headman, with Kam Jalan to interpret for them. He even met
the witchdoctor (if that is what the man was) who seemed
quite an ordinary youth. Burnett had expected a wizened old
sage, with—well, frankly, with the trappings of such people:
skulls, rags and lank, smelly hair. Instead, he was presented
with this young man, hardly out of his adolescence, wearing a
colourful kain sarong and smiling like an idiot.

The villagers themselves seemed a sullen lot, which was
unusual for Malays. They regarded him steadily as he passed,
and then they returned to their chores, but he noticed that

even then their attention was not with their tasks. They were watchful, their brown eyes darting this way and that, as if they were waiting for something to appear.

In the evening he retired to the Headman's hut and sat in the light of an oil lamp to discuss Siana. In the prison of the yellow glow the mood of the conversation began, perceptibly, to change. Burnett could hear the forest moving, hear its multitude of creatures calling. It came home to him forcibly that this was not Kuala Lumpur. Nor was it a hotel. Instead of cockroaches, the floor might be crawling with spiders the size of soup plates. What was there to keep them out? Out of politeness he had left the unloaded shotgun in the Land-Rover.

The Headman's voice lowered to a serious murmur which later fell even further to a mesmerizing drone, and Burnett had to fight to keep his eyes open. Also the smell of the burning oil, thick in his nostrils, was pulling at the wild pig they had eaten for lunch. It had been a long day and he was exhausted. He rocked slowly on his buttocks, listening, listening. Kam Jalan's softly-voiced translation crept in between him and complete unconsciousness.

'... when a woman dies in late pregnancy,' Kam Jalan was whispering, 'the sorcerer waits until three days after the burial, then exhumes the corpse by night. The dead mother offers her unborn child to him, that he might use his magic to make it live again. He takes the child and seals it in a jar of fluid, a potion, until it takes on the squat form of a logi and develops the strength of several men ... '

Burnett's eyes were suddenly wide. He gripped Kam Jalan's arm.

'What are you saying? That Siana's baby is ... has been stolen?'

'Not stolen, sir, for the mother is said to have offered the child after her death.'

'How, if she was dead? How?'

Kam Jalan shrugged in the light of the lamp.

'I am not the sorcerer. I do not know the ways. These are just tales, sir, to impress us. I regret the translation. It was stupid of me not to remember we were talking of Siana, your lover. Stupid of me . . . ' But Burnett could see by his expression that it had been deliberate. Still, he was shaken.

He was revolted but he could do nothing. The Headman's eyes were on him, staring intently. This is insane, he thought. To remove the foetus and bottle it was a disgusting practice, even for primitives.

'Where is the . . . object now?' he managed to ask.

'Why 'object', if it is alive? It is now the property of the sorcerer. He uses it as a slave, to rob from other villages, sending it into their huts at night. . .'

'My child? He uses my dead child to do that?' cried Burnett.

Kam Jalan held up his hand. 'Please, do not shout. These people are most sensitive. You do not need to believe all this. It is a story told to us by the Headman. Often these people do not know the difference between the fantastic and what is real. You and I are civilized men. These people are superstitious . . . '

'This is ridiculous . . . '

'Of course it is ridiculous. You must not mind what I say—'

When the lamp was finally extinguished, Burnett's thoughts were a turmoil of distrust and anguish. Later, in the middle of the night, he awoke from a fitful sleep to hear someone dragging a heavy weight around inside the hut. Then there was silence, and he knew he was being watched. For a long time he lay there unable to move, until sleep overtook him.

The following morning Burnett woke abruptly to find himself alone. An unnatural peace had descended upon the village. With a thick head he staggered to the doorway and looked out. The rains had fallen during the night, leaving the

river swollen and congested with flotsam. The village looked
deserted. Then he saw them, crowded around the chicken
coops on the far side of the open ground.

He made his way to where they stood, gesticulating grimly
at something lying on the ground. On reaching them he looked
for Kam Jalan and attracted the man's attention. No one was
talking much, but there was something very wrong—he could
see it in their faces.

'What's the problem, Jalan?' he asked.

Kam Jalan pointed towards a heap of brown and red lumps
by the wire: the bodies of the chickens. Then Burnett saw the
smaller pile. He felt uneasy.

'Something has torn the heads from the chickens,' said Kam
Jalan. He picked one up and flicked at the wattle.

'What kind of animal would do that?'

'No animal,' replied Kam Jalan enigmatically.

Burnett looked quickly at his face, but it was impassive.

Kam Jalan asked: 'Did you hear the noise? In the hut last
night?'

'Yes, was that you?'

'No, it was the same creature that did this.' He looked
directly into Burnett's eyes. 'The logi.'

'Logi? I don't understand,' said Burnett.

Kam Jalan answered with a nod of his head.

'You do. You do. You understand. The logi is the baby of
Siana. The time for pretending between us is past. You should
face the truth.'

Nearby, the river gurgled through tangled branches of
natural dams.

'It was in our room? My child?'

'Your son.'

Burnett tried to arrange his thoughts in perspective. His
problem was in finding a motive. What did Kam Jalan and
these villagers want from him? The scenario was elaborate and

costly. They must have set it up with a definite purpose in mind. He knew he was to be the victim—but why? His fears, he was aware, were necessary if he were to save himself. He needed to be alert, primed for action. That meant humouring them and waiting until the opportunity arose for escape. He carefully resisted the strong temptation to look towards the Land-Rover. Was it still there? Was the shotgun still on the seat?

He said, 'Whoever was in our room, it must have been adult. That was no child moving around.'

'You don't understand, sir. The logi is small, but very, very heavy. Compressed. It has the weight of a fully grown man.'

Burnett looked towards the edge of the jungle, thinking he saw something move. 'Where is it now? In there?'

'It hides during the day.'

Kam Jalan was silent for a moment. Then he said, 'They want you to do something for them.'

Was this it? The whole village was present, watching him. He looked around at the faces, the expectant expressions.

'Yes?'

'They want you to shoot the logi, tonight.' The words came out in a rush now. 'You have a shotgun. It will be easy for you. Something went wrong, you see—with the magic. The sorcerer is young and a little inexperienced, and the logi runs wild. It should be the slave but it does not respond to commands. The whole village is in fear of it . . .'

'Why . . . ?' The thought was repulsive. To murder. A baby? A pink-skinned little boy? Even if it was smaller than usual. 'Why don't they kill it themselves?'

Kam Jalan's answer filled Burnett with apprehension.

'We cannot catch it. Now you have arrived it will come to you. It knows you . . .'

Burnett felt weak, and his head was beginning to spin from too much sun and too little food. 'It can't know me.'

Kam Jalan smiled. 'You are forgetting, sir, they have taught it who you are. They have taught it your name. It knows how to call you. Last night it came to you. Watched you fall asleep. It sees. It hears. Darkness is no barrier to the eyes of a logi.'

'Why didn't you kill it? Last night.'

'I?' Kam Jalan looked affronted. 'I take the life of nothing. Not even the smallest fly. It is against my religion. You must kill it.' He paused. 'The ceremony today is for you, not Siana. It is the dance of the hunter's moon.'

So, he would stay, it seemed. But one thing was certain. He would not kill—certainly not his own child. What sort of man did these people take him for?

The ceremony was indeed no solemn occasion. They laughed, they performed acrobatics, they showered praises on Burnett's head. At least, Kam Jalan interpreted their shouting and prancing as honouring Burnett's prowess as a hunter. They stalked imaginary beasts and slew them with a gusto and bravado probably never displayed beyond the village clearing. The feasting and dancing lasted until evening, then, when the rain came down as a wall of water, they slunk away to their huts, exhausted.

As darkness fell, Burnett walked across the kampong to the edge of the jungle. If his child was there he wanted to see it. Nothing. Not even the stirrings of animals or birds. But on the slow walk back to the huts he knew he was being accompanied.

Burnett went to the Headman's hut. There the occupants made him sit in the centre of the wooden floor, and the polished leather case containing his shotgun was brought to him. Kam Jalan refused to touch the weapon, but the Headman's son was eager to remove it from its nest of red felt and hold it in his thin arms. Reluctantly, it seemed, reverently, he parted with it, placing it carefully in Burnett's hands. Burnett removed two cartridges from his breast pocket and, aware of the seriousness of the occasion, broke the breech of the Smithfield and loaded it. They left him alone, with the gun across his knees.

Light left the hut swiftly, as if it had been sucked up into the atmosphere by a suddenly created vacuum. With the darkness came the uneasy suspicion that perhaps, just perhaps, he was being tricked.

A board creaked in the doorway.

Burnett slowly raised the shotgun until the barrels were pointing through the open doorway into the night. He could see the stars, but all else was blackness. Then came a shuffling sound and heavy breathing, like a man labouring during a climb.

'Who's there?' said Burnett.

There was no answer, except the loud croaking of a frog. His finger tightened on the trigger. Something was in the hut, crouched in a corner. Burnett relaxed and stood up. He walked slowly to the door, then out into the night, inviting the visitor to follow him back to the Land-Rover. He sat in the vehicle for a few minutes until he felt it move with the weight of someone climbing into the rear. He was afraid, but it was a controlled fear. The supernatural was a terrifying abstract if dwelt upon, but this was his own flesh and blood, not some strange monster conjured up by evil forces.

* * *

The wet smells of the jungle came to him strongly as he sat considering what he should do next. Kam Jalan had the keys to the Land-Rover. Burnett could oblige the villagers, and they would then let him leave. The other alternative was to force Kam Jalan at gunpoint to take him back to Kuala Lumpur.

'I'm not going to kill you, you know,' he said, into the blackness around him. There was no answer.

Burnett made a decision. He jumped out and ran to the main hut and, as he had expected, found the villagers crowded within.

'Kam Jalan,' he called into them, 'drive me to Kuala Lumpur now, or I will open fire on these people. You shall be the first.'

The Indo-Malay stepped from the huddled group and bowed sharply. He switched on an electric torch and led the way back to the Land-Rover. Burnett was nervous, expecting at any moment to receive a parang in the back.

'Just a minute,' he said. 'My things.'

'Sir?'

'My gun case . . . and holdall.'

Kam Jalan shouted something, and a few minutes later two or three figures skulked past them in the dark. Burnett pressed the barrels to the back of Kam Jalan's neck.

'Remember, if they try anything . . . '

'They will not do so,' said Kam Jalan sullenly.

'They had better not, or you'll lose your head.'

Half an hour later Burnett was bouncing on the Land-Rover seat as Kam Jalan drove them recklessly along the potholed track back to Kuala Lumpur. The rain was falling in great swathes of wind and water, but Burnett was determined to reach K.L. by midnight. He was elated at his success. He had never considered himself to be strong-willed or adventurous, and tonight he had proved something to himself.

'The suspension . . . ' said Kam Jalan.

'Keep going.'

The windscreen wipers laboured to keep the windshield clear of the flood.

They reached the hotel at twelve-twenty. The monsoon had ceased and Burnett jumped out of the vehicle, still carrying the gun. Nervously, he searched the back of the vehicle, but after several minutes found nothing. His holdall and gun case were there, and several pieces of equipment, including a box of tools, but certainly no child, supernatural or otherwise. He felt cheated. Had he imagined being followed from the edge of the village to the huts? And then again to the vehicle? What about the movement of the Land-Rover on its springs? Perhaps the child had climbed out again, while he had been fetching Kam Jalan.

Well, it wasn't here now.

'Bring my things,' he ordered Kam Jalan.

Disappointed, he climbed the steps and made his way to his room. There he stripped and went into the shower. He took his bottle of whisky in with him.

Once he was clean he felt refreshed. Wrapping a towel around him he returned to the bedroom. Kam Jalan had been and had placed the gun case and the holdall on the bed.

'Damn the man,' said Burnett irritably. He had expected him to wait.

The bed suddenly creaked.

Burnett looked down. What? There was something most . . . the holdall was creating a depression in the bed far too deep for the weight of a bag of personal effects.

It moved, very slightly. Afraid, yet at the same time fascinated, Burnett crossed to the bed and stared down at the case.

The top had been left unfastened. Slowly the opening began to part, and Burnett cried out as the holdall fell, over on to its side.

The logi was not like a small, pink-skinned baby after all. It was the colour of fungi that squat in deep caves, and it tumbled from the holdall as ungainly as a leaden toad, to roll clumsily on to the linen bedspread.

The bed sagged to form a pit in which the grotesque logi sat and regarded Burnett with a lugubrious expression. Its head tilted to one side as Burnett cried out again, loudly. It was not the repulsive, wrinkled skin of the creature which motivated the shout, nor the lidless eyes with mucus crusting their rims, but the familiar, the caricatured resemblance to Burnett's own features. There was the sound of a bullfrog again, only this time, his senses sharpened by his fear, Burnett recognized the word the Malays had taught it. He reached out for his shotgun, leaning against the wall, as the logi crawled rapidly towards the edge of the bed. The creature dropped suddenly on to his bare foot, crushing it. It dug its hard little fingers lovingly into the pulpy flesh.

'Bapa,' it croaked happily. 'Father, Father . . . '

Burnett's head was awash with pain. He steadied himself against the wall and grasped the gun. They stared at each other for a full minute, then Burnett allowed the gun to slip between his fingers. It clattered on to the floor. The logi pulled the weapon to itself and cradled the present in its arms.

SNAKE DREAMS

When the Dyaks found him, the fever was well into its third day. MacAllen was barely conscious, lying half-submerged in a pool of filthy swamp water, the murky liquid threatening to end the fever in a sudden and dramatic way. Insects were using MacAllen as an island, to escape the long tongues of the frogs, and around him the Borneo forest pulsated and murmured, filling his head with strange, warped visions. That light which did manage to filter through the canopy above was of a greenish, sickly hue, and within it shadows moved back and forth like phantoms on business of little urgency.

He felt drugged, as if his skull were full of some warm, viscous fluid that dulled his thoughts, heavy enough to prevent him from lifting his head. He was sick too, vomiting into the stagnant pool, which attracted other creatures not fastidious about their diet. He felt them slide and crawl over his inert form, their touch tingling his inflamed, sensitive skin.

The Dyaks lifted him up onto bony, strong shoulders. He could hear their voices, but the chatter seemed distant. His limbs were leaden, hanging heavy: logs on the ends of cords. The dark, sinister scenery around him sometimes danced with slow, rhythmic movements constrained by a lethargy of its own. At other times, it pressed against him, its pressure on his brain threatening to squeeze his skull until it burst like a rotten fruit. He remembered taking the company launch up-river for a quick survey. Somehow he had taken the wrong fork and had found himself in fast-flowing water, white water. Panic had set in: he was fearful of electric eels, and those giant fossil-like pythons that basked on the shore. He made for the bank, but a submerged log holed the launch just as he reached it. The rest had been a nightmare: stumbling through the fly-ridden jungle, trying to find a path; drinking dirty water; being driven insane by unremitting noise, the insects, the clammy prison of leaves; and finally, succumbing to the chills, the sweats.

There were times when he felt he wanted to die. He wanted the Indians to finish it, there and then: to slit his throat and so defeat the fever. The peace that would follow seemed to him then to offer such inviting rewards. Death was merely a horizon beyond which lay tranquility.

'I want to live!' he cried, wondering which was lying, his soul or his mouth.

'I'm dying,' he croaked to them, but they took no notice. They continued their chatter, which he often confused with the chatter of the monkeys.

As they carried him within the clammy interior of the forest, through the tunnels of darkness, past the wooden pillars that supported the thick, layered roof, he tried to tell them who he was.

'Engineer,' he murmured thickly, his tongue a lazy, fat snake curled within his mouth. 'Got lost. Susan. Mus' tell Susan, got lost.'

Susan, sweet Susan. Cool, cool Susan.

'Met at a dance,' he told a face near him. 'Nice. Pretty.' The face grinned at him.

He lapsed into silence. Susan danced for him, slowly and sensuously, moving in and out of the shadows. Her movements became sinuous, serpentine. They danced together, holding each other tightly, squeezing one another gently. Then, afterwards, an old, exciting game. A serious game.

'Hot,' he said. His flesh was baking. The face grinned. 'Hot, man!' he shrieked. He would catch fire from within: smoulder, burn. There were drums in his ears, throbbing out a painful rhythm. He thought his skin was splitting down his back and a snake was trying to creep inside him. He hated snakes; loathed them with that unknown fear that grips at the back of the brain, where the irrational lurks. He thrashed, but they held him tightly, dancing with him, as if it were a game. A serious game.

Brown, fast-flowing water slid with a sinuous movement between low banks. His temples pounded as they lay him in a canoe, and his eyes, which seemed to be expanding, were ready to explode. His blood was like boiling mercury in his veins and it seemed that his bones had been wrung, twisted like ropes. MacAllen thought he wanted to die.

The Dyaks would not let him rest. It seemed that no sooner had he been placed in the canoe than he was lifted out again, hoisted back onto hard, bony shoulders. He had not the strength to remonstrate with them. A sudden chill went through him and made him shudder violently. They almost dropped him, but moments later he was carried safely into the darkness of a grass dwelling.

He was in a hut. The cool, reed-strewn earth was underneath him as the hot flushes flooded back, melting the ice water in his veins. A face was close to his: a beautiful, Dyak face. He thought she was going to kiss his cheek, but instead, she whispered close to his ear: urgent, intense words which he did not understand.

'I want to die,' he whispered back, afraid that it was true. Terrified of death, he wanted to be released from the fever, but he did not want to slip away completely. Where would he go? To the bottom of the river? It was important to cling on to the banks, but his fingers felt loose, boneless.

He began to rave as delirium washed over him.

Yellow eye. A distant, wavering yellow eye and the smell of burning fat. Susan was there, moving dimly in the light of the yellow eye. High breasts. Taut, coppery skin. No, not Susan. Someone else. She came to him and smiled down on him with blinding-white teeth. There were markings on her face. Susan, mismanaging her cosmetics? No—no—Susan was blonde. This woman had black hair. Black as death.

'Small lady,' he said, trying to reach up, and again she smiled. The rushes of his bed pressed into his back, leaving it sore and uncomfortable. Why hadn't they used river sand? Sand was soft, warm and comfortable. He tried to turn over, but she held him, stopped him from thrashing. Little, dark lady with the strength of ten men.

As he began to recover, he was aware of the giant length in the shadows of the corner of the hut. She was detached from it, yet part of it. She was leaning over him, her cheek close to, touching, his thigh. There was a thin reed in her mouth. The sharpened tip of the reed was under his skin, deep in his artery, and she was blowing gently. He could feel the fluid entering his system: coolness flowing into the warm blood. His wandering gaze found the thick, long form with its penetrating eyes, staring at him from the darkness on the far side of the hut. His brain reeled.

'What are you doing?' he whispered.

She looked up then, and the other creature which was part of her, slid over the floor and out of the door of the hut. It took a very long time for it to go.

She smiled at him. A bloody smile. But a fly was bothering him, insistent demands being made in his ear. He tried to swat it, failing. He felt weak and helpless. She bent her head again and the reed pricked his thigh. He kept his eyes on the door.

'Will it come back?' he said.

During the day, he would walk through the hospital grounds, sometimes pausing to watch the children of visitors playing in the sandpit. Not far away to the south, the river up which the launch had brought him slid lazily into the forest, its long length disappearing into the thick, green folds. To the north, nearer still, the city hummed with mechanical life. The children irritated him, messing around with the sand. When he came out of an evening, they would all be gone.

The hospital were almost ready to release him and he had an interview with the doctor that afternoon. In the cool office, with its air conditioning, he felt out of place.

The doctor had a smooth face, remarkably smooth. His eyes were brown and his hair was slicked back, like someone from a nineteen-thirties' film. He was explaining how MacAllen had been found.

'Some fishermen saw you, lying naked on the river bank—tourist types,' he grimaced a little. 'They brought you up-river in their boat and we took you in. That's as much as we know. Your fever had broken, but you were still in a very bad state.'

'I told you I was treated by the Dyaks,' said MacAllen.

'Yes. You said that.'

'I want to know what kind of medicine they used on me.'

The doctor shrugged, his small sharp eyes registering discomfort. 'Who knows? They have their own ways. Some of them are quite effective. After all, they've been treating themselves for centuries . . .'

'What I want to know,' cut in MacAllen, 'is what these marks are, on my thigh.'

Again, the shrug. 'They would appear to be needle marks.'

'You mean, they gave me injections?'

'I don't know. As I said, they look like needle marks—some sharp instrument.'

MacAllen realized his fingers were restless and he deliberately entwined them to keep them still. His dreams had been bothering him.

'Doctor,' he said, slowly, 'is it possible for the body to receive, say, injections of blood—from another creature?'

The doctor's head went back, sharply,' and he glanced towards the window before looking into MacAllen's eyes again.

'Creature?'

'What if—what if one were to introduce snake's blood into a vein? Say, the blood of a python?'

'I would say that the system would reject it. You'd be a very sick man.'

'But if one were already sick?'

The doctor picked up a sheet of paper from his desk top and then replaced it on the same spot, very carefully. He had kind features, but there was something a little brittle in his manner, which might have been a dislike of foreigners, or perhaps awkward patients.

'Are you telling me this is what happened? That they injected you with the blood of a python?'

The words were delivered in a soft tone, but briskly, as if time were of the utmost importance.

MacAllen shook his head.

'I don't know. I was confused. The whole scene was confusing. I tried to communicate with them . . . '

'But surely, they did not understand you? I take it you, ah, raved in English?' There was just a trace of contempt in the doctor's enquiry, but MacAllen ignored this.

'Look, all I want to know is, did they poison my blood?'

An impatient sigh escaped the doctor's lips.

'Mr MacAllen, we've done several blood tests. There is nothing to suggest that any foreign agent exists—the virus, of course . . . ' He paused, then said, 'I suggest you try to forget the whole thing. When someone is in a state of high fever, all sorts of delusions occur. As you remarked earlier, things become confused. Dreams begin to merge with reality. You had fever dreams, Mr MacAllen—simply that.'

'Is it that simple?'

The doctor looked up, suddenly, with a sympathetic expression.

'Would you like to see another kind of doctor?'

'You mean a psychiatrist? No—no, I'm not . . . I don't need that kind of treatment.'

'And your fiancee arrives this evening?'

'Susan? Yes, I called her yesterday. She's in Paris, at a conference, but she's taking her private jet across today.'

'She must be a wealthy woman.'

'She is—as well as being my fiancee, she's my boss. She owns the company.'

The doctor looked even more impressed and MacAllen could not help adding, 'Not bad for a lowly engineer, eh?'

He could smell the dampness of her skin: a musky smell that reminded him of a freshly dug claypit. She pressed food between his lips. It tasted gritty, like mashed seeds of some hardy plant, mixed with water. The room still spun occasionally, and he never took his eyes off the door. The snake would come back. He knew it would come back. It belonged there, as much as she did, more than him. He was the outsider, not the reptile.

A man came to the door, holding a bunch of fish.

He held them up. They flashed silver in the white light from beyond. The man laughed. The girl laughed. MacAllen felt the rush of guilt. He was the one that would rob them of their livelihood. He was going to steal their river. He shrank from the girl's touch. She turned and looked at him curiously. Then her eyes changed. They had gone hard, like flints.

She knows, he thought. She's read it in my face.

'I don't want to,' he cried. 'I have to. It's my living—just as fishing is yours. The dam—the river has to have a new course. Nothing I can do will stop that.'

She stroked his head, soothed him, murmuring words that made him feel drowsy. Of course she doesn't know, he thought. How could she know? We don't even understand one another. I'm just being stupid. It's the fever. It's making me . . .

But then he stopped, for he sensed that something had returned to the hut. It had got in without him seeing it: slithered into a corner. He whimpered in fright. The hand stroked him as a trembling fit overtook him, seized control of his muscles. Afterwards he felt weak.

Susan came to his room in the hospital that evening. He was sitting by the window, looking out beyond the gardens at the river, and he had to stay where he was, because she was also there. She was sharpening the tip of a reed with a small, bright blade. Her soft thick lips closed on the blunt end and she blew through the hollow tube, into the palm of her hand. A downy feather wafted up on her warm breath, into the air. Her lips parted and she smiled, redly.

'Hello, Susan,' he said.

The sharp prick again. Cool fluid. He slapped at the spot and looked down, finding he had swatted a mosquito. A red smear besmirched his leg. He was sweating heavily and his blood was throbbing in his veins. He could hear the thrum of his heart, pumping deep inside him.

'Good journey?'

'Darling, never mind about me. You look awful.'

Susan, pale-skinned and soft-eyed, with that bloom on her which reminded him of delicate flowers, closed the door behind her. She moved tentatively to the centre of the room.

'Darling, I want to hug you, but I'm not sure—the illness. Is it all right?'

'Apart from the sallow skin—the dark bags under the eyes, and the loss of weight—I'm fine. You can do what you like with me.'

He trusted his sickness now. He could feel his blood stirring at the closeness of her. Even through the warmth of the evening, the heat of her body came to him. It aroused a new kind of excitement: one he had not experienced before the fever. Through the open window, the scent of exotic, parkland blooms filled the air, mingling with Susan's expensive Parisian perfume, but that was not the cause of his sudden anticipation. He was experiencing a catharsis, finding himself underneath the layers of what he used to be. He felt the surge, the rush of blood.

Susan was regarding him with strange eyes. She looked very vulnerable in her printed cotton frock. She looked fragile. Expensive perfume, but simple, cheap dress. That was Susan. He had always liked that compromise about her. She knew he could not afford costly suits, so she dressed down to him.

He stood up, feeling the soft breeze from the window on the back of his neck. Then he reached out his arms.

She came to him, nestled in the hollow of his shoulder.

'Darling,' she murmured.

His blood was on fire now, burning its own courses through his body, finding new channels. Her hot breath was on his cheek. It came out as a series of quick sighs, close to his ear. He pressed his mouth hard against hers, then his breast against her breast, until he could feel the frantic flutter of her heart, like a trapped, terrified bird, beneath.

She moaned in the back of her throat, then took her mouth from his to say, in a half-playful, half-serious tone, 'Darling—not so tightly. You're squeezing me to death . . . '

His arms felt strong. He watched her eyes open wide and thought they would never stop. Never stop. Never stop. Never stop. Squeeze, became crush. The sounds coming from her throat were taut and high-pitched, reminding him that they were playing an old game, a serious game, which required furtive movements and frantic responses.

WAITING BY THE CORPSE

The pale corpse lay on the shore. The drowning had been within the hour: the body was not bloated or disfigured in any way. A strong current swept around the bend and carried flotsam to this corner of the river, depositing it on the mud as if it were discarding some unwanted luggage.

It was night, the shoreline lit by the ghostly luminescence of the stars. No moon was in sight. I heard the foghorn moan of the ferry. It was as if some leviathan were dying alone somewhere out in the estuary. The corpse did not hear this sound. Its eardrums vibrated with the low note, but the message failed to reach its brain. The path was dead, to the dead organ where once were clustered ideas and dreams by the thousand. The corpse stared upwards at the pointillism above. The gaze was unseeing, uncomprehending of its beauty.

I waited by the cadaver, while the hermit crabs scuttled like small severed hands over the other pebbles nearby.

The limbs of the dead look quite different to those of the quick. They have this porcelain quality and seem translucent.

If one were to lift a lifeless hand and hold it up to some bright light, one would be able to see through it, trace the network of fine blue veins, the skeleton of the fingers. To disturb this body however, was impossible. I did not mind it, waiting with it, but it defied any alteration of its pose.

There was a light at the far end of the beach—one, two, several. People were coming, moving slowly as if searching for something amongst the rocks, in the hollows of the sand. Perhaps the corpse had been missed, his missing reported, and the worst suspected? Well, the worst had happened, and lay at my feet. I hailed the search party, calling them to the spot.

'Over here,' I cried. 'It's over here.'

They did not hurry their pace, as if none of them wished to be first. A corpse is something you have to come upon gradually, not suddenly. You have to know its precise location, the position of the limbs and torso, so that you can recognise it instantly for what it is. Nothing is more worrying than a lump or heap which one cannot identify until the perspectives jump into place, and then suddenly the recoil comes, the revulsion sweeps through one like a shockwave, as one sees that it is indeed a body, twisted into an unlikely geometrical figure. Expectation does not make discovery any easier: in fact it makes it more violent because the heart and brain are primed for shock and react more powerfully. It is similar to being told there is a snake in your bathroom, or a giant yellow-black spider: you go cautiously, wanting to locate the creature but at the same time afraid you will see it much too quickly.

The first torch beam fell on the corpse.

'Good God!' cried the owner of light, and the recoil came as expected.

'I'm afraid there was nothing I could do to prevent this tragedy,' I told him.

There was a shuffling, a surge behind the first man, as others came up, then a swaying back, as if they had blown by a wind coming from the body on the sand.

'Is it him?' cried a female voice.

The man in front averted his face.

'I'm afraid so . . . poor devil.'

A younger member of the party, one with a strong-looking jawline and broad shoulders, stepped in front, crying, 'For heaven's sakes, he might still be alive. Shouldn't we be doing something? Shall I try respiration . . . ?' and he bent over the corpse and grasped the head with his fingers, put his mouth to the blue lips of the corpse.

He dropped his task the instant his lips touched and stepped back again, revulsion in his expression. His face was ashen as he wiped his mouth repeatedly on his forearm, as if trying to take off the top layer of skin.

'Stone cold, clammy . . . ' he said.

'He died,' I told them, 'at least an hour ago.'

A woman wailed, 'Oh no, God no,' and others went to comfort her.

The strong man said, 'At least let's take him up to the house.'

Gingerly, three men took hold of the corpse by its wet clothing, each holding on by one hand, careful to keep the thing from banging against their legs. They held it as if at any moment it might leap into life again, for they seemed ready to drop and run. There was a horror in every breast that was particular to each man, yet all and one the same feeling. I went with them, feeling rather useless, yet unable to help with the load.

We were walking along the river bank when someone screamed.

'It wasn't my fault!'

Immediately the bearers used this as an excuse to drop the corpse and take a rest. They were all perspiring coldly.

Someone else said, 'Of course it wasn't. It could have happened any time. He's tried it before, we all know that.'

'You blame me,' said the grief-stricken voice, 'I know you do. It wasn't my fault, though. I know I told him we were finished. I said it was over . . . but I didn't mean it. I swear I didn't. It was just one of those arguments, you know.' The voice broke into sobs, then came out again, harsh and angry. 'He did this to spite me. Oh, how cowardly can you get? He did this to make me feel guilty, to make me suffer.'

There was a shushing and a murmuring around her, until all sound drifted into a quiet weeping.

The bearers picked up the cadaver, this time more roughly, with a certain contempt, as if they were used to its deadness now and resented its weight. It was no longer an object of mystery, to be held in dread and awe, but ordinary bones and meat, useless without its movement. How heavy a lifeless body can be, its veins filled not with the lightness of blood, but with plumbeous fluids trying to find a lost centre. The carriers were sweating hotly now, cursing silently for volunteering, but not yet willing to yell that it was someone else's turn to help drag the carcass up to the beach house.

'I'm sorry, I'm quite hopeless,' I said, but no one was paying much attention to me, they were all wrapped up in their own private thoughts, so I just shrugged. 'I'm no good at this sort of thing.'

Suddenly, one of than cursed, and turned round to the rest of us. The corpse was dropped again.

'We're not thinking straight. We naturally try to do the right thing by . . . ' he nodded towards the grief-stricken woman, 'but you realise we could be in a great deal of trouble. This fool,' he pointed towards the corpse, 'has got us into one hell of a mess. I'm supposed to be somewhere else tonight.

'And I'm on the run,' said another. 'When they catch up with me, I'll have a lot of explaining to do. I don't need something like this to add to my problems.'

They all looked at the grieving woman.

'Well,' said a man, 'what do we do?'

'Do? What can we do?' she cried.

A thickset fellow stepped forward and shone his torch on the dead man's face. It had changed colour, from slate blue to grey. The tongue had disappeared into the back of its throat and one eye was half-closed now.

' I say we bury him right here,' said the fellow, firmly.

'Here?' came the predictable screech.

'Here. The river sand's quite soft. We can dig with our hands—and before you start ranting and raving, just remember this is partly your fault. If you hadn't drunk so much wine, you might have seen what sort of state the idiot was in. Well, now we're stuck with our mistakes, but I for one am not going to spend the next three years explaining to the police what I was doing here with all of you. I have my reputation to think of. Elections are not that far off . . . .'

'You and your bloody elections,' said another, quietly. 'You and your neck. We can't just dig a hole in the sand, throw him in and then walk away.'

'Why not?' said a small man. 'I'm with him. We've got to stick together on this. I've got enough explaining to do already.'

'Quiet down everybody,' said the grieving woman, in a much calmer voice.

'Yes,' I said. 'Everybody calm down. Let's hear what she's got to say.'

The woman's voice was low.

'Suppose we do bury him here—just suppose mind—what about the river? Won't it wash him up again, or something?'

'Not if we go deep enough,' said another woman, and someone cruelly asked her if she knew that from experience. 'All right, then. All right,' said the grieving woman, 'let's get it done and then we can all get out of here.'

They all dropped to their knees and began spooning out the

wet sand in gobbets. Again, I did not feel I could assist them. I had no part in their fear, either of the police or anyone else. Once they had begun digging they were intent on their task and took no notice of me. I waited, fingering the single coin I had taken from the corpse, watching than work feverishly, as if they were digging not to bury a body, but to find hidden treasure.

'The bottom of the hole is filling with water already,' said one, despairingly. 'The sides are caving in. We'll never get it deep enough. What the hell are we bothering to bury him for anyway? We didn't kill him, after all, he killed himself . . . .'

'That's a matter of opinion,' I said.

He ignored me, but the second woman took it up.

'No, none of us are to blame, are we?' she said in a sarcastic tone. 'She played him false, he cheated him out of all his money, you denied him help . . . ' she was pointing at each of them in turn. I waited for my turn, thinking she would accuse me of failing to rescue him, but she passed me over, 'we're all so innocent, aren't we?' she finished.

The grieving woman's voice was low and penetrating.

'We all know you're the only altruistic one here, don't we? Except that 1 know different. You wanted to help him, all right. You wanted to help him out of my bed and into yours, even though he couldn't stand you. Well look at him, look at the facts. He'd rather be dead than with you. You've got him now. Take him home with you.'

'You disgust me,' said the second woman, but then she started crying softly, and walked further along the bank.

The one with the strong jawline spoke again.

'Look, let's just leave him here. No one will find him until at least the morning and by then we can be a long way away from here. What do you say?'

There were murmurs of assent from the sweating group. They stood up and stared down on the dead person. Then two of them lifted him and tossed him contemptuously from the bank down in the shallow rapids beneath.

One by one they began to drift away, along the shoreline, towards an area of lights. The grieving woman was the last to leave. When there was no one to see, she spat on the face of the corpse.

'You always had to have the last word, didn't you?' she murmured. 'Well that's my final say.'

Then she hurried off in the same direction as the others. I stayed with the corpse, waiting. I wanted to go with the living, but of course I couldn't. I tried to remember my name, who I was, who all those people were. I felt I ought to know all these things, had known them until very recently, but the words were buried in lumps of dead tissue in my skull.

I heard the splash of oars and the slow slide of a small craft through water. There was movement in the corpse now, excited by the ripples the boat created in the shallows. It seemed as if it were trembling back to life. The eddies and currents stirred up gravel, scratching at the dead feet, scouring the mouth, nose and ears. The night hardened around the unfeeling hands. The corpse was nothing to do with me any longer. I knew now what I was doing. The lifeless body had to stay where it was, of course, but I?—I was waiting for the ferryman.

MIRRORS

He found himself in an exotic city, in an oriental country, but was not quite sure which city or which country. Having taken the sleeping pill he had been bemused when woken from a deep pool of sleep, to be told the plane had developed engine trouble and they had to make an emergency landing. The airline had driven the passengers from the airport to a hotel, where a room had been provided. It was the Hilton. One might be in a Hilton in Bangkok, New York or Amsterdam: they all had similar interior plans, similar decor. The hotel was no indication of where he was. Nor were the staff, who simply looked oriental. They might have been Korean, or Thai, or Vietnamese: Walt was no great traveller and could not separate these nationalities from one another. In an American city he had once mistaken a Filipino maid for Chinese.

So, here he was, wandering streets encrusted with neon lights—red, blue, pink, opal—each sign like pouting lips begging him to enter the establishments they advertised. There were bars, night clubs, nude theatres, dancing palaces.

houses of erotic fantasy . . . his mind had stopped on that one, fixed on it. Houses of erotic fantasy! This was a new one on him. At first he had decided he would not go inside one, but simply think about it further in a bar. But sidestreets and backstreets and a long narrow alley had led him to one of these houses of fantasy which unlike the others seemed to be trying to hide itself, down below the street. The sign bidding him to enter was level with his knees and the steps under the sign led down to a basement.

Should he go inside? Did he have time before the aircraft was repaired. Sure, he had the whole night. Perhaps all of next day too! He was lost anyway. It would be necessary to call a cab to get back to the hotel. There was no way he could find it himself. Especially not in the dark.

He descended.

'How much?' he asked the man standing at the open door. 'How much for an erotic fantasy?'

'What one?' came back the reply. 'Ordinary, Special or Extra-special?'

'Will traveller's checks do? American dollars?'

The man smiled. 'Of course.'

'Then I want the best.'

'Extra-special—four hundred dollar.'

'Four hundred?' cried Walt.

The man laid a slim-fingered hand on Walt's sleeve and moved conspiratorially closer, as if about to reveal a sacred trust.

'Listen, mister—you never have something like this again. Four hundred very cheap for this. She very beautiful woman. What happen if you say no? You go home. You sit in chair by fire and make regrets. You tell yourself you would pay one thousand dollar for chance like this again.'

He let these words sink in, then he added, 'Maybe you just want Ordinary or Special—but not so good. I tell you mister, you not want your autumn years to be filled with sadness. Extra-special is best of best.'

Walt knew his own true nature. He knew his own weaknesses. In the past he had bought toys for more than four hundred. That mountain bicycle for a start. That had cost him five-fifty and he hardly ever used it. The chance of an experience like this did not come twice in a lifetime. He really had no choice.

'I'll take the Extra-special.'

The man was effusive.

'You make good choice. This wonderful adventure. Very fantasy. Very erotic.' The man did a little shimmy with his hips and smiled one of those enigmatic smiles that only orientals can seem to produce. 'I guarantee you never have nothing like this before in your life. You not forget this night for a thousand years.'

'I should live so long,' replied Walt, drily.

Walt had never been with an oriental woman. In truth he had not had sex for quite a time, not since his marriage to Jody had broken up a year ago. This would be quite a new experience for him. He believed he liked diminutive females. They appeared to be more submissive. That might not have been true, but it seemed so. Jody had not just been a muscular five-feet-eight. She had also been a work-out freak. When her arms gripped him around the back of his neck, and legs locked behind him, her heels driving him into her, he had felt as if he were in some kind of medieval vice, a fucking-machine built to pummel men's genitals to pulp. He had felt manacled. No need for handcuffs or leather straps: Jody had been a human bondage device all by herself!

He was led through narrow winding passageways, the walls lined with red and gold flock wallpaper, to a large wooden door. The man turned and smiled as he produced a large iron key. The door was opened and Walt pressed gently inside.

'Woman come in a moment. She pretty. You like her.'

'I'd better,' said Walt, staring around him.

There was a musky perfume coming from somewhere. He discovered holes in the sides of the bed and guessed they were vents. The aroma was powerful and intoxicating, with some kind of an aphrodisiac quality. He felt himself being aroused. Walt had heard of certain foods and drinks doing that, but not a fragrance.

He studied the room itself, which was weird by his standards.

Then he inspected the bed, which was large with black satin sheets.

Each side had a huge round red pillow with a hole for its centre.

The headboard was carved with a painted rainforest scene. There was a red monkey motif following the oval shape of the bedhead: mischievous-looking creatures with round quizzical mouths, linking tails. Snakes slid in and out of stylised undergrowth. There were tigers in there somewhere, half in and half out of shadow. Magnolia trees stood leafless and bare, with dark-red cupola-shaped buds on the tips of their branches. Succulent pitcher plants, with deep mysterious recesses, grew from mossy banks. Vines entangled and wound their way throughout the whole scene, binding all the individual beasts and plants together. Incongruously, right in the centre of the headboard there was a long railway train entering a deep tunnel.

When he studied the picture closer he could see death in there too.

There were the symbolic skulls, obvious to any culture. He noticed that these were arranged in casual piles with exactly four skulls to each heap. There were shapes of pale light which might have been severed hands scattered throughout the undergrowth of the jungle, secreted in pockets of dead leaves. White flowers and white feathers decorated the floor of the rainforest. Rib bones curling out of rotten logs, were hung with hair-moss, dripping with a substance that might once have been human skin.

Necrophilia?

'We're having none of that sort of thing,' he murmured to himself, half-jokingly. 'She'd better be alive when she comes in here.'

It was then he turned his attention to the walls, floor and ceiling. These had had of course noticed as soon as he had come through the door, but had ignored in favour of the headboard details. Now that the only piece of furniture had received his close inspection, he could study the rest of the room.

It was all mirrors, mirrors everywhere: on floor, ceiling and all four walls.

Reflections of the bed went into infinity in all directions. When he stepped further into the room, a thousand-thousand Walts went with him, like a curved line of soldiers. When he stood still, he was the hub of helicopter rotary blades made of Walts, which whirled gracefully away into light years beyond. It was while he was thus experimenting with the simulacra that he was aware of another presence. She suddenly appeared by his side in the mirrors, startling him.

'Did you just come in?' he said, looking at the closed door. 'I didn't hear you enter.'

'I am very quiet,' she said, smiling.

She was an enchanting, delicate young woman whose very form and beauty took his breath away. He was not just astonished but shocked by her loveliness. He felt inferior to such a woman. She could not possibly want to stay in this room with a clumsy oaf like him. If she did, there must be something wrong with her, something hidden and perhaps vile.

'Are you—well?' he asked.

'Yes thank you,' she breathed, misunderstanding him. 'I am perfectly well, thank you very much.'

Her breath smelled of oranges and mint, as the words came out of her mouth like invisible bubbles. Suddenly, he did not care. She could be riddled with horrors for all he worried at that moment. He knew this was his one chance to have such a woman, for he would surely never get another. There were drums in his loins. Heavy metal music coursed through his thighs and belly. This was happening to him. Two hours ago he had been just another seedy passenger on a plane. Now he was a king with the most exquisite concubine in the land. He watched as she removed her scant clothes to reveal small breasts with brown tips, a smooth flat stomach with a neat dark triangle below it. Walt swallowed hard and began trembling.

'Shall I—shall I undress now?'

Once Walt had stripped himself, she took his clothes and put them in a box under the bed, as if they were tainted things. Then she lay beside him on the bed, where he was studying himself in the ceiling mirror, his erection somehow larger and more formidable in this looking-glass. Thousands of curved penises went sweeping away in a crescent, like a palisade of sharpened stakes on a medieval battlefield, ready to pierce the chargers of rash knights. Then her rosebud mouth was on his breast and he could feel the dry silkiness of her breast beneath his armpit. A lump came to his throat. He began to cry soft tears. He did not know why. They just came from somewhere deep inside and flowed down his cheeks. She licked the tears from his eyelashes, saying they were deliciously salty.

Then, when she reached for him down below, he felt her fingernails graze his abdomen.

'Ouch,' he said, looking down.

'Sorry' she replied, smiling.

But he was astonished. He had not noticed before now, but her fingernails were about an inch long, and very sharp. Her hands were like those of a goddess from some dark jungle religion. If she wished she could pierce his skin with those claws. It was not a thought that rested lightly on his mind.

'Good God,' he said. 'Don't you ever cut those?'

'My people believe it is beautiful to have long nails,' she explained in a disappointed voice. 'You not like them?'

'I—well—they just look a little dangerous, that's all.'

But then, looking down on her, he forgot about the nails.

They made love not just once, but three times in the next two hours. This was remarkable enough, since Walt was normally a once and then roll over and go to sleep man. But even after the third session he was still ready to go again. He guessed it had something to do with that smell of musk.

Then he found the gun.

He had thrust his hand under his pillow accidentally during a moment of passion to find a pearl-handled automatic there. He whipped it out to study it. It was manufactured in Japan, an exact copy of one of the Colt .38 models. On checking it he found it loaded. A magazine of twenty-seven rounds. Having been a sergeant in the army, he knew how to use it. Its presence in the room gave him concern.

'What's it doing here?' he demanded to know. 'Why?'

'Sometimes in the past we have had robbers,' she explained. 'It is for your own protection, in case we are attacked.'

'Are we likely to be?' he questioned, alarmed, thinking of Chinese triads, or Burmese bandits, or even Indonesian pirates. He did not know where he was. It could be any of them. Perhaps even Cambodian rebels looking for hostages? 'I don't like this—where are my clothes?'

Slim long-nailed hands restrained him, pressed against his hairy chest, forcing him back down on the bed with their sheer daintiness.

'You must not worry. It is all in the past.'

'Are you positive?'

'Yes.'

Her small buttocks somehow worked themselves underneath his hands. The gun was back under the pillow. He was fondling crevices again, finding his potency amazingly fresh. Never had such energy coursed through his body before this night. Jody would have at first been delighted, then not so delighted, then finally weary of him. He always suspected she pretended a high sex drive in order to humiliate him. He could have used this newly-discovered potency to destroy her domination over him.

Where had it been when Jody was at her most demanding? It had not been her fault. It had not been his. It must have been the fault of the time and place. He should have thought of mirrors before. It was, after all, simply Narcissism taken to extremes. It was fun to watch.

He found, after a while, that he enjoyed her mirror image better than the flesh and blood. If she was lovely in life, she was superlative in glass. They tried many different positions and he adored the reflections which tumbled away from him in all directions. Superb forms, equal to those produced by any sculptor he cared to name. Poetry in moving images. He preferred the silence to words or music. This was art. This was profound. This was the sport of angels . . .

'Hey!' Alarmed, he sat up quickly. 'Did you see that?'

'What? What have you seen?'

He stared into the right hand wall. He could have sworn . . . but it was impossible. He was surely drugged by that heavy narcotic called sex.

'It doesn't matter,' he said, resuming what he had been doing, what she had been doing to him. 'I'm seeing things.'

But then it happened again and he was sure this time.

'I did see it,' he cried, pushing her away. 'That—that . . . '

It was the hundredth, no, perhaps even further back than that, about the hundred-and-fiftieth reflection of himself and the girl. This distant set of reflections had been doing something different. Walt and the woman had actually been in one position, and this particular couple, out of the thousands before and after them, had been in another! Surely that was impossible. Unless there was some sort of flaw in the mirror. But wouldn't that affect all the images? He tried to decide whether it worried him or whether he was merely intrigued by this strange phenomenon. Eventually he decided on the latter. Maybe it was because he was sated. Overload? His mind was playing tricks on his eyes. Yes, he was seeing things. It might be interesting to go with it, allow himself to be swept along with the illusion.

He lay back again and she eased herself on top of him.

Walt's eyes scanned the mirrors, watching for the one rebel image to appear. All around him were couples locked in the shape of a reversed T. Wait! Yes, there. One pair on the far wall, way back down the line, had flipped over with the man now on top. Walt stared in fresh amazement as this movement fanned out from this single couple. Forwards down the line the images began riffling, running down towards him like a row of dominoes. Flip, flip, flip. It was a fantastic sight. He had seen computer images do this, but these were simply mirrors. Then the line reached him and his consort.

He suddenly felt himself being flipped over. Their sexual roles were instantly reversed. He was now on top of her.

At the same time as this physical miracle took place he had an orgasm that was like a massive jolt of electricity rushing through his loins.

'Jesus!' he yelled. 'Arrrggghhhh! Christ!'

The sweat poured from his naked body. He had never felt anything like this before, not even his first time over that gravestone at the back of St Peter's church. His head ached from the absolute pure passion of the moment. Semen gushed from him in a torrent. And yet afterwards he did not feel drained of desire. There was still a river of raw lust rushing through him. Her hands were all over him still, rousing him again, bringing him to a new and superhuman state of sexual excitement.

'Again!' he cried. 'Let's do it again. Did you feel it too? You must have done. I heard you yell. You loved it didn't you? Christ I feel randy. I'm ready for half-a-dozen of those. I bet it's better than any drug. What do you say—let's go for another one, eh?'

She smiled at him with small even teeth. Then she worked her contortions to form the two of them into a new inter-locking puzzle. Her body was fantastic. Walt thought she must have bones of rubber the way she was able to arch her back, put her legs under her own arms, bend her waist that way. Eagerly he stared into the mirrors around him, searching for that one set which would herald an unbelievable orgasm.

Yes, there it was, on the ceiling.

'Here it comes,' he yelled in excitement. 'Here it co— aaarrrrhhgggg—oh GOD, GOD, GOD, GOD . . . '

The small three-letter word was appropriate. He was having the orgasms of a young god. The world was not just moving. It was spinning at ten times its normal speed, hurtling through space a thousand times faster than usual. He held her small naked body to his as if they could fuse together, meld, merge. She let out a high tinkling laugh. Incredibly she was enjoying it as much as he was. Oh, he knew that hookers faked it all the time, that they were good at making the right noises at the right moment, but he could tell she was luxuriating in it— not wildly like himself, but sensitively. It was as if she were enjoying a glass of fine Champagne in a hot bubble bath.

'Again?' she said, laughing.

Thrice more they were manipulated by the couples in the mirrors and each time it got better and better. Finally Walt did not think he could stand another one and he suggested they have a cigarette. He went to the box under the bed and found his packet of Camels. He lit one, but she refused, with a little shake of her head. Walt shrugged and lay back on the bed, puffing away contentedly. Four hundred dollars? Christ this had been worth a million. Fantastic experience. Jody would have been proud of him. Or perhaps not? Maybe she would be jealous. That thought was very pleasing to him, since he was the one who had been dumped.

He lay there in a state of bliss, studying a thousand-thousand Walts with lit cigarettes, all in equal states of bliss. He arced his red-ended cigarette through the air, made designs as might a child with a sparkler. The Walts all copied him, faithfully, their lit cigarettes tracing figures of eights, centripetal and other pretty shapes.

Beside the Walts lay the beautiful oriental women, resting like lilies on black satin sheets. Their arms were by their sides, limp and lovely. Their mouths slightly open, revealing a hint of white teeth between the cupid's-bow lips, their eyes closed.

Suddenly, as he stared, there was a tiny movement amongst one of the images down the curving line. The stirring of a butterfly. The flutter of a moth.

What now? He frowned. He was enjoying his cigarette.

A search of the couples revealed nothing at first and then he saw her, way, way back down the long sweep of oriental beauties.

She had opened her eyes.

He glanced quickly at the real woman beside him, to see that her own eyes were still tightly closed. He looked back at the woman in the distance. So, this one was staring out at him from her place in the line, way out in space somewhere. So what?

Then he saw that the Walt beside her was unaware of her changed state. That should not be, for he—the real Walt—was certainly aware.

The next move made Walt start with horror. The distant

female image had used those long sharp fingernails at the end of a flattened palm. Her hand was like a knife with a serated blade. In one swift movement she had slit the throat of the man beside her. Blood spurted up in a fountain, dousing the cigarette. The reflection of Walt made a motion as if gargling and pressed his hands to his gaping wound. To no avail. The blood gushed between his fingers, splashing on the black satin sheets.

And her face was twisted in an ugly triumph, as if she had just performed a great service for herself. She stared out gleefully at the real Walt. It was horrible to witness the savage joy in her expression. It was as if she hated him with a primitive passion, a loathing nursed by ten thousand years of servitude.

He watched horrified as his dying image, deep inside the mirrors, reached out wildly with blood-blinded eyes, seeking a hold on his murderess, only to find its fingers groping between her open legs, scrabbling for a grip on the sparse hair of her vagina. Desperate fumblings, unable to get a hold on that elusive female centre. It was her magnet, yet now she used it to repel what she had once attracted. His hand fell back, clawed at his terrible wound, which opened like a second mouth crying for pity.

She threw back her head and silently laughed.

All this happened within the tiniest fraction of a second.

Then, inevitably, all along the line the women began slitting the throats of the unsuspecting Walts, one after another, slash, slash, slash, slash, slash, with the same reactions, the same twist of the female features. The blood and gore rushed down towards him like a swiftly-burning fuse. In that instant he knew he was going to die. When the line of murders reached the end, the nearest reflections, the woman beside him would wake and then slit his throat with her scissor-sharp claws.

Down the line came that sweep of slashing hands on the

end of white arms, like a sea wave surging down a long curved bay.

'NO!' he screamed.

Instead, he reached under his own pillow and found the automatic pistol. In the next moment, before the line of arms reached his bed, he shot the woman beside him twice in the chest. She did not even open her eyes. There was the faintest of grunts and then she flopped over the edge of the bed, to strike the glass floor with the sound of a dead fish hitting a slab of marble.

Walt sat there trembling, the gun still gripped tightly in his fist. At any moment he expected the door to be flung open. There would be oriental men wielding meat cleavers tumbling into the room. They would see the dead body and set about him, hacking him to pieces, leaving him bleeding from a thousand cuts. In his mind he could feel the cold bite of the choppers and knives now, biting into his vulnerable flesh. Bile rose to his mouth, as the terror of a horrible death washed through his stomach.

He had twenty-five rounds left in the automatic. He waited in abject misery, wondering how he had got into this mess, and how he would ever get out of it.

No one came.

He waited for at least ten minutes, before breaking down and sobbing, burying his face in one of the pillows.

Then he suddenly got angry. Red, misty rage swamped his brain. He sat up quickly. What the hell was all this? They had set him up, somehow. He was a patsy. They had used him to murder a woman whose name he did not know. What would he say to the police? The whole story was so fantastic the cops would laugh at him. Yet it was possible, with modern technology, to arrange something like this. The mirrors could be screens, displaying pictures they picked up through hidden cameras. Once the computers behind the screens had the images, they could do what they liked with them. All right, he had experienced unbelievable orgasms, but those could have been drug-induced, using that fragrance which pervaded the room at all times.

He stared again at the terrible mirrors and another thought came to him.

Maybe it was more devious still!

He remembered they could often hide prying eyes behind them. He finally saw through it their whole filthy deviant scheme now. There was an audience behind those mirrors, paying to watch him make love to, then murder a young woman. Voyeurs of sex and death. The owners were using him to supply their jaded customers, those men who had seen and done everything, with a new excitement, a new experience. He imagined drooling customers watching open-mouthed as he and the woman frolicked on the bed, cried out in ecstasy, desire overflowing. Then the spectacle of the murder, the weapon blasting, the bullets striking flesh, the fear on the face of the murderer, the subsequent show of remorse. They probably loved every twisted minute of it: their voyeurism satiated with visions of fornication and blood.

Well this was Walt Jones they were dealing with, not some nampy-pamby from the suburbs of Suckerville. He was not going to lie down for this kind of manipulation. He was going to make them pay in more than money.

'You bastards!' he shrieked. 'You bloody bastards!'

He began firing then, at random, the bullets shattering the mirrors all around him, above him. Walt imagined the terrified audience behind those mirrors, running for their lives as he pumped rounds into the walls and ceiling. He felt a savage triumph as the mirrors crashed all around him, the shards raining on his bed, some of them lacerating his naked body. It was raining glass and he did not care whether one of those dagger-shaped shards pierced his heart or not. He really deserved to die with them, with her. They had forced on him the role of executioner for their own anomalous cravings and he had failed to see how they were manipulating him.

Finally, he was out of bullets, the mirrors all broken.

He shook his head. Fragments of glass like diamonds fell from his hair. Bits of mirror lay all around him, reflecting parts of him: a foot, an eye, the gun. Debris of his lust, his hunger for secret pockets of flesh. He wondered what made a man risk all to simply merge with woman for a few moments of high pleasure. How deepseated was the desire to perform the act of procreation.

Blood seeped from his wounds, staining the bedsheets. He leaned over to look at the body of the woman. He did not want her beautiful body to be mutilated. He was anxious to make sure she had not been disfigured by the falling pieces of mirror, many of them shaped like silver knives.

She was gone. Her corpse was gone. The space on the floor where she should have lain was simply covered in splinters of glass.

Looking around him at the walls and up at the ceiling, he could see no evidence of hidden recesses from which people might have viewed.

'What?' cried Walt, distressed. 'What is this?'

Frantically he began searching through the shards, thinking the woman's body might be underneath. As he moved the broken slices of mirror around he discovered parts of her shattered image still captured in the glass. Sobbing hysterically, he began to piece her together again, like a puzzle—a pretty brow here, a small breast there, a piece of thigh—and gradually he began to reform her. She was cracked of course, a flawed image, but she remained just as beautiful under the faults and fissures.

Once he had her complete face, she opened her eyes, looked out at him, and smiled a sweet smile.

'Oh, God!' cried Walt. 'You're still alive in there.'

At that moment the door began to open. A high wind suddenly rose from nowhere. Glass began swirling, whirling around the room in a blinding blizzard. Faster and faster flew the shards, until it was as if he were in the vortex of some mighty storm, whose snowflakes were deadly slivers of obsidian. He put his arms around his head to protect himself from the tornado, but the blast around him did not touch. It showered against the bare walls and ceiling. As the fragments flew into the walls and ceiling, they refitted like a self-making jigsaw, until finally the wind died and the mirrors were all back in place, with not a crack to be seen.

'Christ help me,' moaned Walt.

Gradually he unfolded his arms, uncurled himself from the foetal position. Looking down he saw that his earlier wounds had miraculously healed, that there were no cuts or abrasions. It was as if he had never been lacerated in the first place by the falling glass. He was clean in every part.

An oriental man walked in, smiling. The same man Walt had met earlier. He had a drink in his hand. Giving it to Walt he looked around him and his grin grew broader. He shook his head, looking about him.

'All over so soon? You finish quick. You want to go again? Only two hundred dollar this time. Extra-extra-special. Only two hundred. You want?'

Walt whimpered and hugged his knees to his chest.

ACKNOWLEDGMENTS

'Blood Orange', *In the Hollow of the Deep-sea Wave*, The Bodley Head, 1989

'The Cave Painting', *Omni Best Science Fiction 2*, edited by Ellen Datlow, 1992

'The Dragon Slayer', *Dark Hills, Hollow Clocks*, Methuen Books, 1990

'Face', *Traffica*, Autumn Issue Number 1, 1993

'The Hungry Ghosts', *Dark Hills, Hollow Clocks*, Methuen Books, 1990

'Inside the Walled City', *Walls of Fear*, Morrow Books, edited by Kathryn Cramer, 1990

'Island with the Stink of Ghosts', *In the Hollow of the Deep-sea Wave*, The Bodley Head, 1989

'Love Child', *Fontana Book of Horror Stories*, edited by Mary Danby, 1982

'Memories of the Flying Ball Bike Shop', *Isaac Asimov's Science Fiction Magazine*, June Issue, 1992

'Mirrors', *Sirens and other Daemon Lovers*, HarperCollins, edited by Terri Windling and Ellen Datlow, 1998

'The River-Sailor's Wife', *In the Hollow of the Deep-sea Wave*, The Bodley Head, 1989

'Snake Dreams', *Tarot Tales*, Legend Books edited by Rachel Pollack and Caitlin Matthews, 1989

'Triads', *Heart to Heart*, Mammoth Books, edited by Miriam Hodgson, 1995

'Waiting by the Corpse', *Maelstrom*, edited by Malcolme E Wright, 1995